EN... ...RIL

There were more buildings ahead, gray, ghost-like hulks in the deepening evening. Between them was a row of monoliths leaning at crazy angles. But I was barely aware of the temples or the stelae. I was staring at the thing in the middle of the trail.

I turned away, my gorge rising.

"Don't come here," I told Pepper, but she ignored me. Then I heard her give a little gasp.

"Oh my god. Who?"

The only thing I recognized was a fragment of blue cloth from the guayabera now covering white ribs.

I never got a chance to answer Pepper because men with rifles stepped out of the forest then and opened fire. Something slammed my head.

The last thing I remembered was the ground rushing up. Then all the sounds died away and the world went black.

Other Alan Graham Mysteries by
Malcolm Shuman
from Avon Books

THE
LAST MAYAN

AN ALAN GRAHAM MYSTERY

MALCOLM SHUMAN

AVON BOOKS
An Imprint of HarperCollinsPublishers

This is a work of fiction. Names, characters, places, and incidents are products of the author's imagination or are used fictitiously and are not to be construed as real. Any resemblance to actual events, locales, organizations, or persons, living or dead, is entirely coincidental.

AVON BOOKS
An Imprint of HarperCollins*Publishers*
10 East 53rd Street
New York, New York 10022-5299

Copyright © 2001 by Malcolm K. Shuman
ISBN: 0-380-80487-5
www.avonbooks.com

First Avon Books paperback printing: October 2001

Avon Trademark Reg. U.S. Pat. Off. and in Other Countries, Marca Registrada, Hecho en U.S.A.
HarperCollins ® is a trademark of HarperCollins Publishers Inc.

Printed in the U.S.A.

10 9 8 7 6 5 4 3 2 1

*Dedico este libro a Mimi y Rosaura,
con cariño*

ACKNOWLEDGMENTS

The author would like to thank Drs. Bill Ringle and George Bay for allowing him to visit their excavations near Ek Balam, Yucatán, in 1999. He is also grateful to his agent, Peter Rubie, and his editor, Jennifer Sawyer Fisher, and assistant editor Clarissa Hutton. He is particularly thankful for the conscientious editing job performed by one of the unsung heroes of publishing, copy editor Dave Cole, and he owes a debt of gratitude to the artist, who has perfectly captured the mood of the book. The author's wife, Margaret, and his son, Karl, accompanied him back to Yucatán, so this is also their adventure. Most of all, however, he wishes to thank his many Maya friends, too numerous to be named. He is especially grateful, however, to his friends Mimi and Rosaura, for their continued friendship and hospitality, and it is to them that this book is dedicated.

Finally, the site of Lubaanah, mentioned in this book, is fictitious. For the sake of simplicity, I have taken the liberty in the text of condensing the two Maya words *lubaan* ("fallen") and *nah* ("house").

▰PROLOGUE

On the third day of the storm the winds died somewhat and the ocean settled into an eerie calm. The crew, many of whom had been lashed to their posts, allowed themselves to hope that the tempest was over, but the captain, who had struggled beside the helmsman throughout the ordeal, was not so sure. He had seen the eyes of storms before and knew that just because the driving winds had slackened and the thirty-foot waves had flattened into a gray, rumpled field, it did not mean that the storm was spent.

And even if the storm *was* finished, there was still little hope that any of those on the tiny ship would survive. It had been well over a month since they'd last seen terrain they recognized, as they'd sailed south with the land of dark-skinned people on their left side. They'd halted at the mouth of a river to replenish their supplies, and instead of meeting natives eager to trade, they'd been attacked. Two men had been killed and the rest had barely gotten away in the small boat. Even as his crew reached the mother ship, the natives had launched canoes, and the captain had little choice but to put to sea, heading west. He never foresaw the storm that would arise and, after two days of tossing the little craft about, leave them disoriented on a featureless ocean.

That had been another storm. When the waves had calmed and the skies cleared, the lookout sighted an island on the west. Perhaps, everyone thought, it was the legendary isle of gold.

1

But if it was an island, it never ended and the river they came to was wider at its mouth than any they had ever encountered. The land was inhabited but not by any race they had ever seen. These natives were brown, not black, and they carried bows and blowguns. Most faded into the forest as soon as they saw the ship, and only once, when the crew landed their small boat to take on water, were they able to actually meet any of the strange little men. In this case, they seized the native and brought him back with them, hoping he would, after interrogation, prove able to understand their language and guide them. But the prisoner was terrified and, after a day on board, slipped his bonds at night and disappeared over the side.

For the next two weeks they'd cruised north, looking for the end of the island, but the land seemed not to have any limit. The crew was fearful, afraid they would never again see their homes and families. There was discussion, some of it heated, about what course to maintain. But the captain held fast: There was no choice but to continue north, because without any sure way to measure distances east and west, there was no means of knowing how far they had come from their original course. Perhaps, at some point north, this land would become familiar, or join with some island they knew. Or perhaps, if this *was* the fabled golden isle, they would find someone who could speak their language and guide them.

Then, in their fourth week of sailing along the unknown coast, the skies had darkened and the captain had sensed the drop in pressure. They had looked for a safe harbor, but the captain knew that a storm like the one they had already come through would dash them onto the shore and destroy the ship, leaving them marooned. The men wanted to take a vote, but he insisted that they put to sea and ride out the blast.

It had been a mistake.

Within hours the sky had gone from gray to black, with low, streamerlike clouds driving toward them like smoke from hell. The waves began to mount, their tops frothed with white, and the tiny craft began to slew sideways in the huge troughs. From his place on the quarterdeck the captain could see the lips of the crew moving in prayer, though the noise of the tempest drowned out the words.

Not a religious man, he nevertheless began to pray, himself.

Waves smashed over the bow and those men who were not lashed to the masts screamed in terror. When one especially large wave burst over the gunwale, flooding the deck with angry foam, two of the crew disappeared in the receding water as the bow shot upward into the next wave.

Then, on the third day, the winds had weakened as the little vessel moved into the eye of the cyclone. Some of the crew—those that were left—had fallen to their knees in prayer. Others slumped to the wooden deck in exhaustion, too tired to give thanks.

And as the helpless craft floated now on the becalmed slate sea, the captain tried to think what, if anything, could be done.

But there was nothing.

And, just as he'd feared, within two hours the winds began to pick up again and the waves started to batter harder at the groaning wooden spars.

Were they riding into the other side of the storm, or had they just been caught by the fast-moving edge they'd already come through?

It didn't matter: They'd never survive this time.

He should have listened to the men. At least on dry land they would have had a chance. Ships can be rebuilt, even in the harshest places. But lives cannot.

He was still cursing himself for a fool when someone sighted land.

At first the captain thought it was a low cloud hovering at the edge of the horizon, but then he realized that the clouds were moving too fast and that it had to be land. They were driving toward it, too.

Desperate, he gave orders to unfurl the sails. All mariners knew that shorelines had teeth that could rip out a craft's bottom. It was better to stay away from land in bad weather. If he could only keep to sea . . .

But it was too late: The winds shredded the fabric until only rags streamed from the masts. The ship rose and fell, and inexorably was borne toward the shore.

Now the men began to cry out again, some from fear and others with excitement, thinking they might have a chance to touch dry land.

But the captain knew better and at the last minute the vessel struck a reef with a grinding, angry sound and water swept over the decks as the ship disappeared under the waves.

Much later, when he came to, he was in a forest, with water lapping at his body. Tall trees leaned sideways in the blast and leaves drove by him on the way to nowhere. He raised himself onto his knees and staggered forward, trying to escape the tide, which even now was trying to drag him backward into the roiling gray ocean. He grabbed a tree, hugged it, and closed his eyes. When, many hours later, he opened them again, the tide had receded and there was a thin strip of beach visible in front of him. He slumped to the ground and rested. When he'd recovered some of his strength, he rose and went looking for his crew, oblivious to the wind that tried to push him back into the trees.

There were two bodies on the beach, the incoming waves washing over them. The rest of the crew had vanished with the ship.

He was still staring at the murderous waters when he heard something behind him and spun around. It was a human voice and the joyous thought suddenly occurred to him that someone had survived.

But when he turned, he saw it was not one of his comrades at all, but one of the natives of this land, a tall man wearing a loin covering and little else.

The captain pointed at the sea, but the native did not seem to comprehend or even want to. Instead, he signaled with his hand and five more like him materialized from the forest.

The first one said something in a language the captain did not understand, and then they were on him, grabbing his arms and bearing him away with them, to where he dared not imagine.

He cast a final, desperate look back at the sea. He sensed that where they were taking him would make the mercies of the sea seem generous.

That's how I imagined it, after what happened at the Mayan site of Lubaanah, in the year A.D. 2001.

ONE

I checked into the Hotel Colón and wondered if it was going to be the second time a woman had stood me up there. The first time had been fifteen years ago and the woman had been Felicia Esquivel. My wife. I hadn't been back to Mérida or the Yucatán since. This time, Pepper had assured me, things would be different. And they were, mostly: the automated customs procedure, the new Mexican money, the *periférico,* or loop, around the city. The only thing that was the same was that I was waiting for another woman: Pepper.

Coming to Mexico had been a tough decision. There were too many memories, both good and bad. The happiest days of my life had been spent here, as a young archaeologist intoxicated with the history, the culture, and the people. I'd made friends, learned the Spanish and Mayan languages, and immersed myself in the exploration of ancient Mayan sites. I'd also met Felicia Esquivel.

We'd fallen in love and, after a three-month courtship, I'd convinced her to marry me, not realizing the demons that lurked in her tempestuous psyche. Then, one day, I'd waited for her at the Hotel Colón and she didn't come. It was only later I found out she'd been with another man, a German archaeologist.

I'd told Pepper I wasn't sure I was ready to come back, and she'd asked if I would ever be. She'd pointed out that I talked about Mexico frequently and that sometimes at night I shot upright in bed from dreams in which I'd been walking the streets of Mérida and prowling tumbled pre-Columbian ruins. Was I really going to let what was now ancient history keep me away? I'd complained about her going back for summer work with Eric Blackburn at Lubaanah, on the east side of the peninsula. So why not come down and visit? Eric was easy to get along with, and he was eager to meet me. Besides, I needed a vacation—she could tell that by the way I'd been for the last six months or so before she'd left for Mexico in June.

I'd debated it long and hard. The company couldn't survive without me, someone should be close enough to the phone to handle Bertha Bomberg's unreasonable demands when the Corps of Engineers came calling, and there was a major proposal that was still out.

Marilyn, my office manager, told me she'd quit if I *didn't* go, and David Goldman, my main associate, told me he was tired of seeing me moping.

They didn't leave me much choice.

And so, after stalling as long as I could, I'd made reservations for early August, but had found out there were no available seats on the flights to Cancún, so I'd have to fly into Mérida, the old colonial capital on the west side of the peninsula. Pepper had said she'd come up and meet me at the airport, but at the last minute her plans had changed: We'd meet at the Hotel Colón at four, just as the siesta hour ended. That would give her time to drive the two hundred miles from Bacalar, where the expedition was headquartered.

I told myself, as I stood in the cool lobby, smelling a mixture of bus exhaust from the street and bougainvillea from the patio, that I was hypersensitive. I could have made reservations at another hotel, but I'd opted to confront the demons at the beginning and be done with them. Then, too, I was disoriented from the changes I'd already noted: fewer Indian women in *huipiles,* the brightly embroidered smocks that had been common in years before; fewer men wearing sandals, which before had been the sure mark of Indian status for males; a total inability to understand what the dollars in my wallet would buy these days; a pervasive use of Spanish, as opposed to Maya, among the people I'd passed when

I'd walked down to the main plaza to kill the rest of the faltering afternoon. I was going to have to get my bearings all over again.

Where the hell was Pepper when I needed her?

Then I thought of the long, narrow main highway between Bacalar and Carrillo Puerto, the rain forest home of the insurgent Maya of the nineteenth century, and the equally narrow road that arrowed northwest from Carrillo Puerto toward Mérida. There were lots of crazy drivers and even crazier truckers down here. What if . . . ?

I walked back down to the plaza, got an orange juice at an open-air café, and when I came back the desk clerk handed me a note.

It was written in Spanish and he said he'd taken it down word for word from the *Americana* who'd called. I thanked him and moved into the light from the open doorway.

I'm sorry I can't make it. I was supposed to pick up Paul Hayes at a little village called Tres Cabras, just south of Carrillo Puerto, and bring him to Mérida with me so he could do research in the museum. But he never showed up. I'll wait until just before dark and if he doesn't come I'll go back to the camp at Bacalar. If you can rent a car tomorrow morning, I'll meet you in Carrillo Puerto at the Balam Nah at four o'clock. I'm sorry.

Pebel

The clerk had done the best he could with a strange *gringo* name. He was a young man with slicked-back hair and a thin mustache, and he smiled as I stuck the note in my guayabera pocket.

"You ever hear of a place near Carrillo Puerto called Tres Cabras?" I asked in Spanish.

He nodded. "Sure. But that's a bad area. *Muchos narcotraficantes.* Drug smuggling everywhere. I tried to tell the *señorita*, but . . ." He shrugged.

"If this place is so small, how could she have called?"

"*Señor,* almost every village in Yucatán has a telephone these days. You pay the owner a few pesos, and . . ."

"Of course." Why should I be surprised? "Look, did she say anything else?"

He grinned. "I didn't write it," he said.

"Didn't write what?"

"What she said at the end. *Ella le quiere.* She loves you."

That night I ate at Los Almendros, which, to my chagrin, it took me an hour to find. I had *poc chuc,* a braised pork served with black beans and a stack of tortillas, and I washed it down with three Superiores. The place was full of tourists and it seemed to lack the charm I associated with it in my memory. But maybe my memory was playing tricks, and maybe the restaurant had never really been the way I remembered. I tore my thoughts away to the matter at hand.

I knew of Paul Hayes, the man Pepper had gone to pick up at Tres Cabras. Retired now, he was a linguist who'd done some of the early, crucial work on breaking the Mayan glyphic code. Pepper had mentioned him from time to time, but I wondered what he was doing by himself in a tiny settlement and why he wouldn't show up when he should.

I lay in the air conditioning and told myself everything was all right: Hayes was not just a linguist but an epigrapher, and such people were known for their eccentricity. He'd been working in Mesoamerica while I was still in high school, so there was no reason to be concerned. If he hadn't appeared, then Pepper would drive back to the camp. Hayes was old enough to take care of himself. And nothing would happen to Pepper on the highway in broad daylight.

There was nothing to worry about. I was back in Yucatán, where it had all started for me so many years ago, and I was home. Everything would be fine.

I knew it would.

▰Two

The next morning I ate *huevos motuleños* at a café on the main plaza and then walked down to one of the car rental agencies in one of the narrow, brick-paved streets that threaded their way to the main square. I got a new Dodge Neon and a city and state map, and then bought a hammock from a sidewalk vendor. I drove west, to Avenida Itzaes, a four-lane boulevard with frangipani flowers in the median. They were called *flamboyán,* and in May, when they bloomed, the whole avenue would have a row of flame down the center strip. I followed the boulevard south, past the airport, all the way to the highway. The road split, one route heading to Campeche and the other to Muná, and the latter was the one I took, rolling down the window to let the heat blast my face, feeling all the tension of the last fifteen years sloughing off like dead skin. I passed ancient haciendas that had fallen to ruin and saw jumbled heaps of stones in the bare, flat fields, marking the locations of ancient Mayan ruins. In days past, the fields had been sown with green henequen, from which rope was made, but I remembered Pepper telling me that henequen, the economic mainstay of Yucatán for a hundred years, was a thing of the past. It had been replaced by *maquilladoras,* where the former henequen workers produced clothes for the American market.

How many times had I driven this road in times past? How many times had I seen these same stone walls, running alongside the highway, passed the little church shaded by the ceiba tree, passed *campesinos* on bicycles, pedaling slowly toward their villages under the grinding sun?

Now I saw the first cornfields, the crop half grown by now and yellowing in the drought. I was leaving the arid northwestern corner of the peninsula and entering corn-farming country, and even though it was August, I let myself imagine there was still an odor of smoke in the air from the burning of the fields four months before. The man at the hotel said there'd been no real rain for a month, which was unusual. I could tell the corn was suffering, from the yellow color of the stalks. Soon, now, each village would be calling on its *h-men,* or ritualist, to do *Chhachaac,* the rain ceremony. Surely they still did *Chhachaac.*

I came to Muná, a dusty little town nestled at the base of the *puuc* hills, a low range that provided the only topographic relief in the whole peninsula. I found a shoe store and bought a pair of *alpargatas,* or sandals with soles made from old tire treads. Then I went back to my car, removed my socks and shoes, and slipped my feet into my new footwear. My feet would bleed for a week or so until the new leather became pliable, but that was okay: The pain would be one more verification that I was where I wanted to be.

Yeah, I know: just another silly old *gringo* pretending he was young again and that the year was 1986.

I took the highway east out of Muná, running alongside the hills and slowing for a string of towns: Ticul, Oxkutzcab, Tekáx . . . The towns had grown larger, and in Oxkutzcab there was a bypass that I ignored, because I craved the sight of the old market and the people gathered in its shade, drinking *liquadas* and eating tacos from the stalls.

I bought some tacos from a vendor and noticed that here also the people who walked past were speaking Spanish instead of Mayan.

The books of Chilam Balam, the Mayan prophet who had supposedly foretold the coming of the Spaniards, mentioned these towns in their migration narratives. Ticul, the place where the Mayan Itzá kings were seated; Oxkutzcab, the place of good tobacco; Tekáx, the place of the wilderness.

I drank in the sights and smells and wondered if my life at

home, in the States, had been a dream. Because now, as I shot down the two-lane highway, with cornfields and orchards on either side and men on foot carrying stacks of firewood on their backs with the help of tumplines, I felt as if I'd never left.

It was a dangerous mood, because fifteen years ago I'd taken the same road to find Felicia after she hadn't met me in Mérida and when I'd reached the archaeology camp a few miles west of Chetumal I'd found out the truth.

Last night I'd dreamed of her for the first time since meeting Pepper. Felicia was telling me that I'd only imagined my life in the States and that no one I'd met there was real, as I'd find out when I reached the camp.

I shoved the dream out of my consciousness and tried to concentrate on driving.

After Tekáx there isn't much, just a few little towns shimmering in the dry heat. I was headed for the last stronghold of the Maya, in what, a hundred years ago, had been deep rain forest.

At Polyuc I came to the first army roadblock. They were set up to stop westbound traffic and they waved me through, but I saw a Honda they'd pulled over, with its doors open and hood up.

There'd never been army roadblocks in the old days and I had a sense of foreboding.

I reached Carrillo Puerto at a quarter to four and gassed up at the Pemex station. Then I made my way to the old church that dominated the east side of the main plaza.

The Balam Nah, it was called in Mayan: the House of the Lord. The rebellious Maya had built it in the mid-nineteenth century, patterning it after a Catholic church. In it, they'd worshiped God, who revealed Himself through a talking cross. With the help of an interpreter, the cross had advised them on battle strategy and admonished them when they failed. They called the town Chan Santa Cruz, or the Little Holy Cross. And they'd been safe here until a hundred years ago, when a stubborn Mexican general named Bravo had built a railroad from Mérida all the way through the jungle to this town, using the rails to ferry soldiers and ammunition. The Mexican army had entered Chan Santa Cruz early in May 1901, but the Maya had fled. Years later, after the last rebels had been seduced into capitalism by the chicle trade, the town was renamed Carrillo Puerto, after the martyred socialist governor of Yucatán. But the cult of the talking cross still existed in little villages scattered throughout the forest.

Now I waited in front of the old church and wondered if the desk clerk in Mérida had understood Pepper correctly.

When five-thirty came and went, I decided he hadn't.

All I could do now was drive south to the archaeology camp at Bacalar and try to find out what was happening.

There was another army roadblock on the southern outskirts of town and this time they were checking traffic from both directions.

I showed my passport and car rental papers and the soldier nodded and handed them back. As I was returning them to the glove compartment, I noticed a Humvee coming from the other direction. But instead of pulling it over, the soldiers waved it past, and I caught a glimpse of the dark, round-faced driver.

The village of Tres Cabras was so tiny I almost missed it, just a cinder-block store with a Coca Cola sign, a Baptist mission with a basketball court, and a pair of speed bumps. I pulled in at the store and nodded to the big-eyed children who watched me get out of the car. A fat man in a T-shirt was behind the counter. I told him I was looking for a *gringa* and showed him Pepper's photograph. "Her name is Pepper Courtney," I said.

He nodded. "*Sí, como no?* She used the telephone. She came yesterday and waited for a long time and then left, and then she came back again this morning."

"Did she leave again?"

"She took the road to Oxté." He gestured behind him.

"When?"

"Ten o'clock, maybe eleven."

"And she didn't come back?"

"*No, señor.* I tried to tell her it wasn't a good road, but she was looking for the other one, the old *gringo.*"

"How far is Oxté?"

"Thirty kilometers. I told her it wasn't a good place to go." He shook his head. "*Muchas contrabandistas. Es peligrosisimo.* The drug smugglers will kill anyone."

"Is it possible she could have returned another way? A way you wouldn't have seen?"

"This is the only way in, *señor,* and the only way out." He shook his head again. "I told her not to go."

"Where is this road?" I asked.

He left the counter and walked out into the fading sunlight. I smelled wood fires and the odor of pork cooking.

"Over there." He pointed and I saw an unpaved track leading into the trees. "It goes to the coast. Oxté used to be a fishing village. Now . . ." He shrugged. "It isn't a good place to go."

I thanked him, got back into the car, and drove onto the track. Its surface was red earth, stable enough so long as there was no rain. I had an hour at most before darkness. Thirty kilometers was just under twenty miles. I decided I'd go as far as I could in half an hour.

Behind me, at the clutch of cinder-block houses that was Tres Cabras, eyes watched me, no doubt wondering at the foolhardiness of *gringos.* I nudged the accelerator and started down the narrow trail.

The first five kilometers were easy enough and took fifteen minutes, but I knew at this rate I wasn't going to make it more than a third of the way before I had to turn around. Once I saw a boy on a bicycle headed toward me, loaded with palm leaves for thatch, but when I asked him if he'd seen a *gringa* he just kept going. When he was gone I got out and studied the ground. There were fresh tire marks, but I had no idea if they were from her vehicle.

I got back into the car, slapping a mosquito. The shadows were blotting up the last of the sunlight and the smell of night was in the air.

Fifteen minutes, I told myself. Then I'd find a place to turn around and I'd drive straight on to Bacalar. Maybe the archaeologists at the camp would be able to help. Or maybe, despite what the storekeeper had said, she was already there.

After ten minutes of bumping over the ruts, I flicked on my headlights.

And five minutes later I came to a fork in the road.

The storekeeper hadn't said anything about a fork.

Common sense said it was time to go back.

Instead, I got out and tried to make out which way the tire tracks went.

Maybe it was my imagination, but I thought they headed right. I started down the right fork.

I was home, in an area I'd known well, albeit fifteen years ago: Nothing could happen to me here.

I reached a curve in the road, eased my way around it, and saw the ghost.

At first it was just a wisp of fog shimmering in the head-lights. Then it coalesced into a form and the hairs on the back of my neck stood up.

It was the form of a woman, coming toward me, a hand held up to blot the glare of my lights.

An old Mayan folk belief about a witch who snared men sprang into my mind and I tensed.

When the hand came down a fraction I saw it was Pepper.

I jerked my door open and jumped out to meet her and she lurched forward as I called her name.

"Alan?"

I ran forward and grabbed her to keep her from falling.

"What are you doing in the middle of the jungle?" I demanded. "Are you okay?"

"The Rover stuck in a hole," she said. "I've been walking for three hours."

I guided her into the car and handed her a bottle of water from my cache. Then I gingerly maneuvered the car until we were turned around.

"What were you doing back here?" I asked, as she lowered the half-empty bottle from her lips.

"I was looking for Paul. He was supposed to be at Oxté, a little fishing village on the coast. He's trying to find copies of the Chilam Balam books, some kind of linguistic study. Eric dropped him at Tres Cabras a couple of days ago. Paul was supposed to take a cargo truck to Oxté. Then I was supposed to meet him yesterday, when the truck made its return trip. But they said at Tres Cabras he hadn't come back on the truck. He's not a young man. He must be seventy and he had a stroke a year or two back. He could be too sick to go anywhere. I thought maybe I could drive to Oxté and see if he was there and get back to Carrillo Puerto in time to meet you. But the Rover bottomed out in a rut. I figured all I could do was walk back."

"That was crazy," I said. "All by yourself at this time of day, with jaguars and snakes . . ."

"Nobody's seen a jaguar around here for years," she said, then nestled against me.

"Maybe not, but everybody tells me there's a bad situation down here now," I said. "Drug smugglers. There's army all over the place."

"That's what we keep hearing," she said. "But nobody's bothered us."

We came to the split in the trail.

"Shouldn't be too much longer," I said.

Then the men in fatigues with rifles stepped out of the trees and into my headlights, and I knew I was wrong.

▰▰▰THREE

I slammed on the brakes and sat frozen as the figures moved toward us in the dusk.

Then Pepper said, "They're army."

One of them was motioning for me to lower the window.

"Que hacen aquí?" he demanded. "What are you doing here?"

"The *señorita*'s vehicle got stuck a few kilometers down the road," I said. "I went to find her. We're archaeologists."

The soldier's face stared at me without expression and then he moved aside and a man shot a flashlight beam into my face and then into Pepper's.

"Papers," he ordered and we dug out our passports and tourist cards. He handed them to the first man and stepped back. "Please get out of the car."

I muttered something under my breath. But there was nothing to do but comply.

"Your Spanish is very good," the man holding our papers said. I noticed that he was a head shorter than the others, but his sidearm indicated he was an officer.

He turned to Pepper. "Why were you going to Oxté? The archaeologists are working out of Bacalar."

"I was trying to find a member of our crew," Pepper managed in halting Spanish. "An old man, a *viejo*. He disappeared."

"Un viejo, eh?" The officer turned and said something I

didn't catch to one of his men. "You know this is an area of drug trafficking?"

"We're just interested in archaeology," I said. "We don't know anything about drugs."

There was movement in the shadows and another form emerged, as short as the officer but broader.

"I guess I really screwed things up," the new man said in a midwestern accent. *"Teniente, estos son mis colegas."*

"Paul?" Pepper came around the front of the car and embraced the older man. "I've been worried sick about you. Where have you been?"

"Chasing rumors," Paul Hayes said and I caught a glint of his bald head. "When I got to Oxté they told me the old man who had the book was another ten kilometers up the coast and I had to hire a boy with a tricycle to take me there, only when I got there it turned out his Chilam Balam book was just a bunch of patent medicine formulas copied in a school notebook."

"Are they going to let us go?" I asked in English, figuring the soldiers wouldn't understand.

Hayes shook his head. "Afraid not. They're on some kind of drug-raiding mission. They told me they were going to hold me overnight until they do whatever it is they came here for. I imagine that goes for you, too."

The officer in charge let him finish speaking, then turned to me.

"Please turn off the car motor and give me the keys. My name is Tapia. I regret that you will have to stay with us until tomorrow. After that, you will be free to go. If you don't have hammocks and *mosquiteros,* we will loan you some. I wish we could make you more comfortable, but . . ."

I shrugged. It wouldn't do any good to argue. *"Servidor de usted,"* I said. "We're at your disposal."

He responded with a little bow. "You're very understanding. I will do what I can to make your stay bearable."

Which is how, an hour later, we found ourselves camped just off the trail, our hammocks slung between trees as we shared the canned food and chips and mosquito coils I'd brought with the grateful soldier who'd been assigned to stay with us. His name was Raul. He came from Chihuahua and he said he hadn't joined the army for this. We took turns sympathizing and when he nodded off we eventually changed from Spanish to English, talking in low tones so as not to wake him.

"I'm sorry I landed you in this," Hayes told me. "It's a hell of a way to celebrate coming back to Yucatán."

"I'll live," I said, slapping away a bug. I turned down the light of the Coleman lantern and then slumped back into the hammock and let the gauze mosquito net fall over me. "But you *did* have me worried about Pepper."

"Hey, I can handle myself," Pepper protested from a few feet away. "But I thought something had happened to you, Paul."

The old man chuckled in a low voice. "I was tromping this jungle when you were in diapers. Of course, there weren't drug lords then and you never saw the army. You didn't need it. And if there was ever a problem with the law, a few hundred pesos could get you out of it."

"What about this bunch?" I asked.

Hayes sighed. "That's why they're here: The army's less corrupt than the civil police. And the fellow leading this bunch, Lieutenant Tapia, takes himself pretty seriously. I was talking with him after they grabbed me. He has strong opinions. So I didn't even *try* to bribe him." He shifted in the webbing. "What the hell? It's only one night."

"Any idea what they're after?" I whispered.

"They'd like to get Chucho Cantu, but they'll settle for whatever they can find in Oxté."

"Who's Chucho Cantu?"

"Big wheel hereabouts. Owns a lot of land, has his finger in everything. Drives a Humvee with armor and bulletproof glass. They weren't able to touch him while the PRI Party was in. Now there's a new president and a new party, but it may take a while to sort things out."

I thought of the Humvee that had been waved through the roadblock on the outskirts of Carrillo Puerto.

"The next best thing is to try to scoop up some of his men and hope they'll talk. And hope that the new government in Mexico City's telling the truth about wanting to clean things up."

"So until then we get to see them round up the usual suspects," Pepper said, yawning. "I think I'd rather be back in my own hammock."

Hayes grunted. "Where else would you have a chance to be in the thick of things? Enjoy it while you can, eh, Alan?"

"Right," I said and slapped away another bug.

I woke up several times in the night, once in a sweat, thinking I'd heard voices and seen green-clad ghosts filtering past me in the gloom, and then another time before daybreak, when the cold of dawn had sent icy fingers along my chest and arms. I curled up as best I could and heard one of the others shift in the webbing.

I stared up at the milky netting over my head, listening to the cries of birds high above. Maybe I'd dreamed the last fifteen years. Maybe if I got up now, tiptoed to the edge of the camp to obey the urging of my bladder, I would come back and find that I'd only imagined the breakup with Felicia. And that would mean that my whole life as a contract archaeologist was a product of my imagination, and none of it had happened—there was no shabby office on the edge of the university, no scrambling for contracts from nightmare bureaucracies like the Corps of Engineers, no Bertha Bomberg to torment us with niggling regulations, no . . . Pepper.

Suddenly I did not want it to have been a dream.

I forced myself up, unused to the instability of the hammock after so many years, and swept the netting off me. I fumbled on my glasses and shook my sandals. Dew gleamed on the greenery of the jungle and a damp-earth smell permeated the thin mist hugging the ground. My fellow sleepers were wrapped in cocoons, half mosquito nets and half fog, and I cautiously slipped out of my hammock so as not to awaken anyone. Hayes was still snoring, but as I stood in the chill gray air I saw Pepper turn over in her own netting. For a moment I thought she was going to awaken, but as I watched she settled back into sleep, her light blanket wound around her.

The guard was dead to the world and we could have all stolen away, but it made little sense to aggravate the army for no reason. I walked to the edge of the clearing, relieved myself, and then considered my options.

My watch said five-ten. It would be light in another hour. I knew I wouldn't be going back to sleep, but neither did I feel like lying in my hammock wide awake. I tiptoed to the other side of the clearing and stumbled on something in the leaves. I bent and picked it up: a thin shard of pottery with a brown glazed surface and the remains of a glyph. A fragment of a Maya pot, evidence of the brilliant civilization that had once inhabited these jungles and been cut short by the arrival of the Europeans.

I tossed the shard away, for the forest was full of them, and lifted a hanging vine as I sensed movement in the bush beside the trail. A jaguar? Not likely: They'd all been hunted out years ago. And we were still too far north for monkeys. Then I saw the grass move again and froze, waiting. A masked face with a pointed snout and a banded tail peered out from the side of a stump. I smiled. A coatimundi, a raccoonlike creature with a ringed tail. It was scrounging for food and trying to ensure that the tables wouldn't be turned. I'd tasted their flesh. Not bad, but this one didn't need to worry.

I watched it scamper over a square fragment of stone and realized the stone was a portion of a limestone block, once part of an ancient Mayan building. I stared down at it, then scanned the undergrowth. A form took shape through the trees, all chunky blocks and heaped earth, split by roots and half concealed by the foliage. It was a pyramid, stretching above the treetops, possibly never visited by archaeologists and certainly never excavated. Not a major discovery, considering that the entire peninsula was a field of jumbled ruins and some estimates put the ancient population at over a million: There were sufficient ruins in the Mayan area to keep an army of archaeologists busy for the next five hundred years. Still, the thrill of touching something hidden for so long couldn't be denied. I eyed the ground for signs of more pottery, trying to make a tentative estimate of the pyramid's age. Maybe, I thought, if I scrambled to the top I could see if it had any datable motifs, a diving god over the lintel, for instance.

But if I was going to climb the damn thing, I might as well be professional about it and get my camera and notebook and make a few records. And my binoculars, in case the mist lifted and I could see other structures poking above the trees.

I tiptoed back to the camp, assured myself that everyone was still sleeping, and carefully opened the car door and removed my knapsack.

Once an archaeologist, always one.

I scrambled up the side of the artificial hill, careful where I put my hands: The last thing I needed was to grab a sleeping fer-de-lance by mistake. It wasn't a snake I cared to be bitten by, to say the least.

I hauled myself over a fallen wall and a shower of stones shot out from under my feet and went rocketing down the pyramid. I hoped the sound wouldn't wake any of the sleepers, but it was too late now. Suddenly I was twenty-five again, flush with the enthusiasm of my first visit to a land of fable and wonder and nothing mattered except climbing the top of every pyramid, visiting every temple, reveling in the sheer adrenaline rush of excitement at being here.

When I reached the top the mist was just lifting in the east and I sat down on a block of stone, feeling inordinately proud of myself. I was panting and sweaty and felt better than I had for as long as I could remember. In the distance I could see the green carpet of jungle fading into a gray field that turned blue even as I watched and then went gold as streamers of fire from the rising sun branded the sky. I leaned back against the stone, closing my eyes against the glare. Some Mayan priest had stood here a thousand years ago, welcoming the sun god. Waiting, I reminded myself, for the bound captive whose heart he would extract with an obsidian knife. The flip side of romanticism.

When I opened my eyes again the sun was halfway out of the Caribbean, too bright to look at, and the mist had melted into tiny wisps curled around the tops of the trees. I wondered if the others had awakened yet and found out I was gone. But I hadn't heard any shouts. Still, I should head on down. There was no sense provoking the guard. I heaved myself up and heard the first little pop in the distance. I stared into the sun and blinked. Maybe it was light reflecting from the sea, but I thought I'd seen a flash, then another. I dug out my binoculars and slowly scanned the even green carpet of foliage until a thin strip of beach moved into view. I stopped, focused, and saw another flash, then smoke rising up to cloud my view. Here and there brown figures ran across the sand. The popping sounds were regular now and I realized it was the army's raid, being carried out on the fishing village ten miles away.

I watched for a few minutes, until a pall of smoke from burning huts blotted out further images, and I lowered the binoculars. I was aware of voices below now from the clearing, calling my name. I turned to begin my descent and halted.

There, on the mixture of loose dirt and rubble in front of me, was evidence that someone else had been here before me and not long ago. They'd stood here, maybe watching the village with binoculars as I had, and they'd smoked at least three cigarettes, because the butts were under my hand now, cheap Gauloises.

"I'm coming," I called and began my sliding descent to the bottom. Why should I be surprised that *teniente* Tapia had posted a spy here? It was a natural lookout spot.

"Where have you been?" our guard demanded, waving his rifle in a way that made me nervous. "You were to stay here, in sight."

"Sorry," I said. "I heard the firing over at the fishing village and wanted to see what was happening."

"You should stay here," the soldier insisted, calmed somewhat now that he saw I hadn't escaped. "And besides, what happens is what always happens during all the raids."

"Oh?"

"We hide, we attack, and there is nobody there." He shrugged. "Why should this time be any different?"

The guard was right. The soldiers returned at midmorning, their Humvees announcing them half a mile away. Tapia slid out of the lead vehicle, clothes muddied and beard unshaven. Our guard snapped to attention, but the officer ignored him.

"I apologize again for the inconvenience," he said, offering around a pack of Mexican cigarettes and then lighting one himself. "I would advise you to stay closer to the archaeological zone in the future, however. It is dangerous to go off alone in the jungle."

He was red-eyed and I sensed his fatigue.

"Your raid," I asked. "Were you successful?"

He stared at me, and for a moment I thought he was going to answer. Then he threw down his cigarette in disgust.

"Return their papers to them," he told the guard and remounted his vehicle.

"You are all free to go."

▰FOUR

We reached Bacalar just before noon. It was as I remembered it, a dusty, hot little town of cinder-block houses perched on the west side of a narrow lake that stretched for nearly thirty miles north and south between a strip of jungle and the Bay of Chetumal. The plaza slanted, the benches in the plaza slanted, and the streets that paralleled the lake ran at different levels depending on whether you were closer or farther from the lake itself. A bumpy blacktop ran along the waterfront, passing walled estates with frangipani flowers visible through grilled gates. A mile south of town was a picturesque motel, white with blue trim and a red-tiled roof, overlooking the rocky beach. I'd stayed there once, years ago, batting away bugs through the open louvers of the window. It was a place where you got the taste of the country, if that's what you were looking for.

Geraldo Gonzales Pech ran a restaurant and also rented *cabañas* half a mile to the south, on the beach. The amenities were rudimentary, but over the years they'd sufficed for assorted foreigners ranging from archaeologists to researchers at the bio-reserve southwest of Chetumal, and that's where the Lubaanah project had elected to stay.

It's where Felicia and I had stayed during the first stages of our love affair, and it's where I'd gone back to find her after she'd stood me up in Mérida. I wasn't sure how I'd react to the place, but I was about to find out.

It's odd the way memory plays tricks: As we pulled into

the palm-shaded parking area in front of *don* Geraldo's restaurant, which also contained the office and his family living quarters, I looked for the little string of thatched huts. I'd remembered them as perching high on the gray rocks over the lake, like the restaurant itself, and yet now I saw that in actuality they were below us, at the base of the steps that led fifty feet downward from the restaurant patio to the gray rocks of the beach. Strange, considering how many times I—*we*—had descended those steps to go from our host's home down to our *cabaña*, where we'd shut the door and hungrily climbed into each other's arms in the big matrimonial hammock. How many other things was I going to misremember?

As I got out, a gray-haired little man in a white guayabera emerged from the white-walled structure and halted, palms out.

"*Puede ser?*" he asked. "Can it be?"

I stared. Fifteen years ago, the hair and mustache had been glossy black, the frame leaner.

"*Don* Geraldo?"

"The same. *Don* Alan? Can it really be you?"

We embraced, and seconds later I saw, standing behind him in the doorway, a plump woman I knew was his wife, *doña* Martina.

"When you didn't come we were so worried," he began.

"I told Geraldo you may have been killed by drug smugglers," Martina cut in. "Things are so bad these days."

"*De veras*, this is true," the little innkeeper agreed.

"It was *almost* that bad," Hayes declared, breaking out a cigar. "The army."

"*Por dios!*" Geraldo cried. "What happened?"

Hayes explained, Geraldo and Martina shaking their heads in sympathy.

"And of course they didn't catch anyone," Martina said, shaking her head and *tsk*ing. "They never do."

"Of course not." Geraldo rubbed his fingers with his thumb in the universal sign for money. He wheeled and beckoned to a barefoot Mayan boy standing behind them in the shadows. "*Muchacho*, get the baggage for the doctors and take it down to the *cabañas*." He gave me a sideways glance. "You wanted a separate *cabaña*, Doctor?"

"I'll be staying with a friend," I said and he nodded quickly.

"*Como no?* Take their luggage, quick, these poor people have been in the jungle all night. The poor *doctora*." He shook his head at Pepper. "It's a disgrace."

Pepper laughed. "All I need is a bath and a few hours' rest."

"Of course," Geraldo said. "And afterwards, you and *don* Alan must come up to the house. There is much to talk about. And poor *don* Pablo . . ." He turned to Hayes, but the tubby little archaeologist was already climbing behind the wheel of the Neon.

"I think I'll just drive out to the site," he said with a not-very-subtle wink at Pepper and me. "Let Eric know we're okay—just in case he was worried—and that we'll need to go back and drag the Rover out of the ruts tomorrow."

Pepper and I followed the boy down the winding steps to the beach. The iron rails looked the same, and the love seat at the first bend was the same one where Felicia and I had sat more than once. And at the bottom, fifty feet below, was what appeared to be the same old diving board.

"Look familiar?" Pepper asked from just behind me.

I nodded, staring out over the lake, with its blue water, to the far shore, where, on the horizon, someone was burning a field. Burning was usually done in the spring, but I supposed that someone was clearing away jungle growth in order to build. I sucked the fresh sea breeze into my lungs and exhaled.

"We can take a dip in the lake as soon as we change," she said as we reached the bottom. "The *cabañas* still don't have showers."

We made our way across the black, lavalike rocks to the little line of thatched houses with cinder-block sides. The one Felicia and I had shared had been the second. Or had it been the third?

"The first hut is Paul's," Pepper explained as we walked. "Sort of a courtesy to put him closest to the steps. Then there's José Durán, our INAH archaelogist. And next is Minnie, our volunteer, and this one is mine."

She indicated the structure to our left. I looked at the rest of the huts just beyond. There were two the size of the others and on the end of the row was a larger, thatched structure with pole sides. "Who gets the big one?"

"That's the lab, dummy. Eric had it built. Somebody stays back here every day with a couple of locals and washes the artifacts and makes notes on them. Then they're boxed and sent to the INAH regional center in Mérida. That way they never leave the country and the Mexicans are happy."

I nodded. The Mexicans were touchy about their cultural patrimony being stolen, the result of bad experiences with foreigners in the past.

"Eric's *cabaña* is the one next to the lab, and the one between his and ours belongs to April Blake, who's supposed to be a student."

"Supposed?"

"Well, she is, but she doesn't want to be here. She's sick half the time and tries to find excuses to stay here at the lab instead of going to the field."

Pepper turned to our *cabaña,* fished out a key, and opened the wooden door.

"Aquí, señor?" the boy asked, looking at me.

"Sí," I said, and handed him five pesos, which was probably too much, but I knew he was used to dealing with *gringos* and it was always good to have an ally.

I closed the door after me and stood facing her, my heart thumping so loudly I was sure they could hear it up on the clifftop. She smiled and came against me.

"Long time," she said.

"Damned long time," I said.

"We'll feel better after a swim."

"I'm not sure about that," I told her. But she was already delving into the old bureau that stood in one corner on the cement floor. "I hope you brought a suit," she said, stripping off her shirt so that her breasts bobbed free. "I'm told that *don* Geraldo frowns on skinny-dipping."

"Yeah," I said, opening my suitcase. "That was because a bunch of us went out one night fifteen years ago and . . ."

"I see."

I realized at once that I'd said the wrong thing. "Sorry."

"It's okay." She watched me peel off my pants. "You going to be able to wait?"

"We'll see," I said, blushing.

Felicia had always been more oblique, less willing to let her desires be known. Because Felicia was a *Mexicana* and the culture frowned on female sexuality except in brothels . . .

"Let's go," she said, and I followed her out across the rocks.

A smell of grease frying drifted down from *don* Geraldo's kitchen and I knew that there would be fried fish and *papadzules* for lunch and tonight *poc chuc* and *relleno negro,* served with stacks of fresh corn tortillas and all the beer you could drink.

Pepper walked to the diving board, dipped a toe into the green water, and drew it out. "Just right," she said and, skipping to the end of the board, arced up and into the air, vanishing beneath the green surface. I waited, looking out to where the water deepened into a blue color. Where was she? My God, what if she'd come down on a rock? What if . . . ?

A hand reached up over the side of the board and grabbed my ankle.

"Let's go," she challenged and sprayed me with cold water. I swore and danced to get away from it. "No fair."

"Wuss," she accused.

I laid my glasses beside the board, took a deep breath, and dove.

When I broke the surface she was twenty feet away, laughing, splashing water in my direction. I lunged after her, barely catching a foot and tugging her under the surface. Then fingers grabbed me from underwater, jerking down my trunks, and I reflexively reached down to keep from losing my suit.

"You . . ." I sputtered as she laughed from a few feet

away. I grabbed her head, pulled her to me, and pressed my mouth against hers. We did a slow pirouette in the water, our hands roving each other's bodies, and I heard her gasp.

"Enough of this," she sighed. "Let's go back to the hut or I'm going to ravish you on the rocks, and the hell with Geraldo and Martina."

I followed her, dripping, out of the water, and as I mopped myself with the towel, my eyes went up to the love seat. I don't know if I expected to see a disapproving Felicia staring down at us, but what I did see was a man with dark glasses, smoking a cigarette. As we began our trek toward the huts, I saw him stand, propel his cigarette through the air, and lean back against the railing with both arms. I had the impression he was smiling.

But the observer didn't stay on my mind for more than the time it took to get to our *cabaña*, because once there, with the door closed, Pepper was unhooking the hammock from where it hung against one wall, folded and out of the way, and I was watching her carefully slip the hook in one of its rope arms through the circular holder set in the wall and push the netting a few times to be sure it was secure. She turned slowly to face me, her blond hair plastered to her face and rivulets of water running into the cleft between her breasts.

I watched, mesmerized, as she slipped the bra top over her head and then slid out of the bottoms. I dropped my own suit and pushed against her until we were at an angle against the hammock, the netting pressed into a band that was all that kept us from falling backward. Pepper giggled.

"Don't you think we'd better get into this thing?"

She spread the webbing and got in, legs deliciously spread, and I carefully climbed in, my knees pressing down against the net. Suddenly I was inside her and her arms were around me and the hammock was swinging with our movements, and our groans mingled with the gentle creaks of the hammock as it tugged against the sides of the hut.

I was falling, and yet I wanted to reach the bottom, to be swallowed up by the void, but the fall never seemed to stop.

Then, suddenly, I gave a shudder and heard her gasping. For a long time afterward I felt her heart beating against my own and kissed the hollow of her neck. A cool breeze licked in through the open window and cooled the perspiration on our naked bodies, and I didn't want to move.

"Wow," she breathed. "I've never done it in a hammock."

I didn't say anything because, of course, I had, and with my silence our mood was suddenly broken.

She slid out from under me and shoved herself out of the hammock to a standing position.

"I'm sorry," I said.

"Why? You didn't say anything."

"I know."

She went to the window and stared out. I idly wondered if the man at the love seat was still there.

"It wasn't this *cabaña,* was it?" she asked.

"No. At least, I don't think so. It's funny, though"—I tried to laugh— "my memory's been playing tricks. I didn't even remember the *cabañas* were at the base of the cliff."

"But you remember *her.*"

"Yes. But that was then." I pushed myself up and went to her, melding my front against her naked back. "It was a long time ago, another time."

"A better one?"

"I used to think so. But I don't think any time can be as good as this one."

She turned then and looped her arms around my neck. "I've thought about it a lot, you know," she whispered. "About how you'd feel coming back to the same place. If there was some way I could have made the project change locations . . .

"I know. But face it: Geraldo's got the best deal in fifty miles. Besides, how could anybody trade the view, the lake, the Gonzales family? See, there are good memories, too."

She reached down, felt me, and gave a murmur of approval. "You won't be thinking of her, then?"

"No," I lied. "Only of you."

▄▄▄FIVE

Half an hour later, ignoring siesta time, we dressed and wandered up the beach, hand in hand. The observer was gone, but as we reached the landing with the love seat I stopped to enjoy the view and something caught my eye:

A pair of cigarette butts littered the ground in front of the cement bench. But not a local brand: Gauloises.

We entered the big thatched dining area that adjoined the Gonzales house and took a seat at a metal table under a slowly rotating overhead fan. At the bar, twenty feet away, a couple of local men hunched over their beer bottles. The waiter, a fat, dark man in his forties, appeared with a menu.

"Botanas," I ordered. *"Y dos Superiores."*

Two minutes later our waiter reappeared with a tray full of Yucatecan delicacies—*salbutes,* made of fried tortillas topped with onion and pork or turkey; *escaveche,* or chopped sea snails in a saladlike mix; *tacos al carbón,* or corn tortillas rolled around charbroiled pork; and fried chips with salsa, all to be washed down with bottles of *Superior*, Mexico's best beer.

"I should have gone to the dig," Pepper commented, sipping her beer through the foam.

"But aren't you glad you didn't?" I asked.

She nudged me under the table. "What do you think?"

"I think after a few *botanas* I'll be ready for another round."

"Save some energy to meet the others," she said, smiling.

"After all I've told them about you, they'll be expecting Superman."

"Even Iron Man Eric?"

"Now, come on, don't start that. How could you possibly be jealous after . . . ?"

"Easy. He's had you for two field seasons and I have to make do with a field visit."

"Yeah, but he just gets to look."

"You sure?"

"You're going to piss me off."

I sighed. "You're right. You put up with my crap."

She nudged me again. "Anyway, you'll like him. He's got a great sense of humor. But he's totally dedicated to his work and loves this country. He told me it even cost him his wife. She had some high-powered job and didn't want to be separated from him for these long periods. So he doesn't see his daughter very much. But he's become godfather to a little boy in the village where our workers live."

"Sounds like a fanatic to me."

"Give him a chance."

"So what's the story with him and Paul Hayes?"

She shrugged and took another sip of beer. "Hayes was sort of his mentor, helped him get grants and wrote a recommendation to help Eric get his job with the university in Houston when Eric left Tulane. Now Hayes is retired and he's just kind of tagging along to do his own thing. He's not really part of the project, except on paper, to give him legitimacy with the Mexicans."

"So what's he *really* doing?" I asked, chewing at a *salbut* and savoring the greasy taste. "Last night he said something about trying to compare different versions of the Chilam Balam books."

"That seems to be it," she said. "You know, the books were written in European characters by Mayan scribes as soon as the Spanish taught them the alphabet, but most of the books contain fragments from the old hieroglyphic codices and parts of the ancient calendars."

I nodded. The books were named after a famous Mayan

prophet, or *Chilan,* who supposedly had foretold the coming of the Spanish a few years before their actual arrival. Now many Mayan villages, especially in the old heartland of the insurgents, had their own tattered books, jealously guarded.

"He thinks that if he can compare enough of them," Pepper went on, "he can find some insight into the way the calendar changed over time. And that could help solve some of the controversies about the relationship of the Mayan calendar and the Christian one. Many of the Chilam Balam books contain Mayan calendar counts."

"Well, I've read some of his work," I said. "Brilliant—if you can understand it."

She laughed. "I know. But he's really a teddy bear. He lost his wife a few years ago and I think he's desperate for something to do."

"And the others?" I asked. "Are they desperate, too?"

Pepper yawned. "Just April. But I think she's been desperate all her life. Her father's a senior partner in some big Houston law firm. The Blakes are part of the country club set. Makes you want to gag. I think that's why April's so screwed up. She can't figure out why she should do anything at all and her father keeps pushing her. So she's in grad school for right now and he pressured Eric to take her on, figured maybe Mayan archaeology would give her something to be interested in. I think she'd have been thrown out a long time ago except that the Blakes give about a jillion dollars to the university every year."

"Sounds unhappy."

"Yeah. And José hasn't had things any easier, though I'm not sure it's his fault, exactly."

"José Durán?"

"Yeah. Not a bad guy, but moody as hell. I guess it's part of the Latin mystique. I think he and April are getting it on, but she's probably pretty demanding."

I smiled. "I've heard of Durán," I said. "Never met him, but the last year I was down here he was a student, working out of INAH in Mérida. Everybody said he was one of Mexico's up-and-coming archaeologists."

"Well, he may be, but he seems to have slowed down

along the way. My guess is too many women and too little digging."

"Well, that's his business," I said, "just so long as . . ."

"Save your breath. He isn't my type. But if you keep up this way, he might have to do."

My turn to administer a kick under the table.

"Well, at least everybody isn't at each other's throats yet," I commented, remembering expeditions where that had happened.

"No, Minnie keeps us sane."

"Minnie?"

"Minnie O'Toole. I wrote you about her. She's a librarian from Des Moines, retired a few months ago and decided to have an adventure. She's sort of the mother-confessor. One of these volunteers from Earth First, paid her own way—and worth every *centavo*." She sighed. "Eric and I were secretly hoping she'd get together with Paul. I don't think he'd mind, either, except he doesn't stay in camp long enough. Still, when they're together, they make a fun pair. You'd almost think they were old marrieds—or old lovers."

I was about to reply that maybe they were when I heard movement behind me and turned to see our landlord.

"*Doctor, Doctora*," Geraldo Gonzales greeted. "I saw you both here and knew I had to stop and tell you how glad I am that everything is all right. And to see you again, especially, *don* Alan, looking so well, hardly a day older, while my poor hair has gone all gray and I have aches and pains everywhere."

"You look not a day over forty," I lied.

"You're kind. May I join you?" The waiter appeared from nowhere and our host asked for a beer. "And no bill for any of this," he ordered. "These are my guests."

He waved away my thanks. "No, it is so good to see you here, so happy, after such a long time. . . ."

We whiled away the afternoon, talking of old times, and after a little while Pepper rose and excused herself.

"I'm keeping the *doctora*," Geraldo apologized, rising, but she put a hand on his shoulder. "Stay. I just need to take a nap before the others come in."

Geraldo watched her make her way past the empty tables. "A very beautiful young woman," he observed.

"Very."

He looked away. "I wondered why you never came back to visit us."

"I wanted to," I said. "But there were things."

"I understand. I haven't seen her for many years now. She doesn't come here anymore, either. I heard she works out of Mexico City."

I nodded and raised my glass. It was good to know we wouldn't be running into each other.

The old man reached over and patted my arm. "I'm sorry. I shouldn't have mentioned it."

"It's okay. And believe me, I've thought about you and *doña* Martina over the years, and of this place."

He shook his head sadly. "But it isn't the same. Everything is changed. When they built Cancún we thought it would mean more tourists, and there are some. But most of them stay in the expensive tourist hotels." He raised his hands in despair. "*Caráy!* Why would anybody who can pay a hundred dollars a night come down here? But mainly it's the drugs." He pushed his chair closer to mine. "When PRI left power in December and we got Fox as president, we hoped things would change. And maybe they will. But every bunch comes in and promises to clean up and they're worse than the ones before. You know the governor of the state fled just three years ago, because he was implicated in the drug traffic. They recruit the young men out of the villages, even. And now we have soldiers everywhere, because the *policía judicial* are so crooked."

It was my turn to comfort him: "At least you have a wonderful family. How are the children?"

Soon we were looking at pictures of his children.

"Geraldo is an engineer in Mexico City. The pollution is horrible, but . . ." A shrug. "And Tomás is doing his year of social service as a doctor in a clinic in Chihuahua. Martinita is a nurse now, at the big Seguro Social in Mérida, and María is married to an architect in Campeche. None of them have chosen to stay here except Rita, and there is no choice."

"Oh?" Rita, I recalled dimly, was the youngest, a three-year-old with a baggy dress and a smile.

"Doctor," he said, lapsing into formal address, "Rita has been sick for the last two years. There were times when we thought we were going to lose her. I took her to all the best clinics." He shook his head sadly. "They did all the tests. *Caráy,* you wouldn't believe all the things they did to that poor girl, I could have cried. Only eighteen years old, Doctor, and to suffer so much."

"I'm sorry. What's the problem?"

He bent his head, as if merely thinking about it added weight. "Some kind of disease of the muscles. The one that the famous baseball player had."

"Lou Gehrig's disease."

"*Esto.* They say there is no cure." He shoved away his empty beer glass. "She's in Mérida now, at another clinic, for more tests. Martina wanted to go with her, but poor Martina is exhausted. I told her our daughter Martinita could see to things."

I didn't know what to say and my friend seemed to sense my discomfort. "*No le hace, Doctor.* It's what God wants, *verdad?*"

"Yes."

"Besides, if she dies, maybe it's a blessing. Who would want to live in this world we have now? Sometimes I'm glad to be near the end of my run. You remember, Doctor, when it was only *arquéologos* and researchers who came here and some tourists. But now we get the dregs. The police leave us alone because they know we have American professors. It's good for the economy. But now . . ." He nodded over his shoulder and I saw a man with a ponytail seated at the bar. As he turned his head, I realized that it was the same man I'd seen earlier watching us swim. ". . . we have people like that one, who come here just to sell drugs."

"You know that man?"

Geraldo snorted. "His name is Felipe Jordan. I think he's a *huach*—a Mexican—or maybe even from your country. He speaks English. He's been around here for the last three or four months, has no work. I've seen him talking to hippie tourists up in Bacalar. I know he's selling drugs. It's only a matter of time before they arrest him."

"Where does he stay?"

"He rents a room in Bacalar at a place where they don't ask questions."

"Maybe he won't be arrested," I suggested, making the money sign. "Maybe he isn't working on his own."

"That could be, too."

"Don Geraldo, who is Chucho Cantu?"

Suddenly my host's face went ashen and his voice dropped to a whisper. "*Por Dios,* Doctor, I don't know anything about him. He's a businessman, a rancher, very rich." The innkeeper shoved back his chair. "If you will excuse me, I see someone in the office." He tried to laugh. "I can't afford to turn away guests."

I watched him flee and idly shoed away a fly. So was the man with the ponytail working for Chucho Cantu? Was that why he'd been on top of the pyramid, giving some kind of signal to the smugglers? Perhaps. Then why had he been watching Pepper and me?

But I was being paranoid: It wasn't exactly pathological to watch a pretty woman swim. Still, the coincidences of his proximity seemed odd. I was shaken out of my thoughts by the sound of a vehicle on the loose pebbles of the parking lot and doors slamming. I looked toward the entranceway, where *don* Geraldo had his office, and saw shadows blocking the afternoon sun.

Then Indiana Jones emerged.

Six

Okay, so he didn't have a whip.

But the rest of the props were there: battered felt hat, khaki shirt open at the throat showing a tuft of manly chest hair, razor-pressed jeans stuck into expensive full-length leather boots, and a dark beard, besides.

Eric Blackburn. Project director. Associate professor at a respectable university and shepherd of about a half million in NSF grant funds at a time when researchers would sell their wives and daughters for travel funds to a professional meeting.

He moved through the office and into the restaurant like a cyclone, bearing bodies in his wake. The bartender greeted him and even the man with the ponytail managed a smile, though I almost sensed he was smiling at me instead of the newcomer.

"You have to be Alan," Blackburn boomed, sticking out a hand. As I took it I realized that, though I'd imagined him taller than I was, he was really an inch or so below my own height. "Tino, beers for everybody. Put them on my tab."

Behind Blackburn I saw the grinning Hayes, scratching his bald head, and behind him, a man and woman, hanging back.

"And you're Eric Blackburn," I managed, feeling stupid afterward. Who did I think he was, Dr. Livingstone?

"Where's our girl Pepper? You two didn't have a fight?"

"She went down to take a nap."

Blackburn sat down heavily in one of the chairs. "Tino, how about moving these two tables together?"

The bartender hastened to comply and I saw the man called Jordan had turned around on his stool so he could enjoy the show. He half raised the beer the barkeep had placed before him, but Blackburn ignored the salute.

"Do you know José and April?" Blackburn asked, and as I rose from my seat I got a look at the pair who'd been hanging behind.

Durán, a slight man with a thin mustache, stepped forward, giving a little head bow and a quick handshake. *"Mucho gusto,"* he said quickly and then stepped back. The girl, April, tried to smile, but it came out as a sneer. A washed out blonde with a halter top, she looked like she'd been on a diet for the last two years, and her legs reminded me of a pair of matchsticks.

"I'm tired," she announced. "I just want to go down and get some rest."

Durán followed her with his eyes and then took a seat on the other side of the table.

"Where's Min?" Blackburn demanded.

"Did somebody call my name?"

A gangly woman with gray hair appeared in the entranceway, a straw hat in one hand and a canvas satchel in the other. "You didn't want to leave the field notes in the van, did you?" she asked.

"What would we do without our mother?" Blackburn asked. He got up and made a sweeping gesture: "This is Minnie O'Toole."

She gave me a thin hand with just enough pressure and a warm smile. "And you're Alan. All Pepper's done is talk about you. Funny: You're not what I would have expected."

"Oh?"

"Well"—she laughed—"after what Pepper's been telling us, I really expected Indiana Jones."

"I guess they don't have enough to go around," I said dryly.

She put a hand on my arm. "Don't worry, I'd have thought

it was a little strange if you really *had* looked that way. There's something phony about that type, don't you think?"

That was when I knew we were going to be friends.

"Well," Blackburn began, lifting his glass, "here's to Alan's return to the Mayab. Let's hope what happened last night isn't a bad omen. Paul here told us about it. Hell of a thing. Next they'll be raiding our camp."

Paul Hayes picked up a taco. "With that Lieutenant Tapia I wouldn't be surprised."

Blackburn smiled. "So tell me, Alan, how's it go with contract archaeology? Pepper says you run quite an operation."

"We're a small company," I said. "But we've been lucky enough to get a few contracts."

"I doubt it's luck," Blackburn said. "You know, I did some work in the Southeast years ago. Florida. I've always wondered how you guys can figure out the stratigraphy of those dirt sites like you do." He gave a little chuckle. "It's a little easier down here, where we have monumental structures. But I'm not telling you anything you don't know."

I shrugged.

"Well," he said, "come on out tomorrow and you can get back into tombs and temples." He turned to Durán. "José'll show you around, won't you, José?"

The Mexican nodded. "With pleasure," he said without enthusiasm.

"I think Paul and Pepper and I are going to have to go back to where the Rover's stuck and haul it out," Blackburn went on. "We'll be a wrecker service for the day."

Minnie lowered her glass. "I worked for a week on a contract archaeology dig before I came here," she said. "I thought it was fascinating. It's what got me interested in coming here to Mexico."

"Naturally," Blackburn said, leaning back lazily. "All roads lead to the Maya." He smiled wryly. "That's why there are so damned many of us." He leaned toward me. "Seriously, Alan, I'm glad you're here. I really look forward to working with you, even if it's only a couple of weeks. And this is the best crew I've ever had. Thanks for coming, fella."

I nodded, unsure whether he was patronizing me or just being a nice guy.

Okay, I'd give the man a chance.

That night, after a late dinner, Pepper and I walked along the rocky beach, hand in hand. Across the lake the burning field was a red glow and the sweet smell of the burning vegetation was heavy on the breeze. Behind us, the lights of the restaurant shone dim on the clifftop, but the *cabañas* below were dark.

"So what did you think of Eric?" Pepper asked, as we turned back toward the *cabañas*.

I shrugged. "We'll see."

She gave my hand a tug. "Give him the benefit of the doubt, okay? For my sake?"

"Absolutely. By the way, I see what you mean about Durán. He seems like a glum sort."

"But he wasn't like that at first. Well, like you always say, 'Everybody in Casablanca has problems.' "

"Bogie said that, but I'll take credit."

I stopped, cocking my head to listen. From somewhere in the distance came a dull drone. An airplane.

"Somebody's flying late," I said, nodding in the direction of the burning field, where the red glow against the sky picked up a dark shape gliding in low from the east.

"Rumor is every low-flying plane's carrying a drug shipment," Pepper said. "Don't know if it's true, but there are strips all over the jungle where bush pilots fly in supplies. If some of the supplies are drugs, who's to know?"

"God," I breathed. "Everything really *has* changed."

"There's still no place like it," she said and I was about to answer when a sharp little cry split the night. We raced forward and I saw a form on the ground, getting up.

The graduate student, April Blake.

"April, what's wrong?" Pepper asked, as I helped the girl to her feet.

"Nothing," April said, taking quick little gulps of air. "I was out walking and I tripped on a rock."

"Are you sure?" I asked.

"Do I have to account to you?" she snapped, jerking herself free.

We watched her walk unsteadily away, back in the direction of her hut.

"She's drunk," Pepper said.

"Drunk on *something*," I agreed.

We waited until she was gone and then started forward again.

Much later, after a midnight swim, we went back to the *cabañas* and lay together in the big hammock under the *mosquitero*. After a time I heard Pepper's breaths coming in slow, even cadence, but I'd been bombarded by too many stimuli in the last twenty-four hours to be able to sleep.

The breeze ruffled the palm thatch above us and every few seconds I stretched out my foot to give the wall a nudge and send the hammock into motion.

I knew it was the emotional baggage I was carrying that gave me a sense of foreboding. I was the same old Alan, convinced nothing could come out right because it hadn't in the past. I'd scored an incredible stroke of luck finding Pepper and being loved by her, but now I'd tempted fate by coming back to the very place where things had gone wrong between Felicia and me.

But there were also the changes of fifteen years: The general sense in everyone I'd talked to that things weren't right. Drugs, army roadblocks, the desperation I sensed in my old friend Geraldo. . . .

I gave the hammock another gentle push.

It would all work out, though. Pepper was here and so long as we were together everything would come out all right. I closed my eyes and tried to sleep, but just as I was drifting off I heard the sound of a plane motor again. Was it just my imagination, or was it coming in the other direction now, from west to east?

▰▰Seven

The next morning, Pepper, Hayes, and Blackburn took the project van to free the stuck Rover. The rest of us started for Lubaanah just after six in my rented Neon, having breakfasted at Geraldo's on fried bananas and tortillas with copious helpings of black beans and chopped onions, washed down with freshly squeezed orange juice. The archaeological site was fifty miles west of the turn off to Chetumal and south of the highway that, running a hundred and sixty miles from Chetumal on the east to Escarcega on the west, splits the base of the Yucatán Peninsula. Turning off the highway, we went down an unpaved track for twenty-five miles into the jungle, nobody saying anything except for occasional comments by Minnie, who, squeezed into the backseat between April and Santos Canché, the Mayan field boss, kept trying to make small talk. But April just scowled and stared out the window and José Durán, next to me in the front seat, said as little as possible, except for occasional exchanges with Santos.

At eight we reached the tiny village of Ah Cutz, where the laborers lived, and I relaxed slightly as I saw traditional pole-sided thatched houses and women in flowered *huipiles*. Maybe, I thought, there were still a few real Maya left.

The site itself was only a kilometer beyond the end of the dirt road. It consisted of a scatter of jumbled mounds in what had once been a cornfield. Excavation units had been placed atop some of the mounds, with Visquine-roofed shelters on poles protecting the excavators from the brutal sun, which even now was beginning to burn a hole in the summer sky. Most of the fifteen-worker crew was already milling about, gourd water carriers over their shoulders, and after a perfunctory conference between Durán and Santos, the Mayan field boss set out ensuring that each group of workers was in the right place. Then Durán turned to me.

"This was a trading site," he mumbled, as though this were a newspaper interview. "Although there is a late post-Classic component, most of what we have found dates from the late Classic period, about eight hundred years after Christ, and there are features of the Peten Classic sites such as Tikal and Uaxactun but also certain features common to Rio Bec and Chenes architecture. The ceramics . . ."

My mind wandered as he lectured, pointing to an excavation unit here, a collapsed wall there.

Suddenly I realized he was staring at me.

"Pardon?" I said.

"I asked if you had visited this site during your survey of the southern peninsula in 1985."

My mind jerked back to the present. "Oh. I don't think so. I'd remember the name Lubaanah, 'fallen house.' And I'm sure back then the site was just a few piles of stones in the forest."

He nodded. "You are correct, of course. The villagers call the place simply *ti muul,* the place of the mounds, which describes most of Yucatán. Dr. Blackburn was the one who gave it the name Lubaanah."

I smiled. "Well, it's not the first time the excavator's given the place its name. I can't say I blame him for that. It's probably better for publicity."

"Yes," Durán said. "But Eric didn't invent the name."

"Oh?"

"You've heard of John Williams."

"Sure. He was an Englishman, explored lots of this area in the late 1930s and wrote a travel book about it."

The Mexican nodded. "Correct. It was Williams who found a site he called Lubaanah. He said it was a major Mayan ceremonial center, but he never went back there."

"I remember now. Little matter of the Second World War getting in the way."

"Yes. Like most foreigners, he claimed to have discovered the site, as if the people hadn't known it was there all the time."

"A problem," I said, sensing offended Mexican pride.

"Anyway, that's how this site got the name," Durán said and started walking.

We passed a fallen stone column and stepped over a line of army ants on their way to some feast.

"So is this Williams's lost site?" I asked.

"Eric thinks it is. It got him grant money. Who can argue with that?"

"You don't sound convinced."

"It's not necessary that I be. I just have to be sure that he does a good job and that the Instituto Nacionál is satisfied. If the site produces good data, it won't matter."

"I guess you're right."

I wiped the sweat off my forehead and stood beside Durán as he talked to Santos, a squat man in his forties with a face that could have come from the portraits on Mayan bas-reliefs. I edged my way over to an excavation pit where some of the laborers worked to clear rubble from the sides of the unit, while others, above, sifted the debris hauled up in buckets through a wooden frame with window-screen-sized mesh. They were talking among themselves in Mayan and I heard one of them ask the other who I was.

So I told them my name.

Santos smiled, but Durán looked discomfited and I realized it was probably because he was from central Mexico and had never learned Maya.

The remainder of the morning I spent with Minnie, at her excavation unit, fingering ancient bits of pottery and flakes of obsidian that had been tossed out of a Mayan hut over a thousand years ago. Once, a shadow fell into the pit and I looked up to see Santos, smiling a gap-toothed smile.

"Where did you learn Maya, *Nohoch Dzul?*"

"Here," I said. "A long time ago. But I've forgotten most of it."

His smile widened and then he was gone.

*   *   *

The van reappeared in early afternoon, followed by the Rover, and our three companions had returned. Pepper sidled over.

"Is it all coming back?" she asked.

"Little by little," I said.

That night we didn't hear the plane again and there were no encounters with April Blake. Nor did I see the ponytailed man called Jordan, which made me just as happy.

When we left our *cabaña* for a beach stroll, however, the light was still on in Blackburn's hut, on the end, though it was almost midnight. A thin thread of classical music wafted out on the night air and I recognized it as Mendelssohn's Scottish Symphony.

Oddly, we liked the same kind of music. Or was there anything odd about it at all?

We came to the diving board and looked up at the restaurant on the cliff above us.

Pepper gave me a mischievous smile. "Let's," she declared.

"Jesus, there's no telling who's liable to . . ."

"We'll swim out into the darkness if anybody comes. They'll never know."

She was already stripping off her clothes. What else could I do but follow suit? Or without suit, that is.

Nobody discovered us, fortunately, and when we clambered out half an hour later, giggling like children, and headed back to the *cabaña* in our wet clothes, I noticed Blackburn's light was off.

The next day was Saturday. Though it was usually a workday, Eric had accepted Pepper's request for a day off. So, while the others worked, we would have a lazy, late breakfast and then take off in the rental car to revisit some of the famous sites along Highway 186, toward Escarcega.

But it didn't work out that way, because the sun had hardly come up before we were awakened by shouts and Pepper and I had to throw on our clothes and stagger out to see what had washed up on the beach.

≡ EIGHT

The little crowd parted as Pepper and I approached and when we looked down we saw what the furor was about.

It was an orange blob that I realized was a body, floating in the lagoon face down. It nudged the black rocks of the shore, the brightly colored life jacket keeping it afloat. *Don* Geraldo arrived a moment later, wringing his hands and shaking his head.

"Pull him in," he cried. "We can't just leave him in the water."

A couple of his workers dragged the body onto the rocks and turned him over.

I stared down and then turned away quickly. Though the bloated face bore bruises, I sensed I had seen it before.

The innkeeper raised his hands to heaven. "*Caráy.* The *pobrecito* must have been murdered by the *narcotraficantes.* Did anybody see anything?"

Nobody had, it turned out, except for the houseboy, who had been sweeping the steps and had just looked down to see the gruesome cargo bobbing on the waves. I turned around to see if any of our people were present. Minnie O'Toole was hurrying toward us, face worried, but none of the others were in evidence.

"Do you think he was pushed out of a boat?" someone asked.

Geraldo frowned. "*Caráy,* these scoundrels tortured the poor man. They probably threw him overboard like that, be-

48

fore he was even dead. Didn't want him to sink, so they left the life jacket on him so he'd be found."

"Why?" Pepper asked.

Geraldo shook his head. "As a warning to others."

Don Chucho Cantu, I thought. Was that who was responsible?

"This is horrible," the innkeeper wailed. "Now we'll have to call the *judiciales*. They'll be all over the place, asking questions, expecting to be fed." He looked up at me. *"Doctor . . ."* Then he shrugged. *"Desculpe.* Why should I blame you? You didn't do it."

I patted his shoulder.

"What happened?" Minnie asked. "Is somebody hurt?"

Pepper told her and the tall woman winced.

"I wonder who he is?" Minnie asked.

Pepper shook her head. "Probably a drug smuggler who had a falling-out with his friends, right, Alan?"

"Yes."

The federal police arrived an hour later, in the form of a paunchy uniformed sergeant, followed by a pair of detectives in guayaberas. They looked at the body, took pictures, and asked if anyone had seen anything. When nobody answered in the affirmative, they sent for an ambulance, watched while the body was loaded into it, and left with it for Chetumal, the state capital, which was a couple of miles to the south. Nobody had asked me if I knew the victim and I kept my knowledge to myself. I wondered how many others on the beach were doing the same thing.

By the time the police had finished, it was noon and too late for our planned trip to the ruins. The others, meanwhile, had left for the site, except for Eric, who said he had reports to write, and April, who claimed illness. Paul Hayes seemed to regard the incident philosophically, and as for Durán, it was hard to say if he cared or if his mind was on getting to the site as soon as possible to make up for time lost by the affair. Minnie alone seemed truly saddened by the fact that a person had died, and once, just before the crew left, I glimpsed her standing on the patio behind the restaurant,

staring thoughtfully down at the body and the huddle of in-
vestigators.

And Pepper? I'd realized a long time ago that her cool ex-
terior was only a mask for her essential vulnerability.

"I can't help thinking I've seen him before," I said.

"But where?"

I shrugged. "You tell me. Maybe you've seen him, too."

She glanced away. "You're going to laugh."

"No, I won't."

"Promise?"

"More or less."

"I didn't look at his face."

Later that night, while Pepper was sleeping, I went down to
the beach myself. The fire across the lake had burned itself
out and the night was black, except for the few lights from
the restaurant above. I looked up at the stars, icy points on a
dark field, and thought about the Mayan celestial cosmol-
ogy, with the maize god journeying by canoe to the place of
creation, between the constellations Orion and Gemini.

I was still staring at the sky when I heard a noise behind
me and turned.

"Got a match?" a voice asked in English and I recognized
the man with the ponytail, leaning on the iron railing,
cigarette in hand.

"Sorry, I don't smoke."

"Probably better for your health," the man sighed. "But I
can't break the damn habit." He straightened up.

"You're one of the archaeologists. My name's Felipe Jordan. I'm from Brownsville, Texas. Ever been there?"

"Yes."

"Border town. Lots of snowbirds in winter. That's what
we call the retired folks who come down to get away from
the cold weather. Where you from?"

I told him. "I'm a contract archaeologist. I do environmental consulting."

He nodded. "Make money?"

"I get by."

"We all get by. Except the poor bastard on the rocks."

I waited for him to come to the point.

"What do you think happened?" Jordan asked.

"You'll have to ask whoever killed him."

"Yeah, that's right. It wasn't an accident, was it?"

"That wouldn't be my guess."

"I hear some of the snowbirds even come down here."

"Probably. Is that what you are?"

"Me?" he chuckled. "Not hardly. I'm just down here to soak up the culture." He stuck the pack of cigarettes back into his pocket. "Well, good digging. Your buddies are all up at the restaurant getting drunk, if that's who you're looking for. Maybe you ought to go up there and make sure nobody falls down the steps."

He turned and walked away down the beach. I started to follow, then changed my mind. Was Jordan trying to tell me that I should check out the others? Was something going on up at the restaurant? If so, why did it matter to him? Why had he even stopped me in the first place? I didn't for a second believe it was for a match. It was more like he was sizing me up.

I didn't care what the others were doing up at the restaurant. I walked back the way I'd come, fifty yards behind Jordan, until he was out of sight, and then I climbed back into the hammock with Pepper, but even with the door closed and bolted I no longer felt safe.

≣ NINE

Over the next few days the tragedy on the beach receded in significance and I saw no more of Felipe Jordan. I settled in beside Pepper to work in her excavation unit, carefully clearing away each level and placing the loose material in buckets to be screened by workers at the top. Hayes came and went on his own in the Rover, explaining that he was finished with the villages between Bacalar and Carrillo Puerto and now would be concentrating on those to the west. Blackburn, too, came and went, but that was the nature of being project director: The leader never had the luxury of settling into a work routine.

Minnie O'Toole kept up her pleasantness, which lightened the gloom spread by April's surliness on the one hand and Durán's wariness on the other. The workers, once they realized I was willing to try my rusty Mayan on them, began to delight in pointing out trees and plants to see if I knew their Mayan names, and Santos, the crew boss, began stopping by our unit to make jokes and tell me stories that had been handed down in his family. I jotted most of it down, because I realized that in another generation or two Yucatec would be a lost language. Santos seemed to have the same urgency.

"In the old days, during this time of the year, they made rain," he volunteered one morning, squatting in the shade of a ceiba tree while we took a break from the sun.

"Chhachaac," I said. "The rain ceremony."

He nodded. "Now they have pumps. Who needs *Chhachaac?*"

"So nobody does it?"

"Some," he said, then gave me a sidelong look. "Have you ever been to one?"

My turn to nod. "A long time ago, up near Tekáx."

"Ahhh." He got up and the other workers followed, but I knew they'd heard our conversation.

Two days later he stopped and asked if I wanted to go to a *Chhachaac.*

"Where?"

"The village, here."

"Who's the *h-men,* the rainmaker?"

"A man from Chetumal. He was taught by my grandfather."

I said I would be pleased to attend.

That night, at dinner, I told the others.

Blackburn leaned back in his chair.

"Well, everybody's been working pretty hard. And I know once the workers have made up their minds to have the thing, they're going to do it regardless, so we might as well forget about work for the day. We'll just call it cultural anthropology." He sighed. "Besides, I ought to spend some time with Emilio, my godson, and his family. I have to make arrangements for his education. I don't want him to end up as just another *campesino,* with nothing to look forward to but six kids to support."

"What does the rest of the family say?" I asked.

"His father was one of our workers the first year, but now he has a job working construction at Cancún. The family expects me to take little Lio to the States when he's older. Right now they're angling to have me take his older sister, María. For some reason they think the future's brighter in the States."

"Imagine that," I said. "So what will you do?"

He shrugged. "The best I can."

"Well, the rain ceremony sounds intriguing," Minnie said.

"I mean, I've read about Mayan rain ceremonies, but to actually attend one . . ."

"Yeah, well it's really just an excuse to eat a lot and get drunk," Blackburn said. "But as long as they want to kill a few turkeys, I'll buy a couple of bottles of rum."

Durán said nothing and April looked as if she couldn't have cared less. No surprise there.

The surprise was Paul Hayes. He didn't say anything at the table, but when Pepper and I got up he followed and caught up with us on the beach.

"Did I hear you say Santos's grandfather was a *h-men*?"

"That's what he told us."

"Funny he never mentioned it to me. I wonder if the old man is still alive." He clicked his tongue. "I've chased all over south Quintana Roo looking at damned *h-men* books and getting Santos's opinions about the ones I've found. I wonder if the rascal's been holding out on me."

"You'll have to ask him."

"Believe me, I will."

The *Chhachaac* began the next evening. As invited guests, we sat in chairs a few yards behind the wooden table that served as the *h-men*'s altar. The altar table had been placed in the rear of Santos's house lot, near the edge of the village under the shade of some poplars, and at the back of the table sat a small arch of woven vines framing a foot-high wooden cross covered by a tiny *huipil*, or smock, as if it were a woman. In front of the cross were seven votive candles, five gourd bowls containing a liquor from the *balché* tree, thirteen cigarettes, and some leaves.

Santos had met us on our arrival, introducing the *h-men*, a man named *don* Plutarco, who came from just outside Chetumal. Plutarco, he assured us, had served the area for many years.

The rainmaker, a wiry little fellow of fifty who wore shoes instead of sandals, assured us that if he did *Chhachaac*, rain would certainly follow, though I didn't ask him when. He shook each of our hands and then returned to his chair.

"Jesus," Hayes swore, taking a tug from a bottle of Presidente. "This guy's a city slicker."

"They come in all shapes and sizes," I reminded him.

He sighed. "True enough. I met one once in Telchaquillo who wore silk slacks and a gold watch, spoke Spanish and Mayan, and smelled like he lived in the barbershop, but that man could sing a chant to the honeybees like nobody else. And I've run into others in the villages who go around barefoot, can't read at all, and have all their prayers and chants committed to memory."

"I think I knew the one in Telchaquillo," I said. "*Don* Andres Coh was his name. He's dead now."

"Yeah, a horrible death."

"What happened?" Minnie asked.

Paul Hayes shook his head. "He became a *uay-miz*—a were-cat—and climbed on top of somebody's hut and they shot him."

"What?"

"Down here, *h-menoob* are respected, but they're also feared because of what they know," I explained. "Some of them only specialize in certain ceremonies—rain, corral blessing, first fruits—but most heal, too, with herbs and prayers. Yet the power to heal also scares people because it has another side, at least in their imaginations."

"You mean the power to curse," she said.

"That's right. Or to turn into a were-creature. So if a particular *h-men* was especially respected in his lifetime, fantastic stories tend to pop up about him after he's gone. Maybe a kind of tension release."

"Fascinating," Minnie said. She leaned forward and lowered her voice. "You don't think this fellow's going to suddenly turn into a were-something-or-other, do you?" she asked mischievously.

"Not until at least three of these bottles are gone," Blackburn volunteered. "Then everybody'll be seeing all kinds of things."

The girl April got up then, swaying slightly. "So is that the famous talking cross?" she asked, nodding at the little cross on the table with its white, flower-bordered smock.

"Well, just about every village has its own talking cross," Hayes explained. "At least in this part of the peninsula. Trouble is, most of the crosses don't talk very much, because their interpreters have forgotten how."

"But it's wearing a *huipil*," she said.

"That's because to the Maya the cross isn't an object so much as a deity, representing the sacred ceiba tree that units the upper and lower worlds," Hayes went on. "The symbolism far predates the arrival of Christianity. When the friars came, the Maya could relate to the symbol of the cross because they already had something similar. So they just adapted the cross to their own religious system. The cross is feminine in their thinking, hence the *huipil*. And that's why when the cross in Chan Santa Cruz first started to talk in 1850, telling the Maya to rise up and drive out the whites, it made perfect sense: There's an old pre-Columbian tradition of the prophets hearing voices and going into trances. That's how the prophet Jaguar, or Chilam Balam, first predicted the coming of the Spanish. Before they even arrived."

"But that was an interpolation," I said. "Something stuck in after the conquest to validate the old religious system."

Hayes smiled and reached for the bottle. "Are you sure?"

April turned and walked back toward Santos's hut. "I gotta pee."

Hayes sighed. "I'm afraid that girl's father's wasting his money."

"She's unhappy," Minnie said. "She just has to find herself."

"I'm more worried about what she's *already* found," Eric said then. "You see how she's walking?" He leaned toward Durán. "José, is she taking pills?"

The Mexican shrugged. "Who knows what she's taking? She doesn't consult me."

Blackburn leaned back. "Whatever."

By eleven that night, only we, the village men, and *don* Plutarco, the *h-men,* were left to keep vigil. Nothing would

happen until tomorrow; the rest of the night would be given
to storytelling and simply waiting, with a few prayers and
chants from time to time. Some of the men had put up hammocks and a few sat in chairs, like ourselves. A campfire
generated thick clouds of smoke, to keep away the
mosquitoes, though we'd also brought coils and Hayes
puffed on his cigars. April had returned around suppertime,
talked in a low voice with Durán, and then wandered back
away. When I asked, Santos said she was in one of his hammocks, asleep.

"She is not strong, that young woman," he said, taking a
seat near the altar table where the *h-men* sat. He leaned toward the *don* Plutarco. "Can you tell us, *don* Plutarco, about
the *ppuz* men?"

The shaman nodded and took a swallow of rum from the
glass he kept in front of him.

"You want to know about the *ppuzoob*?" he asked. "Yes, I
can tell you."

And, in the light of the flickering candles, he told us the
story, in Mayan, of the little hunchbacked race, or *ppuz* men,
who had lived on the earth until the time of a great flood.
They had tried to escape the waters by climbing into the
grinding stones that lay scattered throughout the fields, archaeological relics of Mayan civilization. But though the
grinding stones bore a superficial resemblance to canoes,
they were too heavy to float and the *ppuz* men drowned.

"*Letié,*" *don* Plutarco finished, "*uch ti u epoca Noe.*"

"What was that?" Hayes asked. "I didn't catch . . ."

"He said it happened in Noah's time," I said.

"I love it." Eric stretched. "One more case of combining
Judeo-Christian and Mayan mythology."

Hayes got up and walked over to Santos. He offered him a
cigar and then gave one to the *h-men*. Both men took the
gifts without words.

"Santos, you didn't tell me your grandfather was a *h-men*,
too."

The Mayan looked away.

"Is he still living?"

"He was my teacher," *don* Plutarco broke in. "A great *h-men*."

Santos said nothing and Hayes got up, came back to where we were, and sat down, arms folded. "Pretty evasive. I caught a glance of this guy's book, by the way. Bunch of scribblings in a school tablet. Not likely to be anything in there."

"And if there were?" Durán asked.

"What do you mean?"

"Would you try to buy it?"

"Buy it? What do you mean?"

"Borrow it, then."

"I'd try to photograph it, of course, just as I have the others."

"Of course." Durán picked up the rum bottle and took a swig.

Blackburn laughed. "Come on, José. Paul isn't a *gringo* imperialist."

Durán rose then and walked into the darkness.

"Touchy national sensibilities," Hayes sighed. "Thinks we're down here to steal the artifacts and rape the women. I thought better of the man."

"He's okay," Eric said. "It's the rum."

I looked over at Pepper, wondering what she made of the exchange, but her eyes were closed.

Sometime after midnight Plutarco began a chant in a high voice, dipping one of the leaves into the gourds and shaking out drops of sacred liquor onto the altar. His words ran together and I'd been away too long to make out many of them, but he was telling the gods that rain was needed.

Pepper shifted beside me. "Have I been asleep long?"

"Couple of hours."

"Missed anything?"

"Not really."

"What's he doing now?"

I told her. "There are four *Chaacs,* or rain gods, one for each cardinal direction. In the old days, the tapir was associ-

ated with water because of its long snout. When the Maya
first saw horses, they thought they were just big tapirs. And
when they heard about the archangels from the Spanish friars, they decided they were the same as the rain gods—they
figured that the Spanish just got it wrong. So now the four
rain gods have angels' names, and the Maya think they ride
horses."

"I love it. I guess that's how the culture's survived so
long."

"That's right," I said. "They adapt. Just like how, in the
old days, they wouldn't have let women this close during the
ceremony and the whole thing would've lasted three days." I
winked. "Imagine: No sex for three days."

"No wonder they cut it down to one." She got up. "I need
to walk around. Will I miss anything?"

"Probably not. There'll just be storytelling and some
prayers until tomorrow morning. That's when they dig the
pib, or earth oven, and put the sacred bread in to bake and
sacrifice the turkeys and hens."

"Sacrifice?"

"Well, they give them some liquor to drink first. Then
they slit their throats, cook 'em, offer some to the gods, and
everybody eats."

"I can't wait." She started away.

"I'll come with you," I said. "I need to stretch my legs."

We walked alongside the hut, with its sleeping occupants,
and out into the narrow lane. Here and there a candle flickered inside a hut and from one or two came the steady glow
of an electric light bulb. I tripped on a stone and a dog skit-
tered away in the darkness.

"Good rum, huh?" Pepper asked.

"I haven't had but three or four glasses. It's customary to
drink on ceremonial occasions. It's, well, *religious*."

She jabbed me playfully. "You're such a spiritual person."

I grabbed her around the waist and pulled her to me. "I'll
spirit you."

She laughed, then suddenly pulled away, and I saw Durán
coming up the lane toward us, his gait unsteady.

He passed us with a nod and headed back into Santos's yard. The spell was broken. Pepper and I followed.

Late the next morning, as the men were removing the bread-stuffs and cooked fowl from the earth oven, Paul Hayes looked around. "Is April still sleeping? Somebody better wake her up and tell her it's time to eat."

Durán walked back to Santos's hut and peered in.

"She isn't here." He turned to one of the women who was squatting outside making tortillas. "Have you seen the young *gringa*?"

The woman shrugged. "When I woke up she was gone."

"Shit," Hayes mumbled. "And where the hell's Eric?"

As if in answer, Blackburn appeared around the corner of the hut.

"Somebody say food?"

"April's taken off somewhere," Hayes said.

Blackburn sighed. "It figures. Well, I guess we'd better find her. There aren't more than a hundred people in this place. Somebody's seen her." He turned to me. "Can you and Pepper take the south half of the village? And José, if you and Minnie can take the other half, Paul and I will check the road to the site, in case she wandered out to the ruins."

Pepper and I decided to take opposite sides of the street. For the first five huts we had no luck. It was in the second block that I found her.

I recognized her by her voice, because she was singing a lullaby. When I stuck my head in I saw two hammocks, both seemingly occupied. The nearer one, though, was gently swinging and I recognized its occupant as April. She was holding a baby close against her breast, while an old, tooth-less woman sat in a chair near the back door, stirring the ashes of a fire. A little girl, eight or nine, stood beside the hammock, looking down at the pale young woman and the infant.

I couldn't make out the form in the other hammock be-cause of the sheets wound around it, but the form wasn't moving.

"Hello, April," I said.

She looked up and I barely recognized her from the radiance in her face.

"Hi. The baby's mother's sick. I went to see Xmari, here." She nodded at the little girl. "She lives next door. She kept saying, *enferma,* sick, and pointing over here."

"And you came to see," I said.

"Yeah. I think the baby's mother has some kind of fever. They were hoping when the ceremony's over that we'd give her a ride to the doctor in Chetumal."

I looked down at the ill woman. Her eyes were closed and she was shivering.

"Malaria would be my guess," I said. "Sure, we'll get her in."

I helped April up and she reluctantly handed the baby to the old woman. "I think this is her grandmother, but she seems to be almost blind. The baby was crying and I asked where its father was, but I'm not sure she understood, because my Spanish isn't very good and she answered in Mayan and she kept saying *kim-in* or something."

"*Cimi,*" I said. "It means dead."

"Oh." She looked back over her shoulder at the house.

"It seems like such a shame. These people are so poor and this little baby . . ." She looked up at me. "I gave the old woman a hundred pesos. Was that all right?"

"That was fine," I said.

"I hope the baby's all right. She was crying so much. So many babies die down here and she's so little." Tears were running down her cheeks and I helped her into the little street. "If I lost another one . . ."

"*Oyé!*" A man's voice broke in and I saw José Durán approaching from the end of the block. Pepper started forward toward April and me, but Durán brushed past her. "What are you doing?" he demanded.

"What do you mean?" I asked.

"You know what I mean." The odor of alcohol engulfed me and I saw his eyes were red from lack of sleep. "First one, and then the other, and now this one, *no*?"

"You're not making any sense," I said.

He reached out unsteadily and tried to knock my arm away from April's.

"Take your hands off her."

"You're drunk," I told him.

"Cabrón!" he yelled and swung at me.

I leaned back, brushed into April, and the blow glanced off my chin.

April gave a little shriek. "José!"

He came toward me then, head down, and I stepped out of the way, but he grabbed me around the waist and bore me back against the stone wall that marked the edge of the street. I kneed him to get free and was straightening when another movement caught my eye.

Two soldiers were standing at the end of the block, automatic rifles cradled in their arms, and a smaller man in starched fatigues was striding toward us.

"What are you people doing?" *Teniente* Tapia demanded.

▰Ten

No one spoke and Tapia stopped in front of us. "I asked a question and I require an answer."

"It was an accident," I began but he cut me off.

"*Señor,* you're drunk," he accused Durán. "I can smell it."

"We're archaeologists, working at the site here," I explained. "We were invited to a rain ceremony in the village. There was some drinking and—"

Tapia exhaled loudly. "And so you decided to act like the villagers. *Señores,* I am not a village policeman. I am here because of reports of illegal activity. But I warn you, this is dangerous country. Behave yourselves."

Durán looked away and I promised the officer it wouldn't happen again.

Durán and I wandered back to Santos's place, taking opposite sides of the little lane. As we got to the front gate we were hailed by Blackburn, coming toward us with Hayes and Minnie. "Did you find her?"

I explained about the sick woman. "Pepper's helping her get the woman to the van. I'll go into Chetumal with them to find the doctor."

Blackburn nodded. "Sure. But what happened to you two? Did you have to tackle the girl when you found her?"

"I tripped," I said.

Blackburn looked over at the Mexican.

"I fell against the doctor," Durán said.

"Look," I said, "what's more important is the army's here.

We ran into a patrol. They claim they have a report of illegal activity."

"Like last time, eh?" Hayes asked, taking out a cigar and snipping off the end. "Who was the leader, by the way? Not a short little bastard who strutted like a turkey?"

"Yeah," I said. "Tapia."

Hayes jammed the cigar into his mouth. "Mark my words, that little bastard's not your run-of-the-mill corrupt official. He has the makings of a fine fanatic or I miss my guess."

"Maybe the country needs a few," I said and nobody disagreed.

It was almost eleven when Pepper, April, and I got back to the *cabañas*. The doctor in Chetumal, a fat-faced little man named Gómez, had given the sick woman a shot of penicillin and some quinine tablets, on the theory that one of the two ought to work. Then we'd picked up some baby formula at a grocery and driven back to the village, where we unloaded the woman, made sure that child and mother were comfortable, and then drove back to the main highway and on to our camp.

"I wonder if she'll live," April said in a faraway voice as we stopped in Geraldo's parking lot. "That doctor didn't seem to know much."

"We did what we could," I said, "and that was the doctor she wanted to see."

"At least she didn't ask to see the *h-men,*" Pepper said.

"He probably wouldn't have treated her," I said. "Some of these guys have a pretty sharp eye for what they can handle."

"You were great with that baby," I told April, shutting off the engine. "You seem to have a way with kids. The little girl, Xmari, didn't want you to leave."

"I've always loved children," she said. "When I was in high school . . ."

"Yes?"

"It doesn't matter. I'm here now. I'm going to be an archaeologist."

"Not if you don't want to be," Pepper said.

April gave a little laugh. "You don't know my old man."

We collapsed into our hammocks that night, too tired to worry about lurking drug smugglers, and I dreamed I was walking along a jungle trail, trying to find Pepper. It was nearly dark and I knew I had to find her before the last light, because there were things lurking in the darkness. I called out, but there was no reply, only a jabbering of monkeys in the branches high above.

The trail split and for a long time I stared at the ground, trying to find signs that would tell me which way to go. But there were no signs.

Most people, I knew, went to the right in such a situation, so maybe she had, too. I started down the right fork.

There, in front of me, was a towering pyramid, dappled with late evening sunlight, and on the temple facade at its summit was a long-snouted rain god's nose.

I called her name again and it bounced back to me from the stone walls. I started forward, toward a low archway into the inner courtyard of the pyramid complex, and as I did a sense of dread overwhelmed me, as if I had entered the den of some indescribable horror.

I came out into the courtyard and saw the low platform in the center: a sacrificial altar. Things were whirring past my head now, emitting a low howling, and I sensed that they were the souls of the sacrificial victims. All at once I didn't care about Pepper, I only wanted to escape. I whirled and ducked back through the archway to the outside and saw her, standing at the place where the trail spilled out of the jungle. She was smiling—not the tolerant, good-natured smile of a woman whose lover has made a fool of himself, but a lascivious smile that grew as she opened her arms and motioned for me to come to her. I hurried forward and it was only as she put her arms around me that I sensed the trap and heard her voice, in Spanish:

"*Alan, creías que me podías escapar?* Did you really think you could get away?"

I felt her arms turning to vines as she drew me against her thorny bosom, and I woke up with a scream.

"What is it?" Pepper was shaking me. "What happened? Is there somebody outside?"

"No, just a nightmare," I said, as the fog fell away. "I dreamed about a *Xtabai*."

"A what?"

I rubbed my eyes. "It's Mayan folklore. A man out walking at night sees a beautiful woman. She calls out to him and when they embrace she turns into a tree with thorny branches and strangles him."

"Did you recognize this . . . *Xtabai*?" she asked.

"No," I lied.

"Well, you're getting back into this with a bang. Get some sleep. I promise I'll keep guard against this bogey-woman."

The next day, as we worked, I thought about the nightmare. The conventional psychological interpretation was that the *Xtabai* represented guilt, because she usually appeared to a man who was where he shouldn't be, like coming home from his lover's house late at night or staggering back drunk from the cantina. So what was I feeling guilty about? I tried to recall the dream exactly. The phantasm had been Pepper—or had it? The more I thought, the more it seemed the image hadn't been clear. Pepper was blond, and the *Xtabai* had had dark hair, like a Mayan woman—or a Mexican.

Felicia.

I was feeling guilty because I was back down here, with Pepper, at the same place where things had gone to hell with Felicia. But why? Was I blocking something out? Was there something that had happened with Felicia that should make me feel guilty, something I'd repressed for fifteen years?

Xtabai, literally She of the Rope, a reference to the ancient Mayan goddess Xtab, the goddess of suicides. For the Maya, the rope was the preferred way of killing oneself, hence the gnarled, strangling limbs of the phantasm.

"What's wrong?"

I realized Pepper was staring at me from her side of the excavation pit.

"You look like you're about to keel over," she said. "Do you need to sit down in the shade?"

I shook my head. "I'm okay."

"Are you sure?"

Before I could answer, Minnie O'Toole appeared at the edge of our excavation, wiping her face with a handkerchief. "Do you want to come see what I found?" she asked.

I nodded and hoisted myself out of the pit, past the two workers who were screening our back dirt.

"José says it's jade. I wish Eric was here to see it, too."

Pepper and I walked through the baking sun to a flat-topped rubble mound with a trench going through the middle of it and a makeshift Visquine cover propped over the end of the trench for shade, while the workers up top stood under a poplar tree, waiting to resume their screening. Durán was down on his knees, carefully brushing something with a little painter's brush, and Paul Hayes stood at the top of the trench rocking slightly on his heels.

"Nice little Classic-period artifact," he said. "May be something to this site yet."

I stood back, not wanting to crowd Durán, but Minnie pushed me forward.

"It's right there, where José's working."

Durán stopped and got to his feet. I saw a tiny, half-moon-shaped piece of greenish stone.

"It's a blade," he said and for the first time I saw something besides resentment in his eyes. "Someone deposited it here as an offering over a thousand years ago."

"Is it part of a burial, then?" I asked.

The Mexican nodded. "I think so. But just now I want to photograph it in place and then we'll clear away a little more of the loose soil around it."

I looked at the area where he'd been working: It was as clean and free of debris as any excavation I'd ever seen, something that would photograph perfectly. As someone who always had trouble keeping his own units clean, I felt admiration for his skill.

"Is that what you would do, Dr. Graham?" His tone was sarcastic and I felt myself flush slightly, despite the heat.

"Arqueólogo," I said, using his professional title, "I don't think I could contribute anything to the fine job you've done."

He gave me a sidelong glance, then nodded. *"Muy bién.* I'll get the menu board and the camera."

I started away and realized Minnie was right behind me.

"I hope you two are making up."

"What?"

She smiled. "I caught a glimpse of that business yesterday, but I didn't say anything. I just went on back and pretended to run into Paul and Eric. I figured José was just drunk. But . . ."

"But what?"

We stopped under a tree beside the van, where the equipment was stored. "I may just be a homely librarian from Iowa, but too much has been happening in the last few weeks for me to take much as a coincidence."

I picked up the camera. "And?"

"You don't have to be on an expedition to see what happens to people under pressure. I saw it happen in my own library. They brought in a new director, cut the budget, and nobody knew whose job would be the next to go. People started acting in ways they never would have ordinarily—and they slept on clean sheets, in air conditioning!"

"Well, I have to admit it seems like José resents me, but I don't know why, unless Pepper's told him so much about me . . ."

"She's been complimentary, of course, but, so far as I can see, perfectly accurate: She said you were a gentleman, 'the old kind,' I think were her words, and that you seemed to undervalue yourself. But she said you'd also managed to start up and develop a business and keep people employed even though you weren't trained as a businessman."

"Actually, my old professor, Sam MacGregor, started the business and his reputation got most of the clients."

Minnie folded her arms. "She also said you couldn't accept a compliment."

I shrugged. "Call it upbringing."

"You know, Alan, she and I have had some pretty interesting girl-to-girl chats."

"Oh, God."

"You don't have to get embarrassed. She just told me you have some insecurities, because you're a little older than she is. And she told me she knew you were reluctant to come down here because you'd had a bad experience here years ago."

"Sounds like you know my life history."

"No, I really don't. But I do know that girl loves you, probably more than you realize, and whatever doubts you have, you need to put them aside. I don't know what happened a long time ago, but this is now. You can't live in the past. I learned that, if I've learned anything."

"Archaeologists always live in the past," I said, trying to make a joke of it.

"You know what I mean."

"Yeah. Well, thanks, Minnie."

"Don't thank me for anything yet. Thank me when it's all over."

"When *what's* all over?"

"The field season. I'm telling you, Alan, I sense undercurrents here."

"Well, it's not encouraging to have the army all over the place and people turning up dead in the lagoon," I said. "But that doesn't have anything to do with us."

"I don't know. I still feel something. Oh, you can laugh and call me a crazy old fool, but I have a good sense of people."

"I'm sure."

She leaned toward me, lowering her voice, though no one was nearby. "I have a feeling that Paul knows a lot more than he's letting on."

"About what?"

"Well, that's the question, isn't it? But all these trips here and there and everywhere, just to look at old manuscripts. I've tried to get him to tell me more, but he always puts me off, says it's too technical. And then there's April."

"What about her?"

"She's not here today."

"She had some stomach problems," I said. "We all get that down here from time to time."

"Eric's not here, either."

"He's the project director. I'm not on site all the time at home, either: You have to write field notes, buy supplies, make calls home, fill out customs forms . . ."

"What I'm saying is, when one's not here, usually the other isn't, either."

I turned slowly toward her, trying to decide how to respond. "You think there's something between them?"

"Would that be so surprising?"

"Probably not. On digs there's a tendency to play musical beds—or hammocks. And it wouldn't be the first time the director moved on some single female."

"No." She smiled and lifted the menu board from its place in one of the metal toolboxes. "And her father's rich."

I hefted the camera and started back into the sun.

▰ ELEVEN

That evening, as we swam just before dinner, I told Pepper about what Minnie had said.

"And their *cabañas* are next to each other," I said.

"I don't believe it. Eric's not, well . . ."

"Anybody can be tempted," I said.

"You're thinking about that Cynthia woman you met during that Corps project in Jackson."

"Sure." The fact was, there was a time when I'd thought about her a lot, though nothing had happened. "I'm just saying Eric's human."

"I'm not saying he isn't," she said, circling lazily in the water. "But I still think if there's any romance in April's life, it's between her and José. All you have to do is look at his reaction yesterday at the *Chhachaac* when he saw you with your hand on her arm.

"Well, maybe he considers himself her protector."

I kicked and rolled over onto my back. In the distance I could see the little line of *cabañas,* first Hayes's, close to the steps that led up to the restaurant and Gonzales home; then Durán's, with the door closed; Minnie's, where I thought I saw her outside in a white smock, probably feeding her cats; then the hut Pepper and I shared; then April's, and finally, at the far end, between our house and the big lab structure, the hut belonging to Eric Blackburn.

We'd looked in on April when we'd gotten back and she'd

71

said she felt better. Blackburn, however, had gone into Chetumal, though for what reason she didn't say.

I tried to envision the two of them together, but it didn't work. For one thing, he was older than she was by at least ten years.

I glanced over at Pepper, ten years younger than I was, and muttered to myself.

"Did you say something?" she asked and swam over.

"No."

"So have you decided if you knew the murdered man?" she asked.

"It hasn't come to me, if I do," I said. "But I keep wondering why he washed up here, of all places."

"They must've kidnapped him from somewhere else," she said, treading water, "and dumped him in the lake. Or do you think he was in a drug smuggling gang and they got into an argument on a boat?" She swam out a few more strokes. "That would mean the smugglers were probably unloading somewhere near here, not up the coast. And why would they be unloading on a lake? That doesn't make any sense. Unless they were landing on the beach, then trekking west across the strip that separates the bay and the lake. But there are still a couple of rivers to cross."

"Don't go out so far," I called.

"Why? It's wonderful."

"Yeah, but you never know."

"Never know what? Oh, you're thinking of those Mayan legends about water creatures that live down in the depths and grab people."

"That's ridiculous. I just meant that if you got a cramp . . ."

". . . you might not be able to save me. What if *you* got a cramp?"

"I don't get cramps. Let's head for shore."

"In a minute."

She was taunting me, of course. I looked back at the *cabañas,* just seven little pebbles now, with Geraldo's skiff barely visible bumping against the diving board.

If someone had dumped the man at the northern end of the

lake, he might have floated down this far, but why would he have been wearing a life vest? He had to have been in a boat. . . . Geraldo was right. It had to have been a warning.

But to whom?

Unless, of course, he'd been killed here and the vest had been a ruse for some reason. In that case, the killer might be closer than any of us thought . . .

At the top of the cliff I glimpsed movement and saw a dark-colored vehicle stopping in front of Geraldo's. The Rover. Eric Blackburn was back.

It was just after dark when we started along the beach for dinner at the restaurant. Blackburn had preceded us, calling cheerily for us to come as he passed our hut, and a few seconds later we'd seen April go past, not walking with him, but close enough behind to have him in sight. I went out onto the beach and looked up the beach at them, waiting for Pepper.

Yes, it was certainly possible. Their *cabañas* were next to each other and that made it easy . . . Well, it was no concern of mine.

A scrawny yellow cat appeared from the bushes and stared at me, to see if I was going to feed it or throw a rock. Then I heard Minnie's voice.

"Kanmiz, where are you? Come to Mama." She appeared from behind her *cabaña* then, something I took to be food in her hand. "There you are, you bad boy."

She saw me and stopped. "Not *you*, Alan."

"I didn't think so."

"I was talking to Kanmiz there. It means yellow cat in Mayan, I understand."

"Well"—I laughed—"actually it means snake cat. You have to give it a hard *k* sound. But then you have to give the vowel the right intonation or you may be saying hammock cat, or hammock broom, or sky broom, or sky cat, or—"

"What an impossible language. It's all I can do to get by in Spanish." She set the scraps down in front of the cat and it considered whether to eat it.

"Well, I'm not so particular," Minnie said. "Ready to go up to dinner?"

Pepper came out then and we walked along together, passing the closed huts of José Durán and, at the end, Paul Hayes.

"I guess Paul and José are already up at the restaurant," Minnie said. "Getting a jump on cocktail hour."

But she was wrong, at least about Hayes, because as we reached the top of the steps we saw him in earnest conversation with the landlord. The American saw us coming, said something, and I saw Geraldo raise his hands, as if in exasperation.

"*Buenas tardes, don Alan,*" he said. "*Señoritas.*" I thought his smile was forced.

Hayes's face broke into a grin. "Well, everybody ready for some *relleno blanco*?" he asked and followed us into the dining area.

I watched the others during dinner, curious both about Hayes's behavior and about Eric and April. Maybe I was just a dirty old man. Or maybe I wanted to think that Pepper's love for me was something special and that, despite absolute knowledge to the contrary, such cases were rare.

But Blackburn and April, though they sat beside each other, showed no signs of affection, though I knew that didn't prove anything. As for Hayes, he drank more beer than was usual for him and by the end of the meal was tipsy, regaling us with stories of a trip he'd once made to Brazil. Durán, on the other hand, drank sparingly and more than once his eyes met mine and then darted away, as if there were something on his mind. Once or twice I saw a frowning Geraldo, bustling about, giving orders to the two waiters but I didn't see the man called Jordan. When the meal was over, I excused myself and started out for a walk on the beach. After talking with Minnie at the site, I had a sense of dread that I needed to walk off. Or was it the talk with Minnie, after all? Last night's dream kept popping into my mind, grabbing my attention with gnarled, rootlike fingers.

I stopped just outside the door, breathing in the warm night air. All at once I sensed someone behind me and turned.

José Durán was standing a few feet away, but when he saw me turn he looked away.

I was about to start toward him when a hand plucked my arm.

"Doctor, momentito, por favor."

I looked down and saw the stricken face of Geraldo Gonzales Pech.

"What is it?" I asked. "Is there a problem?"

"Sí, Doctor." He threw up his hands and I followed him into the little cubicle that served as his office. He shut the door and slumped into the chair behind his desk. "How long have you known me, Doctor? Fifteen years? Twenty?"

"More or less."

"And you know that I'm an honest man."

"Absolutely."

"And I run a good, decent restaurant and I only rent *cabañas* to respectable people and I hire only servants that can be trusted."

"Certainly."

"Then why are all these things happening?" He threw up his hands.

"You mean the dead man on the beach?"

"Sí, but there's more. One of my servants has run away, a little girl I hired just three weeks ago. You try to help these people and look what happens!"

"Probably eloped with her boyfriend," I said. "But surely you can find someone else."

"No one wants to work here now. They're all afraid. And now there's this business with *don* Pablo."

"What business?"

"He's saying that while he was gone today someone broke into his *cabaña* and stole from him."

"So that's what the two of you were talking about."

"Exactly. He was asking about my employees." Geraldo wrung his hands. "He will be telling everyone that it was one of my people who broke into his *cabaña.*"

"Was anything stolen?"

"He only said someone went through his papers. Why

would any of my people go through his papers? Doctor, if the word gets out that guests aren't safe here . . ."

"I'll talk to Dr. Hayes," I said. "Maybe I can find out what happened and calm him down."

"Would you?" Geraldo's face brightened and he shot up from his chair and grabbed my hand with both of his. "Thank you, my friend."

I walked down to the beach. There was a light on in Hayes's hut and a smell of cigar smoke floated out on the breeze. From inside came the sound of a Scott Joplin ragtime tune.

"Paul?"

A second later the door opened and Hayes was inviting me in, his pumpkin face glowing from the liquor.

"Alan, just in time to have a little toast."

He offered me a glass and a rum bottle and I poured in just enough to toast with.

"What are we celebrating?"

"That it wasn't taken." He flopped back into his hammock and I took the single folding chair.

"What wasn't taken?"

He grinned slyly, rocking backward and forward. "What they were looking for."

"Paul, Geraldo's pretty upset. He thinks his business is going to be ruined if people go around saying it isn't safe to stay here."

"Well, it isn't, goddamn it. But I didn't say I suspected any of his people. I just said he needed to put better locks on the doors. He just took it to mean I was accusing his maid. He's like all Latins—sensitive as hell."

"I might be, too, after a murder on my beach. The killers could still be around here."

"That body could've drifted in from anywhere. It was just Geraldo's bad luck it washed up here. Screw Geraldo. He's doing fine from this expedition. I happen to know what Eric's paying him and it's twice what any local would give him for these rat traps."

He must have seen the expression on my face because he reached out then to pat my arm. "Oh, I kr ow he's a friend of yours. Everybody in archaeology rents from Geraldo. Hell, José's known him almost as long as you have. Everybody from INAH in Mexico City stays here when they're in these parts. Geraldo's not going belly up anytime soon."

"I hope not."

"But I'm glad you dropped by. I've been meaning to talk to you." He reached over with the bottle and filled my glass. "Drink up. You're going to need it before the night's out."

▰▰TWELVE

"You'll appreciate it, too," Hayes said, "because you know Mayan." He snorted. "All these other archaeologists, digging down here for almost a hundred years, and how many of them ever took the trouble to learn more than a few words? Is it any wonder they never cracked the hieroglyphs? That it was epigraphers, linguists, people trained in languages, that did it, instead of excavators?"

"And you have something new on the glyphs."

He gave the hammock another shove. "Yes and no."

"Paul, talk plain."

"Can I trust you, Alan?"

"I don't know. Are you going to confess a murder?"

His grin widened. "No. Something worse." He paused to let the statement take effect. "At least as far as the academic world is concerned."

"Oh? Plagiarism? Doctored data?"

"God, no, Alan, much worse than that: *an unpopular theory.*"

"Oh. You think the world was created in six days."

"Don't patronize me, Alan. I may be drunk, but I'm not *that* drunk."

"Sorry."

"Forget it." He swung back and forth for a few seconds, as if waiting for me to try to pry out further details, but I kept silent. Finally he reached over and refilled his glass. I watched him drink and when he'd finished, he wiped his mouth with the back of his hand.

"You've heard of John Dance Williams."

"The British explorer. Sure."

"He visited this area in the years just before the Second World War. He was an Englishman with a Sandhurst education. The army sent him to British Honduras—what's now Belize—but he resigned his commission for reasons nobody knows. Some kind of scandal, probably. Afterward he just sort of went native and roamed British Honduras, Guatemala, and southern Mexico—a kind of soldier of fortune."

I nodded. "I read his travel book, but it was a long time ago. He was a good observer of Mayan life."

"As you know, he picked up a couple of Mayan languages— Yucatec and Mopán—*and* he was fluent in Spanish, of course, though in those days damn few of the Maya in these parts could speak Spanish."

Another world, I thought, without roads, electric lights, telephones . . .

"When the Germans went into Poland in '39 he saw what was coming and went back to England. He enlisted in a regiment as a private, the same way Lawrence of Arabia did after the First War. He was killed during a secret commando operation in Norway."

I waited, knowing he was too wound up now to stop.

"For most of my career," Hayes said, "I've had a certain interest, but I've kept it to myself, because it was a career wrecker. You know the academic world, Alan: People talk about intellectual freedom, but an unpopular idea is a stake through the heart."

"That happens," I agreed.

"But a few years ago a friend of mine in England who knows about my interests found a letter from Williams, written just a few weeks before he died, to a professor at Oxford. He made a copy of the letter and I'm going to show it to you."

Hayes pushed himself out of the hammock, padded across the cement floor to a little metal lockbox, and, with a key that was attached to a cord around his neck, opened the box and removed an oilskin pouch. He opened the pouch, took out a piece of folded paper, and passed it over to me.

I leaned forward to get the benefit of the bare overhead bulb and opened the paper.

It was a photocopy of a document in cursive script, but even as dim as the letters were I could make out the words:

May 21, 1942
Hodder on Binford
Kent

My dear Wilfrid:

I regret that we never had the opportunity to finish our conversation, because I feel that you deserve an answer to some of the questions you posed about what you regard as my "fantastic hypothesis." I shall shortly be shipping out and I have a feeling that unless I set this in writing now there may not be another opportunity.

As you know, while I was in Central America I suffered several bouts of malaria-paludismo, as they call it down there. The last time was in Bacalar in June of '39. I cannot adequately describe to you the sensations that the disease causes. First a malaise, then a fever, then terrible chills, and finally delirium. For a week I lay in my hammock, not knowing whether it was night or day. It is not an experience I recommend. Dr. Carrillo, the local medico, took care of me. During this time he recounted to me the many ruins he had visited in the interior, while making the rounds of some of the villages: The Maya are a very pragmatic people and they will utilize the services of their native healers alongside those of modern medical men without any sense of contradiction. Carrillo had an assistant, a boy named Jildo, who came from the interior and who knew the locations of many of these ruins. When I was sufficiently recovered, Jildo took me by horse to a little Cruzob village forty or fifty miles in-

land. *As I explained to you, the Cruzob are the children and grandchildren of the rebellious Maya who
worshipped the talking cross and tried to drive out the
ladinos in the middle of the last century and they've
stayed pretty well hidden in the jungles ever since, expecting an attack of the dzulob, which is what they call
the ladinos. They are receptive to British and Americans, however, because they have the notion that English speakers will some day bring them guns and
allow them to push the ladinos off the peninsula. Each
of these little villages has its own priest or interpreter
of the cross and each one of these gentleman has his
own sacred book, which is kept in the thatched temple
hut or balam nah, as they call it. The men of the village
serve turns as guards to protect the holy of holies,
though now this is largely a formality, since a sudden
invasion by Mexicans is, to put it mildly, somewhat unlikely. This Jildo introduced me to his uncle, a man
named Eleuterio Euan, the village witch doctor or, as
they term it, h-men. I was only in the village a day before I was struck down by another attack of the paludismo and for the next two weeks my mind is a blank,
unless you count some rather fantastic nightmares of
Mayan gods and goddesses, which stemmed, no
doubt, from an excess of exposure to the culture! I am
told that don Eleut applied herbs and potions, and I
gradually recovered, though whether his medicines
were the reason or whether it was a natural process I
am not able to say. In any event, a friendship developed between us and he gradually came to trust me
and to appreciate my interest in the history and culture of his people. Gradually, he explained the mean-
ings of some of the old prophesies and how an ancient
prophet, or chilan, had foretold the coming of the
Spanish before the actual arrival of the first Conquis-
tadores. One day, which I well remember, we were
walking through the village plaza—really little more
than a cleared space surrounded by pole-sided,
thatched huts—and he volunteered, quite suddenly,*

that I reminded him of the stranger from the prophesies who arrived here from over the water in a remote time. Then, for the first time, he went into the temple hut, brought out his old handwritten book, and read to me how this stranger had come here in Katun 10 Ahau, which is the designation they give for one of their periods of 7200 days, which, in our calendar, comes to a stretch of about 20 years. It said this stranger had come from the east and that he was the vassal of a great king, and that after the stranger had been in Yucatán for a while, he, too, was made a king, because there were no more sons of the royal lineage, and he stayed and married an Indian woman and had children by her. He died, finally, in a great battle, inside the city walls, protecting his people. Then don *Eleut said there was a site in the interior, not far away, where this foreign king had lived and reigned, and he promised that one day he would take me there. I sensed that I could not press him on it and, in fact, I must admit that I wondered if the old man was actually bending the sacred words a bit to flatter me. Maybe he still nourished the old delusion that some English speaker would bring guns and money and he hoped to persuade me that I should be that man! Nevertheless, there was nothing to do but wait until he felt it was time. The time came a week or so later, when we were walking in the forest and quite suddenly came upon a ruined building. This was no surprise, because ruins are everywhere, but this building seemed to be in excellent condition, except for some minor destruction by vines and tree roots. Then, as I stood there, with monkeys chattering in the trees above us, I realized there were other buildings, just visible through the foliage, and I knew that this was quite possibly another great undiscovered site. Many of these ruins, of course, were visited by Gann and others, so I asked Eleut if other English speakers had come here before. He smiled and led me along a trail, past several stone buildings in as good condition as the first one, and he pointed out a raised causeway that resembled a road, elevated about a meter or two above ground level. I can hardly describe to you the eerie sensation, being deep in the jungle, with parrots squawking in the trees above, and the rustling sound of creatures in the underbrush. It was as if this place had been deserted yesterday and all the inhabitants whisked off to some other level of existence. Vines hung like snakes from the gnarled tree limbs and I had the sense of eyes peering at us from deep within the recesses of the temples. At last we came to a central plaza, and I stepped around a line of toppled limestone obelisks, all bearing the carved visages of gods and covered with hieroglyphs. At the end of this plaza, set upon a platform of stone, was a single temple, slightly larger than the rest, with a roof adornment that resembled latticework, disappearing into the tops of the trees. The broad stone steps that led to the top of the platform were broken by the forest growth but, following my guide's example, I managed to scramble my way to the top until I stood on the porch of the temple itself.*

That was when I saw the masques.

It would be difficult to describe the impression this made on me, to see a line of human heads, one above the other, on each side of the central doorway into the inner temple. There were three of these sculptures on each side, and all were remarkable enough that I felt they might come to life at any moment, peering out from the stone framing of the door. These were typically Indian, with almond eyes and the large noses that one sees among today's indigenous inhabitants. All had ear ornaments and some had glyphs carved in their cheeks. It was, however, the seventh head, which was placed directly above the door, that interested me the most. As I stared at it I felt I was looking at my own face. That may sound like a bit of an exaggeration and, Wilfrid, I know you may think I was still suffering from the fever. But what I mean to express is that the features of this sculpture were perfectly European and

it clearly had a moustache and full beard, which, as
you know, is almost unheard of among the indigenous
peoples. I turned to Eleut and saw him smiling and he
told me then that we had reached the site, which he
called Lubaanah, meaning "fallen house" in Maya,
because some of the temples have collapsed due to the
undergrowth. He showed me a mural on the interior of
this porch, and, though the art work was shaded by the
roof and the jungle, I managed to make out a line of
warriors in battle. The effect was incredible—colorful
lines of naked bodies, armed with spears, spear throw-
ers, and bows, in a fight to the death with some Indian
enemy, and there, in the forefront, the king. You will
probably think I am exaggerating, but, Wilfrid, I can
tell you that his face was identical with the one in the
seventh mask. The beard was quite visible and they
had painted his body white, as if his skin were lighter
than theirs.

I had weeks before used the last of my film and so I
was left to make sketches, which is what I did for the
remainder of the day, until Eleut told me it was late
and time for us to return to the village. I did, however,
dig into some of the piles of rubble with the camp
shovel I had with me. Unfortunately, there was little to
be found besides a curious fragment of dark stone
with some strange scratchings on its surface, which I
have sketched in the addendum to this letter. This
stone I brought back to the village. Shortly afterwards
I returned to Bacalar for provisions. But I was still
weak and suffered something of a relapse, so that I
was forced to spend several more weeks resting. I decided at that time to return to England to recuperate
and to raise money for a formal expedition. But before
many days the war intervened and when I returned to
England we were in the midst of hostilities with Ger-
many. It seemed incumbent on me to do my patriotic
duty as soon as my strength was restored and so you
see me now. I shall shortly be doing my own small bit
against the Hun and I have no idea when, if ever, I

shall have an opportunity to return to Central America. Nevertheless, you can now see the basis for the opinion I expressed to you that the sixteenth-century Spanish were not the first white men to arrive in Central America and that even that notable Italian navigator, Columbus, was a Johnny-come-lately.

There were a few words of well wishes and then the signature, in bold, clear cursive:

John Dance Williams

I set the letter down on the aluminum camp table.

"So now you know my secret," Hayes said. "I've always been a diffusionist at heart. There are so many data in favor of it—the Jomon pottery from Ecuador that points to a Japanese arrival two thousand years before Christ, the Olmec heads with their negroid features, the Paraibo stone from Brazil, the various Welsh and Ogham inscriptions from different parts of the New World, the resemblances between the Southeast Asian and Mayan calendars . . ."

He waited for my reaction, but I didn't give him any.

"As far as I'm concerned," he went on, "it's willful insanity to deny the evidence when it stares you in the face. But for a hundred and fifty years, American archaeologists have insisted that, aside from the Vikings, whose colonization they dismiss as a short-term phenomenon, nobody from the Old World could possibly have set foot in the New World before 1492. And anyone who dares to suggest otherwise is branded a heretic and a crank."

I took a deep breath, choosing my words carefully. "I'm not sure anybody says *nobody* from the Old World could have come before Columbus, just that there wasn't any sustained influence."

Hayes guffawed. "Of course. They stonewall until you show them irrefutable evidence and then they say, 'Well, it's possible one or two people were swept up on the beach,' but they don't mean it. It's just too much against the accepted dogma: The peoples of the New World had to have developed on their own, without any help from outside. It's not science, it's a damned *political* position, and if you say anything else, you're called a racist."

"There's truth to that, of course," I said. "But you have to admit, Paul: The evidence for diffusionism is pretty murky. I mean, the Paraibo inscription comes from a piece of stone that was lost, so we don't even have an original, and the Jomon stuff can just as easily be an indigenous development, and as for the Olmec heads—"

"Oh, I know, Alan, you've been indoctrinated, I didn't expect anything else."

"Paul, what I'm saying is it's a question of evidence *and* mechanics. You not only have to show evidence that can't be refuted, but you have to provide a mechanism for it to have gotten where it was, and I don't mean Vikings hiking all over Oklahoma and Arkansas and randomly leaving writings on cave walls that some epigrapher says reads something like, 'Ten men heading north.'"

"Haven't I just showed you evidence?"

"That letter from John Dance Williams? Come on, Paul. The man was already half dead from malaria. He sees a sculptured head and a temple mural and says this looks like a European? How do we know *what* Williams saw? Hell, we don't even have his original letter here."

"No, we don't."

"He says he didn't have a camera, so he sketched the things he saw, but do we have his sketches?"

Hayes shook his head. "The sketches have disappeared."

"And the drawing he says he made of the stone with markings on it?"

"We don't have that, either."

"Then what's left?"

The older man licked his lips and reached into the box again. He removed a small object, wrapped in a soft cloth.

"The only thing we have," he said, opening the cloth with a flourish, "is the stone itself."

THIRTEEN

I stared down at the little slab of green stone. Perhaps eight inches long and three across, it had a dull luster, and on its surface had been scratched what appeared to me to be a random series of lines at different angles.

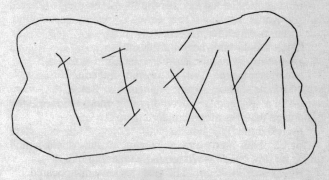

"Where did you get this?" I asked, turning the object over in my hands.

"Same place as the letter. My contact knows the Williams family. John's sister had the original letter and some of her brother's other things and after I'd read the copy of the letter, I called and asked if there was anything else, like maps or drawings and, voilà!"

I stared down at the object. "Looks like random scratchings to me."

Hayes took it back and reverently laid it on the cloth. "That, my friend, is because you aren't a linguist. Very few archaeologists are. Oh, they make the required course or two in historical and comparative linguistics in graduate school, but that's the end of it, and most of them have a very vague notion of the development of ancient writing systems. But, Alan, you have to understand: Ancient writing is my field. That's how I can know what this is."

"And what is it?"

"It's a Canaanite script, relatively late. It was used by trading peoples in much of the Mediterranean area. This particular variant I'd suggest is Punic, originating in North Africa or southern Spain."

"That would make this . . ."

"Mid-second century A.D. is when I'd date it, based on the writing itself. And the fact that old Eleut's chronicle referred to the Katun 10 Ahau. That *katun,* or twenty-year period, would have fallen from A.D. 140 to 160."

"That would have been during the period of the Roman Empire. Why wouldn't the writing be Latin or Greek?"

Hayes shrugged. "Lots of people—especially traders—would have known all three languages. But if they were stuck in a strange place, wouldn't they more likely use the language that was most natural to them?"

I picked up the stone again. "Sorry, Paul, but these scratches look pretty random to me. Some Mayan could have sat down and played around with a flint tool—"

Hayes uttered a snort of disgust. "Alan, you're being bull-headed! Do you think somebody would go to this much trouble just to do the Mayan equivalent of whittling?"

"Well, what does it say, then?"

The little man frowned. "I can recognize certain letters—a *D,* a *W,* and an *H,* the first part of 'Jews' or 'Judea.' If so, then it's possible that this is essentially similar to the Bat Creek inscription, and Cyrus Gordon, the paleographer, reads it to mean, possibly, 'the end for the Jews,' as in the Hebrew concept of the End of Time. It was a popular apocalyptic concept in those days, as you may recall, with the temple having been destroyed in A.D. 70, during the first revolt against the Romans. And there were two other revolts after that. You had lots of turmoil, with Judaism being persecuted and Christianity finally being recognized by Constantine in the fourth century. But in the meantime, people went about their business: They lived, died, and carried on commerce, some of it long-distance, via ships."

I scratched my cheek. "The Bat Creek inscription, if I remember right, was interpreted as Cherokee writing by the man who discovered it."

"Because it was found in Tennessee, where there were Cherokees. But remember, Alan, that little piece of stone was discovered directly under a human skull in a burial mound, during a scientific excavation by the Smithsonian Institution in the 1890s. It's still in the Smithsonian. A number of paleographers have examined it and there is nearly unanimous agreement that it represents a Semitic script of the second century after Christ."

"Unanimous among diffusionists," I said dryly. "Paul, look, I can't argue with you about Canaanite script because I'm not an expert on that. But how many possible letters do we have here? Four? Five? Why *shouldn't* they duplicate some of the letters on the Bat Creek stone? The law of probability—"

Hayes's head jerked up and down. "I know, the argument is that with such a short corpus of writing you could have gotten the marks randomly." He leaned forward then and put a hand on my knee. "That's why it's so important, Alan, to find the supporting evidence."

"And where *is* this supporting evidence?" I asked.

"At the site of Lubaanah," Hayes whispered. "The *real* site of Lubaanah, not the rather pedestrian ruin Eric is investigating." He sighed. "Eric decided to call the site by that name for publicity purposes, but you've seen for yourself there's nothing there that remotely resembles what John Dance Williams described. It didn't matter to Eric, though, so long as he could field an expedition."

"Has he seen this letter?"

Hayes smiled. "Eric and I have agreed to disagree on this. I showed him the letter, but he blew it off. His mind was set.

I was hoping, though, that you might be a little more open-minded."

I thought for a moment. "So what's the next step?" I asked.

Hayes carefully replaced the little object in its box and lifted his glass.

"We have to find the real site of Lubaanah."

"And that's what you've secretly been looking for."

"Bingo." He got up, staggering against the table and then steadying himself. "I've been traveling to all the little villages, trying to find out if anybody remembers Williams's visit. Of course, I know that was sixty years ago, but there's always a chance there's somebody. I've been concentrating on the *h-menob,* the shamans, because one of them could have been the student, or the student of the student, of this Eleut. And I've also been asking about a site nearby that resembles the one Williams described."

"And so far?"

"Nothing yet. I started in the area near our excavation, because that seemed to agree best with what Williams implied about the general area, but when that didn't pan out, I expanded north, all the way to Carrillo Puerto. But I think it's unlikely it's any farther north than that." He gnawed his lip. "The worst possibility is it's across the border in Belize or so far into Guatemala I won't be able to get there without going through a new set of government red tape."

"Well, I think there's a worse scenario than that," I said. "The site could have been destroyed."

"I try not to think about that."

"Paul, you said this inscription dates from around A.D. 150 or so. That's late pre-Classic. But the kind of site Williams described sounds like full-blown Classic, even early post-Classic. The sculpture, the murals, the buildings. . . ."

Hayes turned his back on me. "But the site may well have a pre-Classic component. The descendants of the site's builders, who also lived there, may have remembered a famous king who lived long before and chosen to commemorate him in their sculpture just as they did in their chronicles. By then he may have become mythic."

"Yeah, but remember, Paul, the Maya had a cyclical concept of time: Sometimes they tended to confuse when events occurred, just so long as they could fit them into one of the *katun* periods. So we don't know, when they say Katun 10 Ahau, whether they mean the 20 years that ended in A.D. 160, or the 20-year period that ended 256 years later, in 416, or even 256 years after that, in 672."

"You're forgetting the inscription."

I nodded. "Yeah, I guess I am."

"And you're also forgetting what Eleut told Williams was written in his sacred book."

"Oh?"

"About this white man coming from a place where there was a great king! Doesn't that bring anything to mind?"

"There are always great kings," I said.

Hayes threw up his hands in exaggeration. "Alan, *think*: There were, no matter how you look at it, two great kings in A.D. 150. There was the emperor in Rome, the temporal ruler, and the messiah of the Christians, the spiritual king."

"And?"

"This could refer to either of them. But I'm inclined to think this was a Christianized group."

He went to the closed front door, as if to reassure himself that no one was outside listening.

I shook my head. "You're saying this stranger was a Christian missionary?"

"Spare the sarcasm. Look, I'll spell it out: I'm talking about a Christianized Carthaginian or at least someone from that general area. Someone who probably set out on a trading mission, maybe from Spain—there were Phoenician settlements there and the Phoenicians were just Canaanite traders. But this man and his crew ended up going beyond the pillars of Hercules—the Straits of Gibraltar—maybe down the west coast of Africa, and somewhere along the way he wandered out into the vast ocean."

"And was swept over to Central America?"

"Perhaps. But more likely he set out in this direction on purpose, as part of a planned expedition to trade and convert."

"Across the Atlantic?"

"Alan, have you ever heard of the Piri Reis map?"

"The name's familiar."

"Piri was a Turkish naval officer: Reis means admiral. He lived in the first part of the sixteenth century and he commissioned a series of maps to be made from ancient sources, many of which the Moslems took from the great library of Alexandria, Egypt, which had been destroyed by fire in the seventh century." Hayes suppressed a belch. "The main map was copied in Istanbul in 1513 and it was rediscovered in the old Imperial Palace there in 1929."

"I remember reading something about it."

"It's a very important document. It shows what has to be the east coastline of South America, and the distances from the Old World are too close to be coincidental."

"But you said the map was copied in 1513. That was over twenty years after Columbus came back from the New World on his first voyage. As soon as he announced his return, the knowledge spread."

"Alan, be reasonable. Cortés hadn't even conquered the Aztecs in 1513."

"So you think . . ."

"I'm saying that the map is compelling evidence, for anyone who isn't blinded by current archaeological dogma, that the New World was known to the ancients and that there were trips back and forth."

He stared, goggle-eyed, as if awaiting my reaction, but I only shrugged. All at once the energy seemed to leave him and he grabbed the central rafter to hold himself up, setting the hanging light bulb into a crazy motion that sent the shadows spinning around the little room.

"And if you don't find this site?" I asked gently.

"I will. Look, Alan, I'm an old man. I lost my wife a few years ago. And I've had a couple of minor strokes. But unlike what you may think, I'm not a doddering old fool." He exhaled heavily. "Still, if my time's coming, I want to leave on a high note."

"I understand."

"Do you?" He stepped close to me then and I could smell the rum fumes on his breath. "All my life I've been convinced that there were cultural contacts from the Old World. Call me crazy, call it a delusion. I've kept quiet because when you start talking about it, people's eyes glaze over—like yours did just now."

"I'm just tired," I said, patting his shoulder.

"You're being kind. But I know better." The focus returned to his eyes then. "But when I find the site and when I publish, nobody will be able to deny the evidence."

"I hope you succeed," I said.

"Look, would you do me a favor?"

"What?"

"Would you hold the stone tablet for me?"

"Paul . . ."

"It isn't safe here. Somebody broke in earlier . . ."

"But you said nobody else knows you even have it."

"Oh, it was probably a maid looking for loose change. But there are characters who wander up and down this beach—I was telling Geraldo he ought to hire a watchman. Any beach bum could break in. They don't have to be looking for the tablet, but they might think it was made out of jade or something."

"And you think it would be safer with me? The same people can break into our hut as yours. Remember the dead man on the beach?"

"You're smart, Alan, and you've been down here before. You know how locals think. Hide it somewhere. I trust you."

"Why?"

"Maybe because you're honest about not believing my theory but you don't call me a racist for being politically incorrect."

"Political correctness isn't my strong point," I said. "Look, I can't be responsible for the thing."

"Of course not."

"I guess you have other copies of the letter?"

"Absolutely. And photos of the tablet. But when it comes to an artifact, there's nothing like the real thing." He took the tablet out of the metal box and handed it to me, wrapped in its cloth. "Thanks, Alan. I'll sleep better tonight."

"I don't know if *I* will." I pulled the door open and turned. "Whenever you want this back, just ask me."

"Deal. Oh, Alan . . ."

"Yeah?"

"Our little conversation: Can you keep it under your hat? Well, you can tell Pepper, but . . ."

"Nobody else," I agreed and wondered if the same people who'd killed the man on the beach would think twice about killing for a piece of stone with scratches.

Later that night Pepper and I walked along the beach, hand in hand. The huts, with their lit windows, looked like a string of landing lights. Only April's, between Blackburn's and our own, was dark, and I wondered if April was with Blackburn. I told Pepper about my talk with Paul Hayes and she gave a low whistle.

"It sounds like poor Paul's lost it," she said.

"Yeah. Still, it would be interesting if—"

She jerked my hand. "Come on, Alan, you don't *believe* any of that stuff? *A Canaanite inscription?*"

"It seems pretty far-fetched." We came to the end of the beach, where the steps led up to the restaurant.

"Do you have this stone with you?" she asked.

"In my pocket."

"Can I see it?"

I nodded. "But it's too dark down here. We'll have to go to the top of the cliff, where there's light from Geraldo's."

We made our way up the steps to Geraldo's back patio, where the tables were empty and a lone waiter was sweeping the green tiles. I moved into a pool of light, cast by one of the lamps that lined the side of the area, and took out the little piece of stone. Pepper unwrapped it and turned it over in her hands. After a few seconds she handed it back.

"This isn't anything," she pronounced. "Those scratches could have been made by some Mayan artisan who—"

"I know. But Paul's convinced."

She walked over to the stone wall that guarded the cliff edge. The lake was black as a pit and I found myself thinking about *metnal,* the Mayan concept of hell.

I'd stood here fifteen years ago when . . .

"I mean, even if there's some undiscovered site out there,"

she said, "there's no reason to think it has anything to do with ancient Semites coming here eighteen hundred years ago."

"No." I turned away from the lake, where I was starting to imagine things lurking just under the placid black surface. "I wonder if it's too late for a beer."

"At Geraldo's?" She laughed. "I don't think it's ever too late."

I came back a few minutes later with two bottles and took a long swallow from my own.

"Are you all right?" she asked. "This business with Paul seems to have upset you."

I didn't tell her about the lake.

"I'm fine," I said.

"You look worried. Hey, Paul Hayes is way out in left field on this."

"Paul's brilliant," I said. "I've read some of his papers on linguistics. Not that I understand everything he's saying."

"That was when he was younger," she said. "Before his stroke."

"You think his mind is affected," I said.

"It's an explanation."

"Yeah." I took another sip. "Unless . . ."

"Unless *what*? Alan, you know as well as I do there's nothing to this nonsense. There's not one shred of evidence that Europeans or anybody else came to the New World between the time the first Indians crossed the Bering Strait and the time the Vikings found Newfoundland a thousand years ago, and after the Vikings—"

"There was nobody until Columbus. I know."

"But you sound like you don't believe it."

"I'm just saying interesting things pop up now and again and this is one of them."

"Oh, Alan, you're so exasperating. If I didn't know you better, I'd think you were trying to aggravate me."

"No."

"Look, all these diffusionists seem to have one goal: to prove that the first people who came to the New World—the Native Americans—didn't have the brains to build the complex civilizations that we know existed here. The concept of building pyramids came from Egypt—even if there's a two thousand-year gap between the first Egyptian pyramids and the first Mesoamerican ones. The Mayan calendar, one of humanity's greatest intellectual achievements, was borrowed from the high civilizations of Southeast Asia. The art style of Mesoamerica is really from India. The poor Native Americans weren't even smart enough to invent pottery! That had to come from Japanese fishermen floating down the whole damned coast of North and Central America two thousand years before Christ. Fishermen who just happen to have left no other traces of themselves, probably because the barbaric Indians ate them."

I took another drink of my beer. I knew better than to argue when she was wound up.

"It's just like in the 1800s, when people claimed the North American Indians couldn't have built the Indian mounds, because they were only savages. The mounds had to have been the work of some superior group of mound builders who were wiped out by the savages. Alan, it's nothing but racism!"

"Well, Heyerdahl says the diffusion went both ways, that the South American Indians reached the South Pacific Islands by going west on rafts."

She squinted at me. "You really *are* jerking me around, aren't you?"

"Not in the least." I leaned back against the wall. Through the doorway to the inner dining room I could just make out a few late drinkers at the bar. "I'm just saying it's a question of looking at the evidence, if there is any. I don't see any good evidence myself, but if somebody came up with some . . ."

"Like this lost site of Paul's?" She shook her head. "Alan, even if you had a sculpture that looked like Fabio, it wouldn't prove anything. There are variations in any gene pool. There can be archaic genes that manifest themselves at a given time."

"Right."

"Besides, I doubt there's any site like that *out* there, no matter *what* the sculptures look like. *Chicleros* have gotten to them all and after the *chicleros* the looters. And there's been a hundred years of continuous archaeological exploration."

"But every once in a while you hear about a new site nobody knew about."

"Nobody but the tomb robbers. Chances are if you found it you wouldn't recognize it because everything worth taking would have been carted off."

"A definite possibility."

"And don't forget the *sacbé,* the causeway you say Williams mentioned in his letter: It probably would show up on satellite photos and archaeologists have been scanning those for over twenty years."

"Absolutely."

"Why are you agreeing with me?"

"Keeps you off balance," I said.

She elbowed my ribs. "I'll unbalance *you.*"

Before I could respond, there was movement inside and José Durán came out of the restaurant. He halted when he saw us, frowning, and I sensed he was trying to decide something.

"*Ola, José,*" Pepper said. "Buy you a beer?"

His head gave a little shake. "I've had all I need."

"José," I said. "If there's something we need to talk about—"

"*No hay nada,*" he snapped. "There's nothing." I stiffened slightly. "I regret what happened the other day. I was wrong and I ask you to forgive me. Now, if you'll both excuse me . . ."

"Sure," I said. "Oh, by the way . . ."

"Yes?"

"The other night *don* Geraldo said something about knowing you for almost as long as he'd known me. Did you work in this part of Mexico in the 1980s?"

"As a student only. Very briefly. *Buenas noches.*"

Pepper waited until José had reached the beach. "He never said anything about having worked here in the eighties. I thought that up to the last couple of years, all his experience was in Chiapas and Oaxaca."

I stared back at the lake. This time the spirits lurking under the surface were beginning to take forms.

■FOURTEEN

It was two nights later, on a Friday evening just before dinner, that April and Eric had their fight. By the time it was over everybody else had weighed in.

It started on the patio, while we were drinking beer, waiting for our food. I sat with my back to the lake, because there were still things out there I wasn't sure I wanted to see. It started because Hayes insisted on going to Mérida.

At first Eric tried to talk him out of it. "It's a long trip. The AC is broken in the Rover."

Hayes laughed. "Jesus, I once went from Villahermosa to Mexico City in a bus full of chickens and pigs—"

"—when I was in diapers," Blackburn finished good-naturedly. "But back then you didn't have a heart condition."

"My damn heart's fine. It was a *stroke* I had. A very minor one. Hell, I'm not even sure the doctors were right. They make it up as they go."

"Sure, and when you get dizzy in the sun out on the site, it's just an act."

"Down here everybody gets dizzy from the sun in August."

Blackburn said nothing.

"Anyway, I was planning on going up to the museum, remember? There are some maps I need to look at, but I got sidetracked up near Tres Cabras. Otherwise, I'd have already taken care of this."

"Eric's right," Minnie said. "What if you had a breakdown?"

"Mexican mechanics can fix anything. I've seen 'em rewire alternators and fix head gaskets with asbestos."

"Then why don't you take somebody with you?" Eric said. He turned to April. "How about it? You could stay until Monday and see a doctor in Mérida who knows something. We can't have you staying sick all the time."

"I'm fine," April said. "Besides, the field season's almost over."

"Yeah, but I don't want to send you home sick. Look, there's a guy named Robles, a good internist—he's treated me. I can call ahead. He may even see you on Saturday."

"I'm not going."

Blackburn's face reddened. "You're forgetting who's running things here. I'm responsible for the crew."

"Then fire me."

Eric shoved his chair back, shot to his feet, and stalked off into the restaurant. A few seconds later we heard an engine start in the parking lot and a screech of tires.

"Where's he going at this time of night?" Minnie asked. "It isn't safe after that poor man was killed."

"Don't worry," Hayes assured her. "He'll just drive up and down the highway a little until he calms down." He looked over at April. "He was right, you know: You really ought to get checked out. And I'd like to have the company."

April looked down at the tabletop. "I'm sorry. I'd like to. But I just don't want to go."

"Nobody wants to see you stay sick," José said softly.

"Thanks. But I don't want to talk about it." April got up then and we watched her walk across the patio, down the steps, and across the beach toward her hut.

"A very strange young woman," Hayes said, shaking his head. He squinted over at José. "You're close to her, José. What's all this about?"

The Mexican shrugged. "We're not that close. We've talked, but she is a very private person, this April."

Minnie rose. "Maybe it's a woman problem. I'll go see if I can get anything out of her."

Paul Hayes drained his glass. "Well, with or without her, I'm going to Mérida tomorrow. I can stand the Rover, air conditioning or not, and Eric doesn't need it. I just hope Eric doesn't crack it up with his nocturnal escapade."

"Is it really April's father he's afraid of?" I asked.

"He is very rich," José said curtly. "She's told me about him and growing up. He made a major donation to the project so that Eric would take her on."

"Poor Eric," Pepper said. "A hostage to a rich donor."

"Poor everybody," Hayes said. "Every principal investigator is a hostage to somebody, whether it's the National Science Foundation, *National Geographic,* or their university. There's no such thing as academic freedom anymore. You have to toe the company line."

It was just after midnight when I was awakened by a noise outside. I opened my eyes, trying to remember if my machete was within reach, and then I realized the sound was a tapping on the wooden door. I threw on my pants and went to open it.

Eric was standing in the doorway, face anxious in a way I hadn't seen before.

"Alan, I'm sorry to bother you," he whispered. "Is Pepper asleep?"

"Yeah."

"Good. Have you got a few minutes to walk over to my house?"

I slipped my feet into my sandals and followed him across the beach, past April's darkened hut, and to his house at the end. He opened the door and turned on the light.

"Want a drink?" he asked, reaching for a bottle of tequila.

"Too late for me," I said. "Thanks."

He regarded the bottle for a second, then put it back unopened. "For me, too."

The hut was furnished like all the others, with a camp table and a couple of chairs, and he slumped into one of them.

"Sit down."

I noticed that the hammock still hung, folded out of the way, from one wooden post, and Eric's laptop was set up on the table, surrounded by stacks of papers and drawings.

"I need your help, Alan. The whole project needs your help."

It would be a lie to deny that a little thrill of excitement ran through me. *To be back in the game . . .*

"You saw what happened tonight with April."

I nodded.

"She defied me in front of everybody. She knows her old man can get the president of the university on the phone any time day or night. And, considering how much he gives to the endowment every year, the president will listen."

There wasn't anything I could say to that.

"The girl's been a liability ever since she's been down here. I wanted to get her out of the way for a while—I think José feels sorry for her and he's a good man. But I need him to be clearheaded, not mooning over some little girl with snakes in her head."

"You think she and José . . ."

"I don't know. And I really don't give a damn, so long as it doesn't affect the project. José's a single man, she's a single woman, over twenty-one. But he's a sucker for a sad story. I imagine right now, in his macho Latin mind, he's thinking I was too hard on her."

"I think José can handle it," I said.

Eric stroked his beard. "I hope so. But the point is, I'm tired of April's hypochondria. There isn't a goddamn thing wrong with her except she doesn't want to have to sweat in the hot sun like everybody else. She grew up with a silver spoon, she knows her old man's supporting this project, and she thinks she can do—or not do—any damn thing she wants."

"Tough situation," I sympathized.

"You got it." He bit his lip. "I don't have much time for rich bitch spoiled little girls. I grew up poor, with an old man who wasn't there half the time, and when he *was,* everybody wished he *wasn't,* because he was always looking for somebody to lay into with his belt. My mother died when I was in high school and I worked as everything from a janitor to a mechanic's helper to get through school. Nobody ever gave me a thing. So if an old woman like Minnie O'Toole can work her butt off in Mexican sun, a twenty-two-year-old rich girl can, too."

I kept waiting for him to tell me why he'd asked me here.

"I was thinking about all this while I was driving up and down the highway. Believe me, I considered every possibility you can imagine. See, Alan, April's not the only problem, though she's a big part of it. We've had good weather for excavating, not much rain, but we're still behind. Paul isn't worth a damn in the field—he's too busy running everywhere, doing his own thing. Not that I expected anything else. He's not an archaeologist, anyway, though he's been involved in it a lot over the years. And his health isn't that good. When he disappeared a few weeks ago, I halfway expected to hear they'd found him dead in some village." Blackburn took out a pipe and slowly packed it. He lit it, drew on it, and then exhaled a cloud of sweet smoke. "I hope you don't mind."

"I like the smell of pipes," I said.

"Good. Anyway, you can scratch him, except for consulting on Mayan etymology and ethnohistory. Minnie? Well, she's a great gal, but she had to be trained and that took a little while. Pepper's great, of course: She's picked up this kind of archaeology easily over the last couple of field seasons, even though she was trained as a historical archaeologist. But she's committed to go back to teach the fall semester. It pretty much boils down to José. I know the Instituto Nacional will let me keep him as long as there's a salary, but José can't be everywhere."

"I thought the field season was ending in a couple of weeks. Do you mean you have money left?"

He pointed the stem of his pipe at me. "That's what I'm getting to. See, it all comes back to Miss April Blake."

Gradually it was starting to make sense.

"Her father," I said.

"You got it. After I'd driven up and down a couple of dozen times and passed about twenty slow-moving cargo trucks, I came back to the restaurant and used Geraldo's phone to call Byron Blake. I was going to tell him I was sending his daughter home and he could cancel the whole goddamned project if he felt like it."

"And?"

"I got him. He was at home and still up. And the old bastard wasn't the least bit surprised to hear from me."

"It's happened before," I suggested.

"Yeah. He said he was surprised I'd been able to stand her as long as I had. We actually had a pretty decent conversation. I feel sorry for what the old boy's had to go through. Remind me, if my kid ever gets like that, to smack her in the head. If my wife ever lets me see her again, that is."

"Sorry."

He waved it away. "One of those things. You think of all kinds of things when you're down here. Things you'd like to change, things that happened . . ."

"Yes."

"But I'm wandering. Goddamn project's getting to me, I guess." He rubbed his eyes. "Hell, you know how it is, Alan: While everybody else is sleeping, the director's up writing field notes, going over the expenditures, trying to decipher other people's field notes, going over photo logs . . ."

"Yeah, I know."

"Where was I? Oh, old man Blake: The short of it is he thanked me for putting up with his daughter and asked if I'd do him 'a further favor.' That's the way he put it: 'a further favor.' Real Old South gentry. He asked if I could see my way to keep April to the end of the field season—just another couple of weeks, until the semester starts, and she'd be coming home anyway. And he said that he'd be very grateful. So grateful he'd be honored—that's another one of the words he used—honored to do everything he could to further assist in my important work."

"How much assistance was he talking about?"

"Enough to let me keep the project going to the end of December. Enough to let me tidy up all the loose ends and get some data we need like hell. The outlier group, for instance," he said, talking about a small group of ruins at the south end of the site. "I haven't been able to do anything but a surface collection from that area. When I write the report, you know what people are going to say: 'Why did he leave those? Why did he start near the north end? Why did he do *this*? Why the hell did he do *that*?' Like I had all the frigging time and money in the world. Well, I chose the north group because it looked promising at the time: The surface collection was full of everything from Tepeu to Plumbate. When we finished with the test excavation units, though, everything was all jumbled up subsurface. But that's not something you can predict ahead of time. But the result's still that months were spent on an area that didn't answer any questions at all except that the Maya built the goddamn thing, which we knew before we came here."

"The best part of the site's always under your back dirt," I said, quoting a familiar axiom in archaeology.

"Exactly." He leaned forward, jabbing at me with the pipe again. "But now we've got a chance to do something about that. We can test the southern group and some of the *muuls*—the stone mounds—in satellite areas. We can get some good settlement study material, and with that we can make a damn proposal they won't be able to turn down for next year and the year after that. Hell, this goddamn dig could go on for ten more years."

"That would be great."

"To put it mildly. But you see what I'm getting to, Alan? I've got a commitment for the money: He told me to name a round figure and when I did the old bastard didn't blink. He said to put it in writing and he'd call the president of the university and tell him to hire a temp for my fall classes. And since the university takes forty percent of the amount of all grants for overhead, they aren't going to complain."

"Sounds like you're set."

"Yeah. All I need is another archaeologist."

It was what I was hoping he was going to say.

"I'm listening," I said.

"Alan, do I have to beg you? You made your goddamn bones down here. This contract work you do in the States is something you do to stay in archaeology, but this is where your heart is. This is where you belong. Pepper's told me and I can see it all over you. Hell, people down here remember you. They know what a good archaeologist you were. This is what you want to do. Deny it."

I couldn't.

"Look, Alan, I don't know what all went down here years ago. Pepper said a little about it." He held up a hand. "Not much. She wasn't blabbing. But I've heard a little scuttlebutt from Geraldo. He says there was a woman and I figure you got screwed over by her."

I felt my face redden. "I wouldn't say that, exactly."

"Doesn't matter. It's history. We're talking about now. This year. A whole new damn millennium!"

"I don't know, Eric . . ."

"Why not? Your business at home? Are you that indispensable? You don't have anybody else who can handle your job?"

"Well . . ."

"Call 'em. Tell 'em you'll fly back a couple of times to see how things are going. It's not that far, with Cancún just a few hours up the highway. In three hours you can be at the airport and an hour and a half after that . . ."

"Whoa. It's not that simple. I have commitments, projects. . . ."

"But you're the PI, the principal investigator, right? They don't need you there all the time. And Alan, this *is* the age of the fax machine and the cell phone and e-mail. Hell, they can call you or e-mail you and you can call whoever it is from down here. I'll even pay the cost of the call."

I tried to imagine La Bombast, our contact at the Corps of Engineers, negotiating with me via long distance from Mexico: *What do you mean, you're not in the States? You're where? Alan, if you think you can take the government's money and go spend it on a beach at Cancún, you're way off. I have a responsibility to the taxpayers and I have to tell you that if this is an example of how you conduct business . . .*

But how likely was it she'd call, really? Couldn't I just be out of town when that happened? Or sick? If it was something really important, like a contract negotiation, I could fly back. Or David could fax me all the documents and I could call her from Geraldo's and she'd never have to know I was anywhere but in the office.

Sure.

Alan, what's that music in the background? Are you calling from a bar?

Making contractors miserable was her raison d'être. She'd love having something real to complain about.

"I might be able to arrange something," I heard myself say.

"Damn straight," Eric said, excited. He jumped up and put a hand on my shoulder. "We're alike, Alan. From everything I've heard about you, everything Pepper and Geraldo have said, I knew we were alike. Oh, I don't mean in the little things. I mean in what counts: I love the Mayan people and so do you."

"I love Yucatán," I said. "It may just be my romanticism, though. It's easy to love a place when you can come and go at will. When you have modern transportation and you can get good medical treatment. It's not the same thing as being a Mayan, though—having to deal with the economy down here, trying to make ends meet, having kids die before the age of one, having to walk two miles to a cornfield and carry charcoal back to your house with a tumpline or on a bicycle."

Eric let out a great laugh. "Pepper said you were like this: Full of that damned sixties guilt about anthropology and archaeology being evil because you're exploiting folks by studying 'em. Come on, Alan. I don't think for a minute we don't help the people we work with. We've brought medicines and some damned good-paying jobs to this area. There's nothing to be ashamed of, believe me."

"I'm not ashamed," I said. "I just try to keep my perspective. But as far as staying down here with you . . ."

"It'll be worth your while," he said. "I promise. I've seen you work now. We'll get along. I may be the project director, but I'll treat you like an equal. You can trust me on that. All I want is a good product, a project we can all be proud of. And your name will be on it. How long has it been since you've published in Mayan archaeology, Alan?"

"A while," I admitted.

"Well, we can take care of that. What do you want to stake out? Settlement patterns? Demographics? Ceramics? Name it."

"It's tempting, of course, but . . ."

"But what?" He shook his head. "Alan, for Christ's sake, listen: We're not just talking about a project, we're talking about you getting back into the field you were trained in, the field you love, being able to do what you really want to do for the rest of your life. What's there to decide?"

"Eric, this is sudden. I need to think . . ."

"Sure. But I need to know pretty quickly. I need to start the paperwork. I have to put together a budget, and if you're going to be in it, I need to have a salary figure."

"Yeah."

"And I have to send some paperwork to the university, too, to have you put on."

"What?"

"Research associate. No, better: adjunct professor. I'll need your vita, if course, but that's a formality."

He must have known he'd scored, because his little shrug said I was a fool if I doubted this was only the beginning.

"Alan, look: You know as well as I do money talks. The academic world is no different than anywhere else. You may run a private business, but colleges are big business, too. There's not a chancellor or university president out there who won't bend over and take it in the butt if you bring in the green stuff. The heroes today are the money-raisers."

I didn't dispute him, because what he was saying was true.

"I lucked out with April, as ass-backwards as that seems. If it weren't for her old man, I'd just be another academician trying to keep his head above water. Hell, when they hired me last year they wouldn't even give me tenure, even though I was bringing them a continuation of the grant to work down here. But now I'll get their damned tenure, because I'll be a big hero. And it's all luck of the draw. I'm not stupid: I know there're fifty other faculty members out there with as many publications as I have and with better credentials in their fields. But some of 'em won't get tenure and I will, because they didn't hook up with the Blake family."

"And you're saying . . ."

"I'm saying right now, because I've got a little clout, I can get you on, at least in a temporary position. But that's a foothold. Give it a year and we'll be bringing in more money and they'll change the damn temporary to a funded tenure-track. That's the way it works."

He was right. I'd seen it work before.

"Houston isn't that far from Baton Rouge. Pepper's at LSU. That's just five hours away. Less by plane. Look, we might even be able to swing something for her. I'm thinking of a whole institute, a Mayan studies program, something that could compete with Tulane and the University of Texas. But I just can't do it alone."

"I really need to think."

"Sure. I know this is sudden. Take a day or two. And I can work with you. I mean, arrange time away so you can keep your hand in with your business at home. I'm telling you what I see down the road, but right now we're just talking the next few months, so you don't have to commit yourself for the long term. You can stick your foot in the water and see if it feels good." He gave a nervous little laugh.

"A day," I said. "Give me a day, Eric."

He took a step toward me, hand outstretched. "Fair enough. I hope you'll decide to help me out, Alan. I think we'd make a hell of a team."

"Yeah."

I went back to our hut, my mind swirling. I hadn't expected this and now the images were tumbling head over heels through my consciousness. A chance to reenter the academic world, to be a professor again, draw a secure salary, have students, and, most of all, work in the field in which I'd been trained. To start to make up for all those lost years . . .

But was it too good to be true? In business I'd dealt with a lot of fast-talking promoters. I'd listened to visionaries wax eloquent about malls and residential golf courses and airports, some of which had never gotten off the ground and some of which had proved to be disasters. And I listened to some who'd gone on to bigger things, fueled by the success of their initial projects. I'd seen a few flim-flam artists, I'd seen some true believers, and I'd seen double-talking lawyers who promised the world and then backed out when it came time to pay the bill. I tried to run my impressions of Eric Blackburn through the filter of these experiences, but no red lights went off. The man was enthusiastic and he'd had a few drinks, but in the little time I'd known him he hadn't blustered or expounded grandiose schemes. He seemed, in fact, as surprised as I was at his sudden good luck with Byron Blake. And if he was willing to let some of that good luck spill out on me, why should I question it? It wasn't like I was unqualified or like he was buying me off. I'd been doing archaeology down here while he was in high school. Now he was in over his head with the project and he needed help. It made perfect sense that he should ask me.

I slipped off my clothes and shut the door softly behind me. From under the gauzy mosquito netting I could hear Pepper's breathing, slow and peaceful, from the big hammock. A couple of nights ago, for mutual comfort, we'd agreed that I'd string my own hammock, because the *matrimonio,* while fine for lovemaking, was a little cramped for normal sleeping. I lifted the *mosquitero,* slid into the hammock, and lay there, listening to the sound of waves lapping and the buzz of a beetle against the mosquito bar. But after a time I realized the sound of my heart was drowning out the other sounds. I turned over and tried to make myself sleep, but excitement kept shoving sleep away.

Who'd run the business if I stayed down here? David? He was certainly capable, and Marilyn, our office manager, was the one who handled the accounts in any case. But David had gotten into archaeology for the love of it, not to formulate budgets, soothe clients, and go to meetings.

But maybe it was time for him to learn. Why should I deprive myself?

I must have drifted off to sleep, because at some point I ceased being in the hammock and found myself in a lecture hall, being introduced as the new Nobel Laureate in the field of Mayan studies. I started across the stage and realized, halfway across, that I'd forgotten to put on my pants and I wondered if anyone would notice.

I never knew, because my dream was interrupted by a buzzing sound. The lecture hall vanished and I saw a Mayan priest in ancient ceremonial regalia, felling trees with a chain saw, until even this dream shattered and I recognized the sound as that of a plane coming in low. Then the sound died away and all I heard were the beetles and the waves and, I thought at one point, a door shutting somewhere in one of the other *cabañas.*

▰Fifteen

When we got up the next morning, Paul Hayes was already on his way to Mérida. But, as expected, April was still with us. No one alluded to the scene of the previous night and even though it was Saturday, April climbed into the van without protest as we started the drive to the archaeological site.

I'd slept poorly after the plane passed over, my dreams a bizarre interweaving of imagined future work at the site and pastiches from fifteen years ago, when things had gone to hell. I didn't say anything to Pepper about my talk with Blackburn, but it didn't take more than a couple of hours for her to ask.

"So talk," she said, when she was sure there was no one else near the excavation unit but ourselves and the Mayan-speaking workers above, manning the screen. "What the hell's going on?"

I stood up slowly and wiped a trickle of sweat from my face. Condensation, caused by the effect of the plastic cover above us, seemed to make up in humidity for the loss of glare.

I reached for the water bottle, took a deep swallow, and then told her what Eric had said.

She listened, nonplussed. "Son-of-a-bitch," she said finally. "And Minnie thought he and April were sleeping together."

She sat down on the edge of the excavation and picked up her own water bottle.

"So are you going to do it?" she asked.

"I don't know."

"Yes, you do. It's written all over you. You're just scared of what I'll say."

"Why?"

"Because it would mean living in different cities. Not seeing each other that much."

"That's a long way down the road," I said. "All we're talking about now is the next few months. I mean, if this happens—and I'm not saying it will—but if it does, we've been apart all summer, and you were gone last summer, so it's not like . . ."

"Tit for tat, huh?"

"Jesus, Pepper, that's not like you. I didn't say anything when you decided to come down here."

"Bullshit. I thought I was going to have to get you a therapist, the way you were moping around and looking like a whipped dog. And every letter from you had some little thing about how you guessed you'd make it okay, trying to guilt me out."

"How can you say that?"

"It's true."

"I missed you like hell. Is that so abnormal?"

"So you took up with that widow in Jackson, the one who—"

"I told you all about that," I said quietly, surprised at her vehemence. "Nothing happened. Of course, if you don't believe me . . ."

"Oh, hell," she swore. She got up and walked out into the sun. I started after her and then stopped. Suddenly I felt a petty sense of satisfaction.

All this time I'd been the one agonizing about her being down here without me. I'd been jealous of Eric Blackburn and jealous of her chance to work in Mayan studies. Now, ironically, the situation was reversed and she was the one with the insecurities.

Now she knew what I'd felt. And I realized I didn't want anybody else to feel that way. Not someone I loved.

I was just starting out from under the covering when I saw her coming back.

"I'm sorry," she said. "I was a bitch."

"No," I said. "It's just something we have to work out."

"Yeah. Any ideas how?"

"I don't know just now, but two rational people with doctorates, who love each other . . ."

"Right."

There were steps outside and when I looked up I saw Eric. He ducked down under the canopy, sweat staining his old straw hat.

Oh, God, he wants his answer now, I thought. But I was wrong.

"Anybody seen April?" he asked. "She's wandered off again."

"I went over to the van just now," Pepper said. "I saw her walking down the path to the village. I thought she was just going to use the bushes."

"Jesus," Blackburn muttered. "Probably gone to see that baby again. Well, I was headed over there anyway, to see my *compadre*'s family. Seems they need a few pesos." He shook his head, wheeled, and stomped off.

A few seconds later I heard the engine of the van start and I turned back to our unit.

"So what do you make of it?" Pepper asked.

I shook my head. "April's making him earn his money."

As soon as we returned from the site that afternoon—a surly April included—Eric left for Chetumal, mumbling something about needing supplies, and he hadn't returned when we went to bed. Which didn't matter particularly because, with the excitement, nobody missed him.

That evening, in Geraldo's restaurant, the judicial police arrested the killer of the man on the beach.

Pepper and I had gone for an early swim, joined by Minnie, who, with her flowered bathing cap and one-piece suit, looked like a figure from some fifties-era movie. Neither Pepper nor I had spoken more of Eric's offer and I was still weighing the issues.

It would mean being away from Pepper for another three to four months and people at the office would have to scramble. But it would also free up my salary. And I'd been working nonstop for over ten years now. Surely no one, not even a workaholic like David Goldman, would begrudge me a vacation.

Vacation. Was that what I considered it? Better get that idea out of my head. Working six days a week in the tropical sun wasn't a vacation. Unless, of course, it was what you loved to do . . .

We toweled off as the sun turned the western sky purple and I idly looked up at a contrail high against the darkening field. Last night I'd dreamed of the low-flying airplane again. But no—it hadn't been a dream, it had been real. Had the plane been coming in from the east or headed out to sea? There was no way to tell. He had to be using one of the landing strips in the interior, some swatch cleared from the jungle, for the landing of agricultural or medical supplies.

And that's why he was flying low, and late at night. Sure.

"Paul ought to be in Mérida now," Minnie said, stripping off the latex cap. "If he didn't stop to take a detour into some little village." She folded her towel and we started toward the line of *cabañas*. "I worry about him. He won't stop, you know. It's like he thinks he's a young man, chasing after all these old books."

We halted in front of her hut and Kanmiz came up to rub against her. She reached down to stroke his whiskers and he closed his eyes.

"I'll see you two later," Minnie said. "I think somebody wants supper now."

I nodded and as I did so my eyes went over her shoulder and I caught a glimpse of two people seated at one of the outdoor tables at the top of the cliff. April and José.

"I think you were wrong about April and Eric," I said.

She squinted up at the pair, shading her eyes. "You think so? Well, maybe. I'm just a nosy old busybody anyway."

"No, you're as astute as hell," I said. "That's what bothers me."

Pepper and I went into our *cabaña* to dress for supper.

"So have you decided what you're going to tell him?" she asked.

"I want to do it," I blurted. "I just don't know if it would work."

"Because you're indispensable at the office or because of me?"

"Both. But mainly you."

"Then don't sweat it. I've been thinking about how I acted earlier. You thought you were the only insecure one? Look, Alan, I guess for the last couple of years I've just been doing my thing and kind of enjoying having you around: I've been taking you for granted because you were always there when I needed you. It just never occurred to me that you wouldn't be because you're so steady. I mean, you're my rock, okay? Then, suddenly, this business comes from nowhere and I see everything wavering. I all of a sudden realized, my God, what would happen if I lost you?"

"You won't," I said, reaching for her.

"But we'll be three hundred miles apart," she said, dropping her towel so that she was naked against me.

"That's the distant future," I said. "Now's now. I waited too long for you. You won't lose me, no matter what."

Our lips came together and I reached out to unhook the hammock from its stored position.

"Tell me again, baby," she whispered and I pressed down on top of her in the netting.

So I did, remembering in another compartment of my mind that once, long ago, I'd said the same things to another woman, here.

We went up to dinner hand in hand, as if something might reach out of the darkness and tear us away from each other. Minnie had gone on ahead and I saw her seated alone at the same table where José and April had been, except that now the pair was nowhere in sight.

"You two look refreshed," Minnie said smugly. Surely the sounds of our lovemaking hadn't carried all the way to her hut?

She leaned over the table. "I was talking to Geraldo. Poor man. He's beside himself. That other man is back and it's about to drive him crazy."

"What other man?" I asked and then I saw who she was

talking about. Felipe Jordan, wearing a faded blue guayabera and jeans, sauntered out of the restaurant and onto the patio, beer bottle in hand.

He spotted us immediately and walked over. "*Buenas noches, compañeros.*"

I nodded.

"I'll bet you've all been wondering where I've been."

"Not really," I said.

"No? Well, I guess the archaeology keeps you pretty busy. Look, is anybody going to Chetumal anytime soon? I could use a ride."

"Sorry," I said. "Isn't there a bus?"

"If I want to stand outside here for three hours in the dark."

"Sorry."

"Don't worry about it," he said, waving. He turned on his heel and vanished back into the restaurant.

"I think he's what they used to call a remittance man," Minnie said. "You know, somebody his family sent overseas to get him out of the way, whom they send money every month to make sure he stays gone. He probably has to go into Chetumal to pick up his check."

"More likely Geraldo's right and he's dealing drugs," Pepper said. "You know, small-time to tourists."

"Maybe so," Minnie said and lifted her *gaseosa.* "I wonder where April and José absconded to?"

"So I guess you've gotten rid of the demons," Pepper said later, while we sat in the love seat overlooking the lake.

I shrugged. "I don't know. They're still there. But I know that I'm not as scared of them anymore. I know that coming down here was the right thing to do. I know now I can handle it."

"I'm glad for you."

She sounded forlorn and I put my arm around her. "Hey, it's gonna work out. You think I'd do anything to risk losing you?"

For a long time there was no sound but the music from the restaurant above, drifting down on the breeze. Pepper turned her head away then and stared out at the dark waters of the lake.

"What was she like?"

It was the first time she'd ever asked about Felicia, as if she knew that to bring the matter up would be to open a wound.

"That's a hard question," I said. "She was beautiful and intelligent and determined. A lot like you in some ways, but totally different in others."

"Like what?"

I struggled for the right words. "There was something a little manic about her. Like if she stopped, her world would cave in. It made her intense. I guess that's one of the things that attracted me. But after a while I realized it was because she was scared, being a woman professional in a society where her profession was not only dominated by males, but where there was the element of machismo to deal with."

"Let me guess: She saw you as a steadying influence."

"She said that. She said she was relieved to be around a man who wasn't always trying to prove something." I looked up at the sky, where low-flying clouds were erasing the stars.

"That makes sense," Pepper said.

"It does *now*."

"What do you mean?"

"You didn't know me then."

"What do you mean?"

"I had things to prove," I said simply. "Maybe it wasn't as obvious as it was with some of the Mexican men she knew. But it was there."

"You're beating yourself up again."

"Maybe so." I closed my eyes and the images swam in front of me, grotesque figures like the monster sculptures at Copán, where Felicia and I had gone on our honeymoon.

"There was a procession making its way through the street," I heard myself saying. "We were in the hotel. It was a *gremio,* a church guild, and they were singing the 'Ave Maria,' by candlelight, peasant men and women, mainly. We heard them singing and she wanted to go join them. We dressed and went outside. It was nighttime. I thought she wanted to see them because it was quaint and we were in a tiny village near a great Mayan site. But after a little while I realized it wasn't that at all, when I saw the tears on her face."

"She was religious."

"She was a Marxist, she said. But after all the lip service to atheism there was the old religion right below the surface, and all the guilt that went along with it."

"Was that what went wrong, then? Cultural differences?"

"I told myself that. I don't know if I really believed it, though. Partly it was her. And partly it was because of the way I was." I opened my eyes again and gave her a bitter little smile. "She was my trophy. There were all kinds of men after her, but I was the one who got her. I beat them all out. It was a game. And I convinced myself that she was a prize, and since she was a prize, she had to be the way I wanted her to be instead of the way she was."

"Things happen when you're young," Pepper said. "You can't blame yourself for it."

I shut my eyes again, trying to recapture the almost unbearable sweetness of that warm summer night in Copán, with the procession singing down in the street, and turning to Felicia. And yet, suddenly, I couldn't recall her face.

"I think it was to get back at me that she did it," I said. "Because I expected her to be a certain way and she felt like she couldn't measure up. So she decided to hurt me for the guilt she was feeling."

"What did she do?"

"Found another man," I said. "And made sure I'd hear about it."

"I'm sorry."

"After she left me standing in Mérida, I came down here and found her. I asked her what was going on, and that was when she told me."

She reached over and squeezed my hand. "You deserved better."

"No. It was a call for help and I didn't recognize it. All I could think about was my own male pride. How could she do this to me? I never realized what I'd done to her by not seeing the signs, the calls for help." I removed my hand from hers as the tidal wave of memories bore down on me. "All she wanted was my attention, my understanding. Instead, I was busy flying around, giving papers, lecturing, playing the role of the big-shot Maya expert."

"So when you found out about her and this other man, you broke up?"

"Not immediately. I was upset, hurt, I didn't know what to do. We'd just started another field season. I was the project director, with a grant from a major foundation. She was on the project as the settlement pattern expert. I'd spent my last school year in the States putting together a team of students and professionals. Everything was in place. I meant to straighten things out between us, but I had to fly home to take care of a few last-minute details. I was gone two weeks. And when I got back, everything had changed."

"Did you know the man?"

I didn't want to think about it, but the words tumbled out anyway. "He was a German archaeologist working at an outlier group at Tancah, just up the road. Funny—I don't even remember his name."

"Are you all right?"

"Sure."

"Then why are you shivering?"

"The wind," I said. "Or maybe I'm getting a chill."

"I shouldn't have asked," she said. "It wasn't my business."

"You have a right to know."

"It's over with now."

But now I couldn't turn it loose. "The project went to hell pretty quick. I didn't stay on top of things, let work slide. We got way behind and I started missing deadlines. A couple of the students complained to the university about the way I wasn't on site enough. That I drank too much. They were right."

"You really don't have to explain."

"I guess for a while I was out of control. There's a lot I don't remember."

She reached up, rubbed my back with one hand.

"There are some things I'm not even sure I didn't dream."

"It's *all* just a bad dream," she soothed. "But it's over now."

But it wasn't over, because I was thinking of the *Xtabai*.

* * *

A long time later, when the constellations were high over-head, we started down the steps toward the beach.

My shivering had stopped and I was holding her hand as we descended and that's why we almost fell headlong when the man came leaping past us. I slammed against the stone railing and reached for Pepper as she lost her balance. She grabbed my hand again. "Who?"

But he was already on the beach, racing at full speed over the rocks, toward the end of the line of *cabañas*. I could hear yells from behind and above us. Split seconds later a pair of beefy men in guayaberas plunged past us, guns drawn, and after them came two others in uniform. We watched, stunned, as they loped off down the beach.

Then the door of José's hut opened and he stepped out, a barely visible figure in the little square of light from his doorway. The fleeing man collided with him, and the two went sprawling onto the rocks. An instant later there was a flash and an explosion from where the two men struggled on the ground and the first two pursuers each fired, their pistol barrels spouting flames in the darkness.

There was a cry and the first of the two pursuers fired again. Then there was silence.

Pepper and I stood rooted in shock, our eyes fixed on the forms in the blackness below.

Someone moved behind us and I turned to see Geraldo, his face twisted with anxiety.

"It's just as I said," he complained. "Drugs. They're ev-erywhere and now, in my own establishment. I knew it was only a matter of time before the *judiciales* came . . ."

Two of the policemen were returning now, dragging a man between them, his hands cuffed behind him. As they emerged into the light at the base of the steps I glimpsed a disheveled form in a dirty blue guayabera, with blood streaming from a wound in one shoulder.

They hoisted him up the steps and we stood back to let them pass. As they came level with us, Felipe Jordan's eyes met my own and I saw naked fear.

"Is anyone hurt?" Geraldo asked, wringing his hands.

One of the detectives nodded back at the beach. "The man who came out of his *cabaña*. This *cabrón* shot him before we were able to stop him."

"*Caráy*, you mean one of the archaeologists?" Geraldo cried.

"*No se preocupe*," the detective said. "He'll live. We'll take him to the hospital in Chetumal. And this son-of-a-bitch is going to spend a long time making hammocks in the state prison." He jerked his prisoner's arm and the man gave a groan. I looked away.

A few minutes later the two policemen in uniform appeared, helping José walk. Pepper and I ran down to take him from them.

"*No es nada*," José said, pressing a hand to his right shoulder. "I'll be okay."

Geraldo threw up his hands, placating. "*Arqueólogo*, this is the first time anything like this has happened to one of my guests. How can I ever apologize enough?" He stared angrily up at the disappearing detectives with their prisoner. "But I said from the first that man Jordan was no good, that he was selling drugs, and now they've come around asking if I knew if he had anything to do with the killing of that man on the beach. I told them nothing about him would surprise me. But I told them I hadn't seen him for days. And I'd no sooner said it than the bastard showed up. Only a few hours after they first came, this afternoon, asking about him. Now I look like a liar, as if I'm in with him. And if that's not enough, he shoots one of my guests."

"It's not your fault," José said. He looked to see if the two uniformed policemen were within hearing, but now that we'd taken their charge, they'd wandered on up the steps. "Besides, Jordan didn't shoot me. He had a gun, but he shot at *them*, not me. It was one of their shots that hit me, the *putos*."

"Where's April?" I asked, as Geraldo helped José walk.

Pepper nodded toward the beach.

April, wearing a plain white *huipil*, was standing in the doorway of José's *cabaña*.

▰ SIXTEEN

Sunday fled in a blur. I drove José to the hospital in Chetumal, taking Pepper and April with me. Minnie, it was agreed, would stay behind to inform Eric, when he returned. In the hospital, José was examined by an intense young intern doing his social service year and the wound was pronounced serious but not grave. Two hours later, after a tetanus shot and with his right shoulder immobilized by bandages, José went back with us and we helped him into his hammock, April insisting that she would sling her own hammock nearby and stay with him through the night. Eric, whom we must have passed on the road, could only shake his head.

"Next time," he told José, trying to joke, "let the cops do their own work."

"Then we'd all be dead," José said.

Eric walked out of the hut and we stood on the beach.

"Our talk the other night . . . was that yesterday or the night before? I can't even remember. But with this . . ." He turned toward me, his face haggard. "I need you more than ever, Alan."

That evening, while we were standing on the beach, I told her.

"I have to. With José down for a week, Eric needs me. I know what he's going through. I've been there. If I can help him, I will."

Pepper nodded. "I knew you would even before."

"Are you disappointed?"

"That you're doing what you have to do? What you want to do? No. I'm just going to miss you."

"I'm not gone yet. And it's only to the end of December."

"Yes."

"What he said about getting me on at his university is just talk. I may not even be interested. All I'm thinking about now is helping to get him through this."

"I understand."

"Tell you the truth, this isn't that interesting a site," I said. "I mean, he hasn't found all that much. I can think of ten other sites I'd rather excavate before this one."

She didn't say anything, just stared out over the lake.

"You'll do a good job," she said finally. "Eric's lucky you're here."

"I'll do what I can." I kicked at a piece of shell, crushed by the heels of people coming and going across the beach. "I guess I ought to call David, though. He needs to make arrangements. By the way, has anybody heard from Paul? He was going to call Eric when he got to the hotel in Mérida. He should be told about José."

Pepper shrugged. "I haven't heard anything."

I put an arm around her waist. "Look, I'll fly back a couple of times. You can fly down a couple of times. It won't be that bad and we'll have Christmas together."

"I'm happy for you," she said.

Later, after dinner, I knocked on Eric's door.

"I'll do it," I said.

His face broke into a huge smile and he jumped up to take my hand with both of his. "Alan, you don't know how good that makes me feel. I have the budget page right here in my computer. I was just waiting to fill in the figures for your salary. Look, I don't know what you're used to getting, but this is what I had in mind." He pulled a sheet out of his briefcase and I saw, to my surprise, that my name was neatly typed out, with a summary of my credentials, and the title *Assistant Project Director*. Under this was a salary figure substantially larger than what I paid myself at home, when there was work.

"That's fine," I said.

"You're sure?" He asked. "I mean, I could do some more finagling, maybe squeeze out a few more dollars."

"No, this is fine," I repeated.

He stuck out his hand again. "Great." He delved in a backpack and came out with a bottle. "Black Label Jack Daniel's," he said. "I've been saving it for the end of the field season. But I think this is a better occasion. We'll toast the success of the project."

I took the glass and lifted it.

"*Salud*," he said.

"By the way," I asked, "has anybody heard from Paul?"

Blackburn shook his head. "No. I told him to give me a call when he got to Mérida, but you know how he is. He probably got involved in his research and forgot all about it. He'll be back Monday or Tuesday." He started toward the door, looping an arm around my shoulders. "Now I need to get this budget revision in the mail and call the graduate dean." He chuckled. "He won't like getting a call at home on Sunday until he hears about the money. Jesus, college administrators are such whores."

I laughed. "Nothing new about that."

"Well, thank God things turned out okay," he said as I walked out into the failing light. "José wasn't hurt too badly and April can spend all her time watching over him. That way she won't be wandering away or getting in anybody's hair."

"I think it'll take a while for Geraldo to calm down," I said. "He's convinced this fracas has wrecked his business."

I walked out, leaving him to his work. The decision was made.

The *Xtabai* was waiting for me when I crossed the plaza of the tiny village. All around, the thatched huts were dark and people were asleep. I wondered why I was here, because there was no reason for me to be alone in this village at night. I should be somewhere else, but with whom?

The witch beckoned, smiling with crooked teeth.

"Felicia?" I called.

But Felicia had beautiful, even teeth

"You're not Felicia," I said, but no words came out.

"*Coten uaye,*" the spirit said. "Come."

"No," I said, but again no sound emerged, and my feet moved as if they had their own mind.

She opened her arms and I saw dead leaves on her *huipil.*

"Stay away," I warned soundlessly.

She was coming forward now and I knew what would happen.

Terror seized me and I knew I was going to die, crushed into the bosom of the creature.

"*Coten. A kat dziz ten uetel?*"

She was inviting me to make love to her and all I wanted was to turn and run.

The other man saved me. Just as her arms were reaching for me, he rushed into her embrace and her branch-arms closed around him. He screamed in pain as she drew him against her, his flesh rending, and I saw blood spurt from his ears and then from the pores in his body. His bones snapped with a crackling sound and his body went limp. The *Xtabai* released him and he collapsed onto the rocky ground.

The moon cast the only light in the plaza and, against my will, I stepped forward and looked down at his face.

It was José.

The next morning, Monday, after we'd arrived at the site, Eric took Santos and me on a hike across a burned field and away from the site of the excavations. The trail led across an open expanse of red earth with limestone poking up through the soil. The sun beat down like a hammer and bounced back at us from the rocks.

"This was the cornfield of one of the village men a couple of years ago," Eric said as we walked. "It's fallow now and just as well, with this drought. It's a good thing the government's put in irrigation programs. At least they have some fruit trees."

But there would always be corn, the giver of life, I thought. When there was no longer any corn, there would cease to be Maya.

I saw a copse of poplar trees half a mile ahead of us, an oasis in the island of sun. When we got near I realized they were surrounded by high weeds, and Santos pulled out his machete to clear a path.

"The south group begins in the trees," Eric explained as we followed the guide. "But we've never really determined how far it extends. Hell, it may go on forever. That would be a discovery."

We reached the shade of the first trees and Santos waited for us to catch up. "*Aqui está*," he said, pointing.

Within the trees was a circular depression a hundred yards in diameter and as I looked down I saw a trail winding its way along the sides of the sinkhole to the bottom of the pit. I stood transfixed and Eric chuckled under his breath.

"I thought you'd like it. There's a wall in the bottom that closes off a cave entrance and a few crude pictographs on the sides of the cave. I took some pictures when we discovered this during the first season and I've always meant to get back here. But we had other work to do first."

"This is part of the south group?" I asked.

"Yup. And it's all yours."

"I want to go down there," I said.

Eric slapped my shoulder. "Then we will. And afterwards I'll take you to some of the other ruins just south of here. You can decide for yourself how much you think you can do in two months. I say *two* because I have two months of catch-up on the rest of the site but this needs looking at. It's been here for a thousand years, but with so many sites being looted, we had to document it while we can." He motioned to Santos and the Mayan started down the narrow trail, hacking at vines in some places, and grabbing nearby roots to keep from falling. We followed, earth sliding from under our feet as we picked our way down. Finally, at the bottom, Eric took out his canteen and handed it around. When we'd all drunk he pointed to a wall of limestone blocks that extended from one side of the overhang to the other, with just a couple of feet between the top of the wall and the roof of the cave.

"There's some wax on the rocks in front of the wall," he said. "Santos told me people still came here until fairly recently to pray to the gods of the underground. Lord knows how long they've been doing that here." He stepped under the limestone overhang and I smelled the dankness of the cave. He kicked at the ground. "Ought to be some deposits here. A test unit where we're standing might show some interesting things."

"If this place isn't sacred," I said.

"He says they don't come here anymore," Eric said. "I don't think you have to worry about that."

I examined the wall. It was solid. Someone had wanted to keep people out of the cave. Or else, I reflected, they'd wanted to keep something inside the cave from coming out.

"The pictographs are just inside, on the side of the cave," Eric said. "I scrambled over the top of the wall when we found this place and looked around, but there's debris blocking the inner part of the cave."

I measured the wiggle space at the top of the wall with my eyes. "I think I can make it."

Eric laughed. "Hey, it's your site now. I say go for it."

The two men made stirrups of their hands and hoisted me to the top of the wall. Eric handed up a small flashlight and winked. "I had a feeling we might need this, so I brought it with me."

I lay on my belly atop the narrow wall and transferred the light from my left hand to my right. I flicked it on and scanned the wall.

The pictographs were crude, all right, nothing like the spectacular, multicolor murals of Bonampak. Instead, these were stick figures, smudged into the wall by fingers dipped in ochre and charcoal.

"Well?" Eric called. "You see 'em?"

"Yeah." I handed him the flashlight and then lowered myself back down. "I wonder when this wall was built."

"Who knows? Maybe you can tell us in your report. When you write it. By the way, as editor-elect of the *Mayan Journal,* I get first dibs on publications."

"Understood."

I turned to Santos. "*Yan mas muulob ti nohol?*" I asked. "Are there more ruins south of here?"

"*Yan,*" he said. "There are."

Eric frowned and I realized he hadn't understood.

"I was just asking how far south this all goes."

"Ask away. Maybe you'll get a different answer in Mayan than I do in Spanish."

"How far south do they go?" I asked Santos. "More than a kilometer?"

"*Ma tech,*" Santos said. "One kilometer. That's all. Not much past the end of this field."

My spirits started to fall and then I caught myself. What was I thinking? A kilometer—over a half mile—of scattered mounds which had once been temples and pyramids. Not to mention this cave, which might hold archaeological materials of incredible richness. It was an area almost as large as what Blackburn's team had excavated in bits and pieces over the last two field seasons.

"I can give you four workers," Eric said. "I can free up two and I talked to Santos and he knows two villagers who need work. He says they're good men. One of them we used last year and he's reliable. The other I don't know, but you can probably train him. What do you think?"

"Can I use your total station and the EDM to map?"

"You don't have to ask."

"Because that's all we'll be able to do this year, make a good map of this area. Then maybe a controlled surface collection of certain areas if we have time, to supplement the collection you made earlier."

"Keep talking."

"What about processing? Who's doing that?"

"My contract with INAH is for them to do the final analysis, cataloging, and curation. That way the artifacts don't leave the country and there's no offended national pride. We do the initial processing in the field lab and then I take the artifacts to Mérida every couple of weeks for the final processing and cataloging. I spot-check their results at that time to satisfy myself they're on track and we try to reconcile any differences. It's worked pretty well."

We climbed back out of the hole and I followed them through the trees to the south edge of the field. I stared across half a mile of moonscape, with the green fringe of jungle shimmering in the distance. Here and there were scattered humps of stone, where houses, temples, and pyramids had once been. Not much now, I thought, but once this was the site of a teeming metropolis with artisans, kings, priests, and the ever-present peasants who raised the food and paid the taxes.

I didn't feel the pounding sun then, because I was thinking beyond this moment, both to a thousand years in the past and years into the future. It was mine. Eric had promised. I could direct the investigations here, mapping and collecting this year and then, in the next field season, do test units, strategically placed one- and two-meter-square excavations that would tell us the story of different portions of the site. And then, in a year or two or maybe three, I could be back with a full crew, excavating large blocks, reconstructing, gathering the million tiny bits of data that would tell the story of this place.

I reached down, picked up some of the rich red earth in my fingers and then let it drift back to the ground as dust.

This was where I belonged and I didn't want to leave. But finally I turned around and saw the other two men waiting in the shade of the trees.

"Seen enough?" Eric asked.

"For now," I told him.

"I thought you might be interested," he said. "Well, back to the grind."

We were halfway back to the main group when Eric stopped to wipe his forehead with a bandanna.

"I'm worried about Paul," he said. "Last night, late, I called the hotel where he usually stays and he hadn't checked in."

"Maybe he's staying somewhere else."

"I hope so. I'm going to try again tonight. I'll call some-body I know at the museum and see if he's turned up. Hell, he's supposed to be back today or tomorrow."

"Is there anywhere else he could be?"

Eric chortled. "With Paul he could be any-damn-where. You saw what happened when you came down here. There's nothing I can do—he's old enough to be my father and he's helped me in the past, so I can't very well order him around. But the man worries the hell out of me. He's not in good health and he drives like a bat out of hell."

"I'm sure he'll turn up," I said.

But he didn't. No one at the museum had heard from him. Eric told us he'd give it another day, because Paul Hayes was capable of appearing as if from nowhere and asking why people were concerned. But on Tuesday, by late morn-ing, thick clouds drifted over the area and thunder began to rumble in the north.

"Old man Chaac," I said. "The rain god."

The farmers would be glad the drought was ending, but rain would turn the back roads into sloppy mires. Our progress would come to a halt, because with the onset of the rains we'd lose every afternoon and the next morning we'd have to bail out our units. And if Hayes was in some remote village . . .

"So are you going to dig at the cave first?" Pepper asked, carefully sketching the floor of the excavation unit on the paper in her clipboard. There were a grinding stone, a flint blade, and several fragments of colorful pottery spread throughout the one-meter area and we'd mapped in the loca-tions of each, using distances from the north and east walls of the unit. Not a treasure to the popular imagination, but enough to tell an archaeologist that a family had lived here a thousand years ago and had carried out the mundane tasks of grinding corn and preparing food.

"I have to do mapping first," I said.

"I mean after that. Next year."

"That's a long way off. I'm not thinking that far ahead."

"You're not?" She looked me in the eyes and I blinked.

"Well, maybe."

She stooped with the tape and remeasured the distance from the north wall to the flint blade. Reassured, she started to draw it on her graph paper.

"Have you called David?" she asked.

"I was going to, but all this business with José and then Paul . . ."

"You know I have to leave Saturday. You want me to tell them?"

It was a barb and she knew it. "I'll take care of it."

"What do you think's in the cave?" she asked.

"I don't know. Probably artifacts from ceremonies. More pictographs. That's what they found at Loltún and Balancanché. But there could be a burial or two."

"It'll make a nice publication. It could even become a tourist attraction."

"I can't control that. If the government decides . . ."

"None of us can control anything," she said.

"It'll work out."

"I know it will," she said and went on sketching.

Ten minutes later Minnie O'Toole appeared at the edge of the unit and ducked under the canopy. "Alan, I'm so excited," she said. "Eric just told me."

I jerked around. "What?"

"That you're staying and the project's being extended for four months. That's great. I told him if that was the case, I'd stay on, too, if I'm not too much of a bother."

"That's great," I said without enthusiasm.

"I'm sorry," Minnie said. "Did I talk out of turn?"

"No," I said. "It isn't your fault. I just didn't know things were set yet."

"He said he'd gotten his dean's approval and he said there was a promise of a lot of money from an anonymous donor. And we can get the permit extended, I know."

"Yes."

"Not that it takes any intelligence to figure out who that donor is."

"I'll be glad to have you here, Minnie," I said.

"Thanks. And Pepper . . ." Then she saw the look on Pepper's face and understood. "Well, I better get back to my own little excavation. Your floor here looks so pretty. I feel like such a klutz. It takes me half a day to just clean up the thing for photographing."

At lunchtime, with the clouds darkening and the rumble of thunder ever closer, Eric left to try to call Mérida again. I found Minnie and walked back with her to her own excavation unit.

"I'm not sure Eric didn't jump the gun a little with his announcement," I said.

"It's his enthusiasm," Minnie pronounced. "He's really excited about having you here, Alan. And I'm the mother goddess, you know. Everybody feels like they can confide to Minnie."

"Well, I haven't made any commitments beyond the next four months," I said. "I just agreed to help out in the crunch."

The older woman nodded. "Look at this," she said, pointing to her unit, where excess dirt had been swept into little piles. "Sometimes I think I'll never get the hang of this."

"It just takes time," I said. "And a sharp trowel helps."

"Do you think that's it?" She picked up her own trowel, a spade-bladed Marshalltown. "Maybe that's what I need to do."

"Bring it by when you get a chance," I said. "I have a file at our unit."

"Thanks, Alan." I started away, but her voice caught me. "I gather Pepper isn't very happy about this latest development."

"No."

"She really loves you, you know."

I wasn't sure what to say, so I said nothing.

"She couldn't wait for you to come down. She was so scared that at the last minute you were going to change your mind."

"The two of you must've talked a lot."

"Pretty much. There isn't a lot else to do. You know, you're lucky to have somebody like her."

"I've often thought so."

"Would you be surprised if I told you I was in love a long time ago?"

"No." I glanced up at the clouds, trying to decide if the thunder was nearer or whether the storm was beating itself out fifty miles to the north.

"I met him while I was at the university, working on my master's in library science. He was a lawyer. He was into all kinds of environmental causes and always taking cases that didn't make him any money from people who couldn't have afforded a lawyer otherwise."

I lowered my eyes from the sky to the tall, thin woman beside me, trying to imagine her young and in love.

"But he didn't want to stay in Iowa. He couldn't make it on the work he was doing and he absolutely refused to start chasing ambulances. Then he got an offer from a major citizens' action group in California. They were willing to pay him a good salary and provide benefits. Not anything like one of the major private law firms, of course. But enough to live comfortably on, and he could practice the kind of law he loved, helping people."

"What happened?" I asked, interested despite myself.

"I'll never forget the day he came and told me about the offer. He was so excited. He wanted me to come with him, of course, right then."

"But you didn't."

"I couldn't. That's what I told myself, anyway. I had to finish my coursework, about another year in residence. Then I'd join him."

"And?"

"We wrote back and forth—this was before e-mail, of course—and we ran up huge phone bills. And I even flew out to visit him over Christmas. But it was funny—I noticed a change. Nothing big, just little things, like he wouldn't meet my eyes, and sometimes he smiled or laughed too much. He seemed to be involved in his work, because that was all he wanted to talk about, almost as if it kept him from having to talk about *us*."

"Was there somebody else?"

"You know, I never found out for sure? I just know I went back and the letters got fewer and fewer and it got harder and harder to get him on the phone, and when I did he always seemed preoccupied. He still loved me, he said. But there was always some case he was involved in, some deadline, some poor soul who was about to go under for the third time because of a greedy big corporation or government incompetence. I began to wonder after a while if he was using his work to keep me at arm's length or whether he really was so wrapped up in what he was doing. All I know is his feelings toward me had very subtly changed. And when the year was up there was no reason to go to him."

"I'm sorry."

"Don't be. Some things aren't meant to work. Some things are beautiful while they last, but they're too fragile to stand the strain, sort of like a blossom with the first frost. It takes a very strong love to survive separation for long periods."

"Is this a message for Pepper and me?" I asked. "Or maybe just for me?"

"I'm sorry. I tend to babble. I need to stuff a cork in my mouth."

"It's okay," I said.

"And I've been worried about Paul. I do hope he's all right."

"Me, too," I said and walked back to our unit. The storm, I decided, wasn't going to reach us. The farmers would have to wait until tomorrow for rain.

When Eric got back at three o'clock he said that Paul Hayes had still not turned up and he was about to notify the U.S. Consulate that a citizen was missing.

A little chill ran through me. Surely if something had happened the police would have reported it by now and the consulate would know.

Unless he'd been robbed and murdered and his body dumped in some out-of-the-way place. It wasn't something I wanted to think about. It wasn't the same Yucatán I remembered.

We were packing our equipment to leave when Santos sauntered over.

"*Don* Alan," he said and I waited, knowing he had something to say.

"Is it true *don* Pablo has disappeared?" he asked in Mayan.

"I don't know," I told him. "But he should be back now."

"He's your friend, *masimá*?"

"He is."

"He talked to me about the ruins," the other man said. "He was looking for a site."

"Oh?"

"I told him there wasn't any site like that around here."

"Well, you'd know," I said.

He gave a little nod. "I showed him the cave, too."

"What did he say about it?"

A shrug. "He was looking for something else. A site with big buildings."

"Maybe he found it," I said then. "Maybe that's where he is. Maybe he found the site with big buildings somewhere north of here."

Santos gave a little smile and walked away.

Late that night I was routed from sleep by a pounding on our door and when I roused myself I found a wild-eyed Eric Blackburn.

He told me they'd found Paul Hayes. His car had missed a turn near Peto and turned over. Because of the fire, it had taken them a while to identify the body.

▰ SEVENTEEN

No one wanted to work the next day but we struggled out to the site anyway, all but Eric, who used my rental car to drive up to Mérida for the myriad arrangements that attend the death of a foreign national in Mexico. José, arm still in a sling and assisted by a solicitous April, insisted on going with us to the site, but once we were there it was difficult to think about work.

Early in the morning hours, after Eric had told everyone about Paul's death, he'd taken me aside. "I'd like you to take over while I'm gone. It should only be a couple of days. Alan, I really need you now."

And for some reason all I could think was, *Everything was going well enough until I came. Fifteen years ago a project went to shit, and now . . . Maybe I bring my bad luck with me.*

It's easy to be irrational at two-thirty in the morning.

Now, at the site, I stared dully at our excavation unit, trying to remember what it was exactly that we had to do. My hand went into my pocket and touched something hard. I drew out the little stone tablet Paul Hayes had given me to guard.

He wouldn't be needing it now. I might just as well throw it away.

Maybe if I hadn't been an archaeologist I would have.

"You don't have any choice now," Pepper told me, standing up from the excavation. For the first time ever I noticed dark

135

smudges under her eyes. "I guess I was thinking about myself before. But Eric really does need you."

I nodded.

"Have you talked to Minnie?" I asked.

"I tried, but she's pretty upset. I think she really cared for Paul."

Half an hour later I picked my way over the open field to Minnie's excavation.

"How're you doing?" I asked.

"Not worth a damn," she said and threw her trowel halfway across the unit. "Goddamn it, Alan, *why*?"

Then she was hugging me with both arms and crying and I was trying to tell her it would be all right, but I knew the words were meaningless.

It was an hour later, while I was searching in the back of the van for a line level, that Santos approached me.

"A terrible thing about *don* Pablo," he said.

"Yes."

"We talked many times, *don* Pablo and I, about the books and the old stories and about the site with the *nohoch muul,* the big pyramid. He told me about a man who came here a long time ago, an American, I think."

John Dance Williams. Well, it was easy to confuse the two English-speaking countries.

"He met an old man, *don* Pablo said, and this old man showed him this place, deep in the forest."

"That's what he told me, too," I said.

Santos nodded. "*Don* Pablo said he didn't tell any of the other *dzuulob.* But he would have told you. You know Mayan."

"And did *don* Pablo?"

"Not as well as you, but more than the others. And he had books in the old Mayan writing, that he brought from his country. He showed me. But many of the words were different. He said they spoke differently then, in the time long ago."

I didn't think I could explain the principles of linguistic change, so I just nodded.

"He knew many of the *h-menob*, too. He used to copy down their stories and their prayers and their chants. He had a little *grabadora*, a tape recorder, and he played some of them for me and I helped him translate them into Spanish."

On an impulse I reached into my pocket and took out the little stone tablet. "Did he ever show you this?"

Santos took it and turned it over in his hand.

"He showed it to me," he said. "He said it had ancient writing, but I didn't understand it. Do you?"

"No."

Santos exhaled and took out a cigarette. He squatted and took out a match and I sat down beside him. "*Don* Alan, many people have come here looking for the ancient sites."

"Many."

"It's a good thing. Once, all the sites were hidden in the jungle. Now there are great tourist centers, like Tulum and Kohunlich and Becán and Xpujil and Cobá."

"Yes."

"When the *arqueólogos* come to excavate a site, they hire men and that means good pay. In the old days, when there was a drought, like this year, there was no corn and the people starved. In the *días de esclavitúd*, the slavery days. Now, when a site is opened for the tourists, they hire guides and groundskeepers and guards all year 'round."

"It's a good thing," I said, reflecting that my own nostalgia was of little consequence when it came to the survival of a people.

"*Don* Eric pays me well for what I do. I am very grateful. I would not do anything to upset him."

"Why would anything you did upset him?"

Santos shrugged, face impassive under the red baseball cap.

"He's spent two years here at this site," Santos said finally. "Much work, much money."

"True."

"He asked me how far to the south the ruins went."

"And you said a kilometer."

He drew on the cigarette. "*Don* Pablo asked me the same

question. He was looking for the site with the *nohoch muul.*
I told him there wasn't any."

"And?"

"*Tuzcep,*" Santos said finally. "I lied."

I stared at our guide. "You mean this site continues into
the forest?"

He nodded. "It does. Small *muulob,* heaps of stone, for
another five kilometers, maybe more. I'm not sure."

"Well, I'm glad you told me now," I said. "At least we
can plan for next year. But Santos, why did you hold it
back?"

He didn't answer for a long time, just continued to smoke
until the cigarette was a stub and then he flicked it onto the
ground.

"Some of the *h-menob* thought *don* Pablo asked too many
questions. They've met foreigners before. At first they
thought the foreigners would bring things to help them, but
now they see that the foreigners just want to ask questions.
But I should have told *don* Pablo. I should not have lied."

"*Maalob,*" I said. "It's okay."

"I told him this site ended a kilometer to the south. I
didn't tell him that it went farther because I was afraid he
and *don* Eric would want to go there. And then, if they went
too far, they would find the site with the *nohoch muul.*"

I waited for the import of what he'd said to sink in. Maybe
I'd heard him wrong. My Mayan was rusty and I was tired.

"There's such a site?" I asked slowly, this time in Spanish.

"*Sí, hay,*" he replied. "The place with the heads."

"The heads?"

"Yes, of the ancient kings. There is a door with seven of
them."

I tried to contain my surprise. "Have you actually been to
this place?"

"A long time ago," he said. "When I was young."

"And it's not far from here?"

"Twenty kilometers, maybe thirty, to the south. *Pura
selva.*"

All jungle. Which meant it was probably still hidden from

the satellites that had been photographing this area for decades now.

"Who knows about this place besides you?"

"Villagers, but there aren't so many these days. Sickness drove them out years ago. *Paludismo*. And *chicleros*."

"And it hasn't been looted?"

"Sure, parts of it. But the heads are supposed to still be there. That place is too overgrown. Only jaguars can get through the vines."

"How do you know, if you haven't been there?"

"*Be bin*," he said in Mayan, looking away. "That's what they say."

I tried to think how to proceed. He'd obviously told me all this for a reason. Maybe it was guilt, a feeling that Paul Hayes would still be alive if Santos had told Paul what he was telling me now. But I also sensed that his mind was not completely made up, that he was testing me to see how I responded.

"What do you think we should do?" I asked in Spanish.

"*Quien sabe?* Maybe sometime, though, we should go there."

"Maybe," I agreed. "When do you think that should be?"

"I don't know. When you have time."

"Is there a road to the place?"

He shook his head. "*Ma tech.* You have to walk. There's a trail through the jungle."

"Can we do it in one day?"

"One day, maybe less."

"Will you take me and *Doctora Pimienta*?" I asked, using the Spanish translation the workers used for Pepper's name.

"Sure."

"When?"

He looked up at the sky, where more rain clouds had gathered, accompanied by rumblings.

"*Zamal, uale.* Early. Before it gets hot. Before the rain."

"And if anyone else wants to go?"

Another shrug. "Why not?"

* * *

That evening, at dinner, I told the others about the site, holding back only Paul Hayes's fantastic theory about pre-columbian visitors.

"José, I'd like to have the Instituto Nacional represented."

The Mexican sighed. "Doctor, I'd be more of a burden than a help. Besides, I've heard stories like this before. You may just be going for a long, thirsty walk."

"It occurred to me," I said.

"No, April and Minnie and I will stay here and do the work we're being paid for."

"But if I find it—" I began.

"—I'll expect a full report for INAH," the Mexican said dourly.

"Of course."

Minnie reached across the table then and put her hand on my own. "Alan, I want to go."

"You?"

"Why not? I'm in good physical condition. And I cared about Paul. I feel like I owe it to him to carry on somehow."

I looked over at Pepper, but she was already nodding.

I turned back to Minnie. "All right," I said. "Tomorrow. We'll see if there's a lost site out there in the jungle." I raised my beer glass. "Meanwhile, let's drink to Paul Hayes."

▰ EIGHTEEN

We left at five, while the mist still wreathed the *cabañas*. Geraldo wished us well and wrung his hands a few more times about Paul. Twenty-five miles west of the Chetumal turnoff we passed a roadblock and I saw Tapia sitting in one of the Humvees, looking his usual glum self. But they were checking traffic headed east from Escarcega and paid us little attention.

In Ah Cutz village, Santos was waiting for us, his machete slung over one shoulder in a leather scabbard, *chiclero* style, and a gourd of water hanging from the other shoulder by a piece of cordage.

We drove the half kilometer to the work site, started the Mayan crew to work, and then said our good-byes to José and April.

"If we're not back by tomorrow," I joked, "you can send the army."

José's eyes met my own. "If you're not back tomorrow, I'll come for you myself."

I wasn't sure if it was a promise or a threat.

The trail, Santos told us, led south, across the vast open space of the fallow field, past the grove of poplars with their sinkhole, and into the forest beyond. Where we were going was shown on the map only as unrelieved green, and the GPS I carried on my belt was little use in pinpointing a location we didn't know, but I took coordinates at the edge of the forest, marked them on the map, and then gave a last look across the open space to the shimmering green of the grove.

It was eight-fifteen and Santos said we had ten to twenty kilometers—six to twelve miles—to go. I hoped the first estimate was closer to the truth, but there was only one way to find out.

"*Co'oneex,*" I said to Santos, readjusting the straps of my backpack. "Let's go."

We headed into the jungle.

For the first two hours, as we followed a narrow, winding trail, I noticed heaps of stone on either side of us, half hidden by the vines and undergrowth. The overhead cover was too thick for me to get an accurate satellite fix, but I judged we'd made about three miles. Under the leafy umbrella, we were spared the full heat of the sun, but the canopy sealed in the moisture so that our clothes stuck to our skin and sweat rolled down our faces. Three times Minnie called a halt and we waited while she drank from her canteen.

"Are you all right?" I asked, after the last halt.

"Just a minute to rest," she panted.

Santos looked over at me and I knew what he was thinking because I was thinking it, too: This was a bad place for someone to get heat exhaustion.

"Should we go back?" he asked.

She took off her straw hat and fanned herself. "I'll make it. I'm sorry."

"Sure you will," Pepper reassured her.

"How much farther?" I asked Santos.

He looked away and gave one of his little shrugs. "Far," he said.

"Two hours?" I asked. "Three?"

He nodded. "Maybe more. It's been a long time."

I tried to calculate: If we ended up on the trail at night, we could sling our hammocks, which each of us carried in our packs, along with provisions. But if it took us more than a day's walk to get there, it would take us more than day's walk to get back. And if Minnie was about to give out this early on, how could I expect her to make it the rest of the way and return?

I was beginning to berate myself for having given in to her request to come.

"We'll go slower," I said. "Anybody who's thirsty or tired, say so and we'll stop."

Minnie nodded gratefully, her face flushed.

"I'm ready now," she said.

An hour later I noticed that the heaps of stone had become less frequent, so that now we seldom saw them. Santos was using his machete now, clearing a way along a path that had degenerated into little more than a game trail. Ahead, through the trees, I saw an opening, and when we reached it Santos considered it for a moment and pronounced it an old cornfield, now fallow and grown up in weeds.

"Whose?" I asked.

"I don't know."

I left the others to rest under a ceiba tree and walked out into the open space to get a GPS reading. Ten minutes later I returned to the shade and took out the map.

Minnie sat on the ground, eyes closed, back against a tree, but Pepper peered over my shoulder as I plotted our location and made a little X on the map, sweat dripping from my arm onto the paper.

"Shit," I said and pointed to the spot I'd marked.

In three hours we'd gone just eight kilometers—a bare five miles. And our pace wasn't getting any faster.

Then Santos told me he wasn't sure we were on the right trail.

"But how . . . ?" I demanded.

"I said it was a long time."

"What other trail is there?"

"There was a fork half a kilometer back. I'll go and see and come back."

I sat down with my companions and closed my eyes.

There was nothing to do in this situation but wait.

"Maybe there isn't any site," Minnie said. "Maybe Santos doesn't remember right."

Ordinarily I would have argued, but not now.

I'd let my enthusiasm get the better of me. I'd been so excited over the possibility of a new find I'd forgotten the lessons of the jungle, the first of which was to not go into it unless you were fit. And it wasn't just Minnie who was wearing down—I could feel my own fatigue now, my energy sapped by the humidity. Our water supplies were low, and, though I carried a bottle of purification tablets, finding more water depended on discovering a *cenote* or sinkhole, because the only river was the Río Hondo, the border between Mexico and Belize, and it was fifty miles to the east.

If there was a site of any size, of course, there would be a *cenote,* because the Maya only built their cities where there was a source of water. But now I was beginning to wonder if there was, indeed, such a city at all, and, if there was, whether we would find it.

I opened my eyes and stared up at the foliage that hid the sky. Sweat rolled down from my forehead and stung my eyes. I checked my watch. Three-quarters of an hour. Santos had been gone long enough to decide whether we were on the right path. Or had he? Maybe he'd decided to follow the other fork for a ways, to see if he picked up any familiar landmarks. Or maybe . . .

I didn't want to consider the *maybe.* Santos's behavior during all of this had been strange. First he'd told Paul there was no such site, then he'd revealed to me that the site existed and offered to take me there. But now, halfway along the trail, he'd vanished, claiming he wasn't sure we were heading in the right direction. My assessment of the man was that he was hardworking and honest. Now, though, I wondered if he hadn't determined to lose us in the jungle all along.

But if so, why?

Then I caught myself: What in the hell was I thinking? There was no reason to distrust Santos. He'd told me he hadn't been to the site for a long time. He was just trying to help.

"Maybe we ought to think about turning around," Pepper said. "I mean, if Santos isn't back in half an hour. He could have been bitten by a snake or something."

"Yeah," I said and closed my eyes again. A mosquito buzzed around my face and I halfheartedly waved it away. The jungle was lush, the rotting vegetation smell permeating the air, and I knew it was the odor of growing things and life, but it was also the smell of death for those so careless as to take it for granted.

I heard footfalls on crushed grass and opened my eyes again.

Santos was back.

"Ahead," he said simply. "This is the way."

"Are you sure?" I asked.

"This field wasn't here before."

"When was it that you last went to the site?"

He waved his hand to show the passage of the sun many times. "Long time. Maybe twenty years. There were more people living back here then."

"And is the site much farther?"

"If we leave now we should be there before dark."

It wasn't what I wanted to hear. Today was Thursday. If we reached our destination at dark we'd have to spent the first part of tomorrow in the ruins, taking pictures and making sketches, and that would mean spending a night on the trail and getting back to the site of the dig on Saturday. Not only would it cause worries, but Pepper was supposed to fly out of Cancún on Sunday, and that was three hours north along the east coast highway.

Coming here hadn't been a good idea and I said so to the others.

Pepper shrugged. "I can always catch a later flight if it comes to that. It may cost an arm and a leg and I may have to fly to Houston or Atlanta, but it can be done. I think Minnie should decide."

The tall woman heaved herself up. "Then I say let's go. I feel better now after the rest. I think I'm getting my second wind."

I pointed to the trail ahead and Santos started forward resignedly, machete slicing through a low vine.

It was the second bad decision I made that day.

The next three hours were the hottest part of the day. After a while the unremitting sameness of the jungle blurred into a green tunnel, with the buzz of insects almost indistinguishable from the heat-buzz in my head. I kept looking for a clearing, someplace where I could use the GPS to get a fix on our location, but the cover was absolute. When we halted for lunch—twelve-fifteen, according to my watch—nobody was hungry and we carefully marshaled our water. Conversation had dropped to an occasional monosyllable and even Santos seemed grim.

In an hour I judged we'd come a mile and a half, what with the frequent rest stops. That put us between six and seven miles from our starting point—maybe ten kilometers in. And according to Santos, our destination could possibly lie another ten kilometers farther on.

By midafternoon the trail began to wind slowly upward, the gradient barely perceptible at first. Santos turned, nodding, and I sensed he was telling us he recalled this part of the journey. I called a halt and we rested for a few moments.

"Close?" I asked, half afraid of his reply.

But this time he nodded assent. "Close," he said. "Maybe five kilometers."

Minnie groaned under her breath. "Did he say what I thought he said? Another three miles?"

"Can you make it?" I asked.

"After coming this far?" She gave a dry little laugh. "Hell, yes."

Slowly, almost imperceptibly, as we walked, the jungle light began to turn to a rich gold and I realized the sun was burning itself out in the west. The mosquitoes were worse now, despite heavy applications of bug spray, and we were all cursing and batting them away except for Santos, who'd broken out a pack of cigarettes and handed a couple of the smokes around. We'd torn the cigarettes open and rubbed ourselves with the tobacco, while Santos had lit up.

"I never thought I'd see a use for cigarettes," Minnie said, watching Santos puff out smoke to drive away the pests.

"Well, if cigarettes kill people, just think what they do to bugs," Pepper said.

Minnie shifted her position on the ground. "Ow. This place is full of rocks." She reached down and brought up a hard, gray-colored object. "Hey, this isn't a rock."

She handed it to me and for the first time in hours my heart started to race. "It's a piece of Mayan pottery," I said. "Post-Classic, from the looks of it."

I held it up for the others to see and the Mayan's face cracked in a thin smile.

"Are you sure there's a *cenote,* with water, at this site?" I asked him, daring now to believe we'd actually get there.

"Yes," he said simply. "There is."

An hour and a half later we saw the first ruin.

The trail curved right and there it was, just around the bend, half concealed by the foliage. Nothing spectacular, just a set of stone blocks erupting from a small hill of earth split by tree roots. I sagged against one of the trees.

"Is this it?" I asked.

But Santos shook his head. "Maybe a kilometer more."

"We're still not there?" Pepper asked.

"Probably an outlier," I said. "We should start seeing more and more ruins."

She consulted her watch. "We'd better hurry or we're going to get caught in the dark."

"Minnie?" I asked, but the lanky woman didn't answer, just nodded ahead at the trail, and we started forward once more.

If I'd been more alert, less tired and thirsty, I would have noticed that the trail was wider now and less overgrown, and I would have asked myself why. Then, failing an answer, I would have asked Santos.

My third mistake of the day.

But Santos had noticed, because he called a halt on his own and told us to wait while he went ahead.

We were all too tired to ask him why.

An hour later the shapes of leaves and trees had become indistinct.

"It's going to be dark in half an hour," Pepper said. "What's going on with Santos?"

I forced myself up. "I don't like it. Before it was to see if we were in the right place but this time it doesn't make sense."

"Should we go on and try to catch up with him?" Minnie asked. "He said we didn't have but half a mile. Shouldn't we try to make it to the ruins before dark? At least there'd be water."

"You're right. If we meet Santos on the trail, fine. If not, we'll at least be where we can fill our canteens."

"If there *is* a site," Pepper said then.

Minnie and I both looked at her.

"What I mean," she explained, "is maybe this is just an isolated group of ruins, a couple of little temples, and he was wrong. Maybe he mistook these for the beginnings of the site and it turned out there wasn't anything else. Maybe he went three or four more kilometers looking for the main ruins and never found them. Maybe he's lost, or as confused as we are. Or maybe he's scared to come back and tell us."

"Maybe," I said, not wanting to admit she could be right. "Another half mile and we should know."

But it didn't take half a mile for us to find out.

We began to smell it only a hundred yards farther on.

"What's that?" Minnie asked, nose wrinkling. "It smells like . . ."

"Something died," Pepper said. "Maybe a deer or a big snake."

I stopped to listen. There was a buzz in the undergrowth ahead and then I heard movement, like something scratching.

"Wait," I told them. "I'll go see."

"I'm coming," Pepper said, but Minnie slid down into a sitting position against a tree trunk.

Too tired to argue, I pushed forward, stooping under a low vine and then halting as a scamper of feet made off into the jungle.

There were more buildings ahead, gray, ghostlike hulks in the deepening evening, breaking a background of green, and between them was a row of monoliths leaning at crazy angles.

But I was barely aware of the temples or the stelae, because I was staring at the thing in the middle of the trail.

The scavengers had left little more than bones, and a trail of ants were still feasting on what was left.

I turned away, my gorge rising.

"Don't come here," I told Pepper, but she ignored me and then I heard her give a little gasp.

"Oh, my God. *Who?*"

The only thing I recognized was a fragment of blue cloth from the guayabera now covering white ribs.

"Felipe Jordan," I said.

"But how?"

I never got a chance to answer because the men with rifles stepped out of the forest then and opened fire and something slammed my head.

The last thing I remembered was the ground rushing up, and then all the sounds died away and the world went black.

■■Nineteen

When I opened my eyes everything was still black and I thought for a moment I was dead. Then I heard my name, whispered rather than said.

"Alan." Hands touched me and I tried to think where I was.

"Alan, it's Minnie. Can you hear me?"

I started to groan and a hand went over my mouth.

"You have to keep quiet. They may be nearby."

My head throbbed with pain. Something nearby stank and flies buzzed. The hand moved off my mouth and I took a deep breath.

"You've been shot," she whispered, mouth close to my ear. "We need to get you out of here."

My lips moved, but no words came out.

"I heard the shots and hid in the jungle. When they were gone I came to see what happened and found you."

"Pepper . . ." It was more a croak than a word.

"I think they took her. We have to get you out of here. It's night. They won't see us now unless they come back this way, and I don't think they will. But if we're still here when it gets light, they may kill us both."

She put something against my lips and I tasted wetness.

"Drink. Just a little bit. There." She lifted the canteen away. "If we can get you far enough away from here, maybe we can find a plant or something with water in it, like in the movies. Can you move at all?"

I tried and felt my toes move inside my boots, but when I

tried to move my body my head felt like it was inside a tornado, twisting and whirling.

"I'm going to feel your wound. I'll try not to hurt you."

Her fingers touched my head, felt backward, and I gasped as pain stabbed me. She moved her hand away.

"I don't know," she said. "I think you were shot in the head, on the left side. But I can't tell how badly because it's dark and I don't want to probe and make things worse. It may have just grazed your skull. I hope that's all, anyway."

"I feel dead," I said.

"But you aren't, and that means something: There are places a bullet can go and miss everything. I read about it in a medical book once."

"A medical book?"

"You'd be surprised what all I read while I was a librarian."

I lifted my own hand then and tentatively touched my wound. My fingers came away sticky and a wave of nausea rocked me.

"Can you stand?" she asked.

She reached under my shoulders and helped me sit up. The world started to spin, concentric waves of black against the even darker night.

"Hell," she said.

"You'd better leave me here," I told her.

"You're crazy."

"I can't do anything. I can't walk. I can't even stand."

Silence, and I heard her panting from the effort to pull me upright.

"Who do you think they were?" she asked. "Guerrillas? Part of that uprising thing in Chiapas?"

"No. They don't ambush foreign nationals. And they sure don't kill DEA agents."

"What?"

"Jordan," I said. "Everybody thought he was a drug peddler. I think he was DEA."

"I thought there was some sort of law about them not operating in Mexico."

"That was under the old regime. Who knows what's really

going on now? Or what secret arrangements have been made? I think Jordan was down here trying to get the goods on this *don* Chucho character. But Jordan was supposed to contact somebody and there was a screwup." I gulped in the warm, moist air, trying to maintain my train of thought. "He thought I might be his contact. So he tried some kind of recognition code using the expression *snowbird*. When I didn't pick up on it, he knew I wasn't his man."

"Who *was* the contact?" she asked.

"I don't know. I don't think the contact ever got here. I think they found out the real spy, killed him, and left the body where it would wash up on the beach to warn Jordan and anybody he might be working with. That's why Jordan wanted to get to Chetumal: He needed to get away, slip over the border into Belize. I should have taken him."

"And the policemen who arrested him?"

"Bought off by Chucho."

"And the policemen killed Jordan?"

I thought about the body a few feet away. Of course it had been too dark for her to see it. She probably thought the stench came from a dead animal.

"Forget Jordan," I said. "See if you can drag me off the trail into the jungle a few feet."

She rose and then, stooping, reached under my shoulders and began to pull.

I felt the ground moving under me and after a second or two I lost consciousness. When I came to again there was something tickling my face and I smelled the chlorophyll odor of plants.

"Alan?"

Whose voice?

Then I remembered and reached out. My hand touched something pliant and I realized it was a fern frond.

"Alan, can you hear me? We're off the trail. I got you into the jungle, I'm not sure how far, maybe fifty feet. I couldn't drag you any farther, but maybe they won't see us."

I didn't say anything because my mind was spinning, and after a while I left the old, familiar earth of my physical existence and floated into space.

* * *

When I opened my eyes again I was having a chill. The darkness was lighter and I dimly realized I was soaked with moisture. I tried to move, but nothing happened.

"Minnie?"

"I'm here. You've been asleep."

"What time is it?"

"Just after five."

"When it gets a little lighter you have to try to get back," I said.

"And leave you? Don't be crazy. Besides, Santos may come back with help."

"Santos may be dead," I said. *Or, worse,* I thought, *he's sold us out.*

"But I can't just leave you."

"Yes, you can. It won't do any good for us to go down together. If you can walk while it's still cool, you can make it most of the way back." I licked my lips and felt a dry crust sand my tongue. "Reach into my left shirt pocket and take out the little notebook. I wrote our last coordinates in it. Take the GPS off my belt. Get them to Tapia if he's still got his soldiers on the highway." I coughed. "Remember: Tapia, not the judicial police."

"But Alan . . ."

"I'll be okay. I'm still alive, so it can't be that serious. I can hold out for a couple of days."

"Alan . . ."

"Please. It's the only chance." I reached up and my hand touched her arm. "Tell them these people are using the site as a drug depot. And for God's sake, tell them they've got Pepper and to go easy."

I closed my eyes and waited. A minute later I heard her sigh and her fingers started to unbutton my pocket, slipping out the notebook. Then I felt her unbuckling my belt and a second later the GPS receiver was gone. Her lips touched my forehead for the briefest of instants.

"I'll be back."

"I'll be here," I said.

And knew it was a lie.

* * *

You never think you're going to die until that day.

I figured that day had come.

I was shot in the head and I didn't know whether it was a minor concussion or whether my brain had been damaged. I remembered what had happened just before I'd been hit, and that was good. Or maybe I *didn't* remember and had invented memories to fill in the gaps.

Maybe any damned thing. I was dehydrated and going into shock, with no real prospects for rescue. Minnie had as much chance of making it back as I did of hauling myself to my feet, dragging myself into the drug runners' camp, and forcing their surrender.

And they had Pepper, which I didn't even want to think about.

I was dying and I knew it.

But the odd thing is that after a little while it doesn't seem so bad. The body releases endorphins that ease you toward the realization that annihilation is imminent. And your mental computer starts looking for programs that can divert it from the fact that it is shutting down.

I began to imagine I heard music.

Not an angelic choir but some kind of reggae, rising and falling in volume, and it made perfect sense, because Bob Marley had gone before me and maybe this was some kind of homing signal.

I jerked back to consciousness, staring up at a monster.

The monster crawled across my glasses and down the side of my face and was followed by another. Ants.

I tried to brush them away.

You little bastards, just wait a couple of hours and you can have all of me, I thought and then, taken by the notion, began to laugh silently at the humor of the situation.

The ants started to talk back.

At first I wondered why they were speaking Spanish, but then I realized it made sense, because this was Mexico and everybody spoke Spanish and I was even thinking in Spanish as I lay there.

"Be quiet," I told them. "Have some respect for the dying."

But they ignored me and I turned my head to blow on them, because I was tired of their using my body for a highway. But when I looked, I saw they were larger than I expected, and were walking upright, and instead of mandibles they carried submachine guns and rifles.

"*Puta madre, porque no echaste este cadaver mas lejos? Se apesta, hombre.*"

"*Me dijiste que lo lleve afuera. Nadie anda por esta senda.*"

"*Nadie mas que los gringos, idiota. Y donde está el hombre que tiramos?*"

"*Ya esta muerto, hombre, no te preocupas.*"

I realized the ants were discussing what had happened to me.

"*Busca en el monte,*" the first man ordered. "See if you can find his body."

He walked away, leaving his companion, whom I could make out only as a blur through the vines.

The second man waited until the first man was gone and then ambled to the other side of the trail and parted the branches with his gun barrel. Then he came back, toward where I lay. I thought he saw me and I wanted to call out, to ask him if he was blind, and then to laugh as he shot me again, because I knew I was already dead and more bullets would only be a waste of ammunition.

But after a glance he shrugged and turned around again, slapping a mosquito with a curse.

I heard the music again and realized it was coming from a radio somewhere in their encampment. I tried to raise my arm to see what time it was, but the parts of my body didn't want to work.

My brain began to run another program.

The *Xtabai* was bending over me, her long, vinelike arms caressing my body.

"You can't run anymore," she said and I thought it was odd that she was saying it in Spanish instead of Mayan.

But instead of strangling I felt a wetness on my face and realized she was crying.

"Why?" she asked. "I wouldn't have done it if you'd been there."

Then she buried her head against my chest and my whole body became soaked with her tears.

I opened my eyes and saw that it was raining.

I opened my mouth and let the runoff from the treetops tantalize my parched lips and throat. Soon the water bore me up and I was floating, a sailor on a stormy sea, and even though I knew I was dead I was afraid.

The boat was being driven toward a beach and I saw the froth breaking on a reef. There was a grinding sound and I pitched forward into the waves, water filling my mouth. I started to choke, and lashed out, desperate, but all I grabbed was water.

When my eyes opened I was on the beach and the natives were looking down at me.

"*Ma cimi?*" one asked and the other, an incredibly ancient man with white hair, shook his head.

"*Cuxaan,*" he pronounced and I knew he was telling the younger man I was still alive.

They should have been almost naked, I thought idly, but the young man was dressed like a Mayan peasant of modern times, down to his baseball cap, while the older man wore a white cotton shirt and a blue-striped *delantal,* or apron, a traditional style of dress I hadn't seen in fifteen years.

They were lifting me now, despite the rain, and my head flopped as they bore me away down the now-muddy trail.

I tried to tell them I was dead, but no one listened.

And when they came to a resting spot under a dripping oak, the old man wiped my face with a cloth and Santos told me I'd been saved by the rain.

▰▰TWENTY

When I opened my eyes again I was in a hammock and the old man was leaning over me. I heard rain beating down on the grass roof and smelled smoke from a cooking fire.

"Where am I?" I asked.

"My name is Leodejildo Chim. You are in my house," the old man said slowly in Mayan, making sure I would understand.

"Where?"

"In the forest. My grandson and I brought you here."

"Your grandson?"

"Santos."

"But—"

"Don't talk."

The old man lifted something wet from the side of my head and I saw him place it in a zinc bucket. Some kind of dressing. He went to the fire, which was under a thatched canopy just outside the rear door of the hut. I saw him stir a pot and then dip a strip of cloth into it. He fished out the cloth with a stick, waved it in the air a few times to cool it, and folded it into a square. He placed the new dressing on my side and I flinched as the heat started to spread through my face.

He reached down, picked up a gourd, and lifted it to my lips.

"Drink," he said. "But not a lot."

I swallowed the lukewarm liquid and then he took the gourd away.

"Enough," he said. "Sleep."

"You don't understand. There's a young woman. She was taken—"

"We know. My grandson will be back soon."

They bore me from the beach inland, to a temple, and soon a crowd had gathered to stare down at the stranger. A child poked at me with a stick and earned a slap from his mother. A priest with sharp-filed teeth and dark, blood-clotted hair came to appraise me. He said some words I didn't understand and I gathered he was telling them I should be sacrificed, because I was a danger to them alive. But another man, middle-aged, with an air of command, confronted him and, muttering, the priest backed down.

The leader bent over me and said something. I shrugged. He struck me a slap across the face and then motioned for me to rise.

It was dark outside when I opened my eyes again. The rain had stopped, succeeded by a slow dripping from the trees. How many days had passed?

I tried to get out of the hammock, but pain rocked my head.

"Not yet," the old man said, from his place on the little wooden stool by the fire. "These things are slow."

"But I can't stay here."

He sighed and I thought I detected a smile. "You are like the other one. Everything must be fast."

"I don't understand."

"No?" He stirred the fire and then, lifting a pot, spooned some beans onto a tin plate. He opened a folded handkerchief and I saw a stack of tortillas.

"Here," he said, making a spoon of a tortilla, and scooping up some of the beans. "Eat."

He watched me swallow the food, nodded approvingly, and fed me another helping.

"The other one had fever. But he was still very much like you."

"What other one? Who?"

"The man who came here when I was young. The other *dzul.*"

I turned my head to look at him again. Yes, he was old enough now to have been a young man in 1939 . . .

"What did you say your name was, *Tata?*"

"*Leodejildo in kaba.*"

"*Leodejildo,*" I repeated. "Jildo."

He nodded. "The same."

"And the other *dzul* who came here . . ."

"His name was *don* Juan. I met him in Bacalar. He was sick and Dr. Carrillo was taking care of him. Dr. Carrillo was very interested in the old ways. He spoke Mayan and he traveled to the villages. People trusted him, even the *h-menob.* The doctor told *don* Juan about things he had seen and then brought me to take *don* Juan there, because the doctor knew I was the nephew of the famous *h-men don* Eleuterio Euan."

I thought back about the letter Paul Hayes had shown me.

"When *don* Juan was well, we went on horses because in those days there were no roads like today. It took us a full day to arrive at the village."

A world without electricity or televisions or airplanes, where the Mayan villagers still lived in the shadows of the Caste War, when they'd risen to drive out the Ladinos.

"In those days," *don* Jildo said, as if reading my thoughts, "things were different in the villages. There was still talk of driving the *dzulob* from Yucatán. The chiefs had taken money from the chicle companies and many of them were no longer interested in war. But in the villages there was still talk about the old ways. There was still a *guardia,* men of the village who kept watch against the Mexicans, and there were still ceremonies to honor *la santa cruz.*" I thought, as he talked, that he was looking beyond me and into the past. "There was still reading from *le huunobe,* the books."

"*Don* Eleut had a book," I said.

He nodded and spooned out more beans with the tortilla.

"He had a book," the old man confirmed. "He kept it in the *balam nah*—the lord's house—which was what we used to call the temple, where we kept *la santa cruz*. My uncle would bring it out on special occasions. He would read from it after the holy cross spoke."

I tried to imagine it, the men in their white shirts and *delantales,* just like the ones this old man wore now, and the women in their flowered *huipiles,* gathered respectfully around the thatched, pole-sided house while the cross spoke inside to its interpreter, *don* Eleut.

"You introduced *don* Juan to your uncle," I said.

"Yes. But my uncle knew he was coming."

"Oh?"

"The cross told him. The cross knows everything. It even knew before the first *dzulob* came from across the sea. The cross knew they would come. It knew about the god they would bring with them, *jesucristo,* and it knew he would come back."

"So your uncle became friends with *don* Juan because *don* Eleut was expecting him."

"Yes. Because the prophesy said the one who came once would come again and *don* Eleut thought this was the man."

I waited. My mind was reminding me that Pepper was in danger and I had to force myself up, go find her, free her from the killers who had her. But on a deeper level it was telling me to be patient, there was nothing I could do. This old man seemed to understand the situation better than I, and he was calm.

"Tell me about the god who came a long time ago," I said.

Don Jildo lifted the poultice from my head, examined the wound, and then replaced the wet wrap.

"He was a king in his land. He lived here with the people for many years, married, had sons, and he led the people in many great battles against their enemies. When he died he was buried underground and a temple was built for his *chibal,* his lineage." Jildo struck a match and a little candle began to dance its light off the pole walls.

Seven kings. Seven masks. The seven faces on the temple.

"*Don* Jildo, is there a building . . ."

He smiled. "You are like him. You are in a hurry. All the *gringos* are in a hurry."

Don Jildo took out some cigarette paper and a little tin of tobacco and began to roll himself a smoke. He lit it from the candle and puffed.

"He was sick, too, when he came to the village."

"*Don* Juan?"

"Yes. He already had the fever when he dismounted in the plaza. My uncle and I took him to my uncle's house, to my uncle's hammock, and he was sick for fifteen days."

"*Paludismo*," I said, but Jildo shook his head.

"No, it only looked like *paludismo*. It was a *susto*. Something had frightened that man's soul."

"What?"

"Something in his own land. It was what brought him to us. He was running away from something. But a man cannot run forever. When he reached this land it caught him."

"But he survived."

"No, he died."

I turned my head to stare at him. "What?"

"My uncle did a ceremony to purify him, to satisfy the gods of his own land, but those gods are different than the *balamob* of the forest. They were far away, too far away to be reached, and when he came here he had the *susto* already in him. My uncle was able to help him for a time, but after *don* Juan was gone my uncle told me that he would surely die, because what was making that man sick was something no *h-men* could cure."

He smoked thoughtfully.

"And later, when my uncle saw him die, he told us all."

"He saw him die?"

"*Ich zaztun*," the old man said. "In his crystal."

Of course. Every *h-men* had a stone—a *zaztun*—that showed him the future.

"When *don* Juan was better," Jildo went on, "my uncle talked with him to see what kind of a man he was. To see if the sickness he carried inside him was something that would hurt others or just himself."

"And?"

"Only his own soul was being eaten. So my uncle showed him the book and told him what the cross had said and how it had made the ancient prophesies that had been written in the book. And when he was sure that *don* Juan could be trusted, he showed him the place of the heads."

"*Don* Jildo, what was the name of this place?"

The old Mayan threw his cigarette out the front door of the hut and walked back across the dirt floor and took his place on the little wooden stool, his face flickering in the firelight.

"We call it Lubaanah."

Lubaanah—fallen house. The real *lubaanah,* not the place where Eric had been digging for two years. The place that Paul Hayes had told me existed, because he had a letter from the man who'd found it in 1939. The site with the seven masks.

"That's where they're holding my friend," I said.

"It is."

"How can you be sure she's all right?"

He got up from the stool and walked over to a small wooden table in the corner, where I saw a *huipil*-clad cross and several unlit votive candles. There was a small metal box in the center of the table and he brought it over to the hammock.

"Look," he said and lifted the lid. I looked into the box and saw a translucent stone lying atop a sheaf of yellowed pages.

"I saw her in the *zaztun,*" he said. "They have not done anything to her yet."

"*Don* Jildo, thank you for everything you've done. But I can't leave her there."

"She's your woman."

"Yes."

He sighed. "When *don* Juan came here my uncle looked into it and saw the thing that was eating his soul. He saw that *don* Juan was not the man whom it was prophesied would bring freedom, because *don* Juan had this sickness in his spirit."

I waited for him to go on, impatient. All I could think about was that Pepper was being held.

"I learned what my uncle had to teach. Long ago the cross ceased to speak. But I have his book and his *zaztun*. And when I looked into the *zaztun* I saw another man coming."

"Another man?"

"Yes. And I thought, *Perhaps he will be the one. My nephew and I will help him.*"

So that's why I'd been saved . . .

"But then I looked into the *zaztun*."

I waited, but he didn't say anything else, just closed the box and replaced it on the table.

"What did you see?" I asked finally.

"Nothing. The *zaztun* was dark."

"What does that mean?"

The old man sighed. "It means that the evil wind inside that man will never go away. It means that the people near that man will be caught up by it and they will suffer, too."

It wasn't what I wanted to hear.

"There's nothing that man can do?" I asked, my head swimming. Had he put something in the water I'd drunk?

"*Mixbah*," the *h-men* said. "Nothing."

When I awoke it was daylight. There was no sign of the old man and Santos was seated beside my hammock.

≡ TWENTY-ONE

"You're awake," he said simply. "Good."

I blinked in the sunlight. "Where is he?"

"Who?"

"*Don* Jildo. Your grandfather."

Santos frowned slightly and then picked up his gourd and offered it to me.

"Drink."

"I don't want to." I shifted in the hammock, aware of a dull pain in my midsection. "Santos, where is this hut? Are we close to the site where they're holding *la doctora*?"

"It is ten kilometers north," he said. "This is a part of the old *poblado* I told you about. It used to be a village, but the fever drove the people away. Now no one lives here. This hut is used by hunters and sometimes *chicleros*."

"But your grandfather . . ." I twisted my head to look at the wooden table. The little cross was there, with its embroidered *huipil*, and so were the votive candles, but the metal box was gone.

"Your grandfather stayed with me all night. He treated my wound. We talked."

Santos nodded. "Good. Now we must help *la doctora*."

"How are we going to do that?"

Santos rubbed a hand across his grizzled jaw and I saw that his eyes were red from lack of sleep.

"I don't know."

"Have you seen her?" I asked.

Santos nodded. "Last night, late, I got into their camp. It was wet and the guards were staying inside one of the old buildings. They have her inside a stone temple. She's all right."

"How long has it been since the ambush?"

"Two days. You've been here one whole day."

"You and your grandfather brought me here. I remember some of that."

"The rain saved you. Because of the rain they didn't want to come out and search for you. It has rained for two days."

Two days. "And *la señorita* O'Toole?"

He shrugged. "*Quien sabe?* They have been looking along the trail we used to come here, because they didn't find your body. They may have killed her. I don't know because I knew that the only way to save you was to take you in the other direction, south. I knew about this house and that they didn't know it was here."

I felt an emptiness. It was too much to expect that Minnie could have made it.

"What happened, Santos? All I remember is that we stopped and then you went ahead and never came back."

"*Sí.* After I went forward I saw a body by the path. I decided to go a little farther to see what was happening, to see if the men who killed him were still in the area. I crept into the site and that was when I saw the *bandidos.* I heard some of them talking about the man they had killed." Santos frowned. "One of the *cabrones* was laughing about how the man had begged for his life and then had begged for them to just kill him. *Hijo de puta, don* Alan, these are bad men. Then one of them said something about the *jefe,* the chief, and how this time he was coming himself to oversee the transfer. I think they were talking about drugs. I looked around, to go back, but some of them had come out behind me from a side trail and there was no way to return, so I decided to go forward and try to see where the drugs were being held."

"And did you?"

"*Como no?* There's a stone building, on the south side of the main plaza. They have guards with *ametralladoras,* submachine guns, guarding it. That has to be where the *drogas* are."

"And the boss?"

He shook his head. "They said he was coming in an *avioneta,* a little airplane."

"That means they have a landing strip. Did you see it?"

"No. I was going to look for it, but I heard shots back along the trail. It was almost dark then and I had no light except matches and I couldn't afford to make a torch to go looking for you. I thought you had all been killed until I saw them coming back with *la doctora.*"

"She wasn't hurt?"

"No, *señor.* But she was angry. She was telling them what was going to happen to them, but they just laughed and said she should worry about what was going to happen to her now that her friends were dead and she was in their hands. After that the anger seemed to go out of her, like nothing mattered anymore."

"Bastards," I swore.

"Some of the men wanted to kill her right there, and there was an argument, but the one in charge—I heard them call him Jorge—said that she was worth more as a hostage. Then some of the men wanted to use her, you know . . ."

I felt sickish.

"But this Jorge said there was time for that later, and that anyway nothing should be done without the permission of the boss, and the boss would be there soon."

"Did he say who this boss was?"

"No."

But he didn't have to because I already knew: *don* Chucho, the man who ran all the drugs in this part of the world.

"Santos, do you know if they have a radio?"

"Just a small one that played tunes, but not a two-way."

"Interesting," I said. When I saw that he didn't understand, I tried to explain. "A radio transmission can be picked up by satellites. In the United States they can listen to what's being said, figure out where the radio is."

"*Mare,*" Santos swore. "They can?"

"Yes. Look, did you see any tents or temporary buildings?"

"*Nada.* They were using the old buildings entirely. They
had barely cut any brush from the plaza area, just enough to
be able to walk from one place to the other."

It confirmed what I thought. Chucho was taking no
chances with satellite surveillance. The same satellites that
could pick off a radio transmission or see tents and clearings
could pick out an airstrip in the jungle. So if Chucho was so
cautious, how was he hiding the landing strip?

"I stayed in their camp all night," Santos went on. "Only
when it was raining the next afternoon was I able to sneak
out."

"But how did your grandfather know? How did you find
him?"

He ignored my question.

"I brought you here because it was the only place I knew
would be safe. Then I went back to the *bandido* camp. I have
been there all night, listening to them. I came back here
when it got light because there isn't any more time."

"What's happening?"

"I heard them say the airplane is coming. It would have
come last night except for the rain. When it leaves they are
going to put *la doctora* on it. Then, somewhere over the
water . . ."

He didn't have to say more.

I pulled myself upright in the hammock. Oddly, my
headache seemed to have dulled somewhat.

"But you can't walk ten kilometers," Santos said.

"Help me up." I put out my arm and he took it, hoisting
me to my feet. For an instant I tottered, then grabbed the
main rafter for support.

"Your grandfather—" I began, but Santos was already
shaking his head.

"It will be hard for you to walk that far. And once we get
there . . ."

"We've got to get her loose and sneak her out," I said simply. "You have to get us back into the camp."

"*Sí,*" he said finally. "There is no choice."

"Where's your grandfather?" I asked. "I know it's a long way, but we need someone to go for the soldiers."

"He's not here," Santos said simply. "*Don* Alan, it is time to go."

I nodded. He was right. He handed me a gourd. "Water. And I have some *pozole.*"

"Good." I wasn't fond of the corn dough that Mayan farmers dissolved in their water as a noon meal while working, but it would have to do.

I followed him into the early daylight and froze in surprise.

I was staring at a village of huts, ghosts wreathed by the mist, and as I stared around me, saw the caved-in roofs, the missing thatch, the yawning doors, I realized that ghosts were exactly what they were.

"But these houses are all deserted," I said.

"I told you: The people died a long time ago and the rest left. It was the fever. Nobody lives here now."

"Nobody?"

"*Nadie,*" he said in Spanish. "No one."

■■■TWENTY-TWO

We reached Lubaanah at just after five in the afternoon, approaching from the south along a trail I didn't recognize. The trek had been endurable only because I knew that it had to be made, and after a while I felt like an automaton looking down from outside myself, even during our frequent rest halts.

Two hours along, my dizziness had worsened and I found myself lurching for branches to grab. Santos cut a sapling and I used it as a cane, leaning ever more heavily on it as we went.

The first man, who'd come, long ago, was a god. He'd lived among the people, fought their battles, died, and been enshrined as the first of his lineage. The people thought he would return one day.

John Dance Williams, a blond foreigner, had appeared from across the sea and at first it had been thought he was the god returned. But he had brought with him his own destruction, a sickness that no medicine or magic would cure. *Don* Eleut had recognized this sickness and knew that Williams was not the man.

Then, years after *don* Eleut's death, when even his nephew had grown old, another man appeared and hope flickered once more. But this man brought an inner darkness so profound that it threatened to suck in the people around him.

I remembered what had happened with Felicia. I don't know when it came to me precisely, because it emerged, like the birth of a monster, over the course of that walk, and perhaps that was why I was unconscious of the physical pain. The pain of memory was greater.

When we halted that afternoon and Santos told me we were only a kilometer from our destination, I wondered if anything I could do would make a difference.

Maybe, I thought, we were trapped in cycles of Mayan time. Maybe it was all ordained and nothing I or anyone else could do was capable of altering what would happen, because it had all happened before and would happen again until the last age of the world.

I heard the radio, tinny and distant, and Santos pointed to show that he heard it, too.

"When it is a little darker we'll sneak in close," he said. "I know a way they don't guard."

I nodded. We would do what we could, but there was no power that could change what was already set.

"In Katun 8 Ahau the Itzá were always driven from their homes," I said.

Santos frowned. "What?"

"It's a prophesy from the old books. Katun 8 Ahau was the unlucky period for the Itzá Maya, the ones who built Chichen Itzá. Every two hundred fifty-six years, when this twenty-year period came, something bad happened to them."

Santos handed me his gourd. "Drink," he said.

"Every Mayan group had its own lucky and unlucky twenty-year period," I said. "Good events and bad events repeated themselves. Maybe this is our unlucky *katun.*"

"*Don* Alan, you have a fever."

"Right." I touched my face and my hand came away hot. "Can we get to where they're keeping her without being seen?"

"*Ojalá!* I hope so."

I sank back against the tree trunk, shutting my eyes against the dizziness, but that only made the spinning increase.

When I opened my eyes again, Santos was shaking me gently and it was dark around us.

"It's time," he said.

I roused myself, but his hand stayed me.

"Perhaps I should go in, try to get her out and bring her here," he whispered.

But I shook my head. "No. I have to go."

"*Don* Alan, you're weak."

He was telling me, in his indirect way, that I would be more of a hindrance than a help. And maybe, if I'd been thinking rationally, I would have agreed.

"I'm going," I said and he turned away, resigned.

I followed him toward the sound of the radio, fronds and vines brushing my face as we crept, hunched over, through the forest.

Pepper, are you still alive?

Santos stopped suddenly and I blundered against him.

"*Mira,*" he whispered. "Ahead."

It was a light, barely visible through the cover.

He put his mouth against my ear, cupping his hand. "*Es-pérame,*" he ordered. "Wait. I'll see where the guards are."

And then he was gone.

I sank onto the ground, eyes fixed on the light. It blinked once as something crossed my line of sight and then remained steady. A mosquito landed on my cheek and I felt the sting as it drilled into my skin.

An inner darkness, I thought. The unlucky *katun*. I knew what had happened with Felicia and maybe it was going to happen again.

But Felicia was still alive. So maybe . . .

My dreaming was shattered by a yell.

I held my breath, expecting a shot or a scream, but there was nothing, just the same music, rising and fading in the sultry night. Someone laughed and I let some of the air out of my lungs.

I detected the odor of meat frying and wondered where they had the fire. Probably, I decided, it was inside one of the ruined buildings, where infrared satellite photos wouldn't spot it.

But the activity of men on the ground and the heat inside the buildings could be picked up by heat sensors. And the radio receiver could be detected by the special sensors in NSA spy satellites.

Except that there was no way to show what it all meant. People in the jungle playing a radio could be a chicle camp, or naturalists doing a biological survey.

Only aerial photos that showed armed men and a nearby landing strip would be definitive. Or some radio transmission that could be decoded. But *don* Chucho was too wily for any of that.

How the hell were we supposed to get Pepper back?

Bushes rustled in front of me and my muscles tensed. Then I heard my name whispered: "*Don Alan, donde estás?*"

Santos was coming back.

I felt his breath on my face and his hand touched me to reassure himself that I was there.

"Are you all right?" he asked.

"Yes. Did you see her?"

"No. She's inside one of the buildings. There are two guards outside. I couldn't get past them."

"Are you sure she's in there?"

"She was when I saw her before."

"Then we have to get past the guards."

Silence, except for the distant radio.

"*Sí,*" Santos said at last. "You're right. But not yet."

"When, then? We can't just—"

His hand touched my arm again, reassuring me.

"Some of the men are drinking. They're talking about when they get out of here, the women they'll have, the money they're going to get from their boss. The more they drink, the more careless they'll get. *Me intiendes?*"

"Yes," I said. "I understand."

He broke out the *pozole,* mixed it with water in the gourd cup he carried, and handed the cup to me. I drank, forcing down the thick gruel.

"Santos, your grandfather looked into his *zaztun.*"

The other man chuckled nervously. "There is no such thing as a *zaztun.* It is only a piece of stone."

"He said there was something dark—"

"*Don Alan, no te preocupas.* Don't bother yourself with such things. You're sick."

"Yes."

I closed my eyes again and a second later he nudged me.

"It's time."

"But—"

"You've been asleep. It's late. Listen."

I lifted my head and was aware of a distant thrumming sound: a generator, probably run by car batteries.

"We must go now because they said the airplane will be here at midnight."

I forced my eyes down to the glowing face of my watch: It was almost eleven. He was right. Back at the *cabaña*, I'd heard the plane going over around midnight. If they kept to schedule, that meant we had an hour, no more. And, with no way to recharge the batteries, they'd only start the generator that powered their lighting system when the time for meeting the plane was at hand.

"It will take us almost an hour to get where she is," Santos explained. "We have to go very slowly, crawl like the jaguar. And when we reach the place where the guards are we must spring out quickly. We must get the *doctora* away and hide her in the forest."

I knew what he was thinking because I was thinking it, too: It was going to be all I could do to get there, much less jump out and disable an able-bodied man.

"Here," Santos said and I felt something cold being pressed into my hand. His sheath knife. He was telling me that merely disabling the guard wasn't an option.

"Let's go," I whispered.

I crawled behind him, my body rubbing against the ground and my head starting to swim again.

Don't worry about how bad the head wound is, about clots in the brain or permanent effects of a concussion. You have an hour to get into the camp, kill the men guarding her, and then get out with her. You'll probably be killed. Don't even think about survival.

What will happen will happen because it is fated, and the cycles of Mayan time are inexorable, grinding the affairs of men into a powder as fine as cornmeal.

I shook my head to clear it. *Get rid of those thoughts. Your mind's wandering, you're already giving up. Focus on this moment, not on fantasies.*

So, was the old man who'd helped me a fantasy?

Ahead of me, in the brush, the movement stopped and I sank to the ground and waited, aware that the thrum of the generator had grown louder.

A light stabbed out, hit the trees three feet above our heads, and then shifted away.

"*Hombre, que haces?*" A man's voice, maybe twenty yards away.

"*Oí algo por allá.* There was something moving over here."

"*Fue zorro. Olvidate de este. Ven acá.*"

The man with the flashlight shot the light in our direction once more, then gave up and walked away. Santos started forward again.

As we crept toward the first building I saw lights ahead, flaring and then going dark as men came and went in front of them.

Santos tugged at my arm. "This way."

I dragged myself after him, trying to keep my balance. We were behind one of the ancient temples now, and its bulk cut off the lights in the plaza. I walked like a man underwater, lifting my feet slowly and then carefully setting them down so that I didn't stumble over a piece of rubble. We came to the corner of the building and I looked over Santos's shoulder.

A makeshift lighting system of bulbs attached to wooden poles shed a surreal light on the plaza area, and the leaning monoliths striped the ground with grotesque shadows. A handful of men in jeans and T-shirts milled about, rifles and submachine guns slung from their shoulders.

"Where is she?" I whispered.

Santos put his mouth against my ear again. "*Allá.*"

He nodded across the plaza to a hill of jumbled stones and

I realized that the darker spot in its center was what remained of an ancient doorway.

As I watched, something in the darkness moved: *Pepper.*

But then the form shifted again and I saw it really was a man. One of the guards, squatting inside the entrance.

"*Hay otro arriba,*" Santos whispered. I looked up and for the first time realized there was a man seated atop the structure, his back against a tree root, rifle across his knees.

My hopes crashed. How the hell were either one of us going to get up there?

Santos seemed to sense my despair, for his shoulders gave a tiny shrug.

We were still pressed into the shadows, mulling our options, when, over the thrum of the generator, we heard it: It started as a deeper hum, as if the generator were laboring harder, died away, and then emerged stronger.

"*Dios,*" Santos swore under his breath. "*El avión.*"

The plane was on the way. Early.

I grabbed his shoulder. "Where's the generator?"

"They keep it in a little house they built." He pointed to the left side of the plaza, where I saw a small box on poles.

"We have to get to the generator," I said. "If we can destroy it, they won't have any lights."

"*Sí.*"

The hum of the plane's engine grew louder.

A man as careful as *don* Chucho wouldn't have hacked a runway out of the jungle. The landing strip, wherever it was, had to be well camouflaged. Suddenly I remembered something from the Williams letter.

"Santos, does Lubaanah have a *sacbé,* a raised causeway?"

The Mayan nodded. "*Sí, hay.* It's on the other side of the plaza."

A *sacbé* was about fifteen feet wide, not much room for error, so it would have to be widened and the top smoothed, loose stones removed. Still, I couldn't think of any other answer.

"That's where they're landing the plane," I said.

"*Puede ser?* Can it be?"

And maybe, just maybe, they'll have strung lights along the runway to guide the plane in . . .

"Can you get to the generator?" I whispered. "That's the only way we can get to her."

"I can try," he said simply and started forward, but I caught him with my hand.

"Santos, there's no way we can be sure of meeting up together afterwards, in the dark."

"No."

"*La doctora* and I will try to head north, along the trail we used when we were ambushed. We'll try to make it back to the village and find the soldiers. But if we don't, we just have to stay in the jungle."

"*Claro.*"

"Don't worry about looking for us. Find your own way back the best you can. Understood?"

"*Sí, señor.*"

"Then *vaya con Dios, amigo.*"

I sensed rather than saw his smile as he said a formal Maya farewell: "*Bin Xicech yetal yaab hach utz.*"

He removed the machete from the leather scabbard that hung from his shoulder and then he was gone.

I was alone again. I leaned against the cold stones of the building, trying to keep my focus. There seemed to be more activity in the camp now, the previously milling men alerted by the sound of the airplane. The plane seemed to be circling now and several of the men headed for the far side of the open space. The guard just inside the doorway of Pepper's prison came out, his submachine gun hanging down like an extension of his arm, and the man above him shifted restlessly on his perch.

What was the old expression for futility? A snowman in hell?

I looked back over at the generator and I thought I saw a new shadow.

My hand tightened around the haft of the knife.

The shadow grew into a form.

And I realized that if I could see him, so could anyone else who looked in that direction.

Santos, for God's sake, be careful . . .

It was too late. One of the men in the plaza pointed at the generator and the others turned.

"*Mira, quien está?*"

I saw the gun barrels swing in Santos's direction.

And the lights went out.

There were yells and then shots. I hesitated, then plunged forward, all too aware of my weakness. Halfway across the plaza I collided with someone and heard a grunt.

"*Oye, quien es?*"

I didn't answer, just kept going toward the spot where I reckoned the doorway to be.

The somebody turned on a flashlight. I saw its eye flare on my right and then dart about, picking out bodies in motion.

I tried to hurry before it stopped on me.

I was too late.

The beam touched me, fell away, then came back.

"*Allí esta! Tirale!*" the man with the flash shouted.

A body emerged from the gloom in front of me, a rifle in his hands. The rifle came up, leveled at me, and the man gave a gurgling cry as something struck at him from the darkness. He dropped the rifle and went down.

"*Don Alan, appurate.* Here." It was Santos, machete in hand.

I stepped over the body as the guns opened up.

Red and blue flames spouted in the darkness, and then a succession of automatic bursts. Hornets buzzed around my head and I heard chips flying from the stone facade. There was more yelling now and gunfire from all sides. Someone cried out and I sensed that one of them had been hit by his own people.

"Santos, where are you?"

"*Don* Alan, here. Be careful!"

I wheeled and an avalanche of dirt and pebbles cascaded onto me from above. I jerked my head up in time to see a form grow out of the blackness.

The other guard.

I swung my hand upward as his body slammed against my

own and as we toppled onto the ground I heard a grunt. I pulled the knife free and crawled from under him, hand shaking.

The shooting had stopped and other flashlights were probing the darkness. Above the trees I heard the loud throb of the airplane's engines now as it circled. I heaved myself up, feeling for the doorway of the old structure.

"Pepper!" No answer.

My hand touched something solid, and I felt my way along it.

Then a match flared and I saw Santos's face.

"In here, *don* Alan," he hissed.

The match went out, but had been sufficient for me to see the open portal. I ducked through it and recoiled at the odor of human feces and urine.

"Pepper!"

The match flamed again and our shadows danced off the walls.

"*Don* Alan . . ."

He didn't have to finish.

The room was empty. Pepper was gone.

TWENTY-THREE

We stared at each other in the flickering light.

"She was here before," Santos said. "They must have taken her away."

The people near that man will be caught up by it and they will suffer, too.

The vacuum sucked at my soul and I tottered.

No. Don't give up. Even if . . .

"We have to get to the *sacbé*," I said. "If she's alive, they'll be putting her on the plane."

"*Don* Alan . . ." His hand touched my shoulder, gently, telling me that it was a fool's errand, and that it would be all we could do to get away from here ourselves.

I shook him off. "Santos, we have to try."

"*Sí*." There was sorrow in his voice. He turned around, resigned, and headed for the door.

The beams of flashlights danced through the plaza and I knew it was only a matter of a few seconds before they touched the bodies of the dead guards.

"Go," Santos said. "I'll be behind you."

I lurched forward, trying to keep low, hugging the protection of the next slumped ruin.

The *sacbé*, the raised causeway, was somewhere in front of me, but there were shapes moving in the night and I would have to either go through them or crash into the jungle and try to get around them.

A red flame blazed through the trees, and then another.

Railroad flares. With the generator down, they were going to mark the landing area with flares.

"*Quien es?*" someone in front of me demanded and without stopping I answered, "Jorge."

"Jorge?"

Before he could argue, Santos's machete hacked down and the man gave a little cry.

We were out of the trees now and I glimpsed stars overhead. Before us, the causeway was a dark wall, with red fires sputtering along its length. The plane's engines had changed pitch and we stepped back into the cover of the trees.

The plane was just out of sight now, skimming in low over the treetops, aiming for the double line of fires. Its engines drowned out the tumult on the ground and for an instant all attention seemed focused on it, as its bulk appeared, blotting out the moon, and then whipping past us in a hurricane of prop wash.

Somewhere out of sight it touched down and I heard the engine pitch change.

Someone was yelling now, about how they were under attack, and Santos pulled me down as a pair of bodies raced past us.

The engine noise had almost died away and I gritted my teeth. If we had to go all the way to the end of the causeway . . .

But then I realized the engine sounds had changed pitch, were increasing. The plane had turned at the end of the causeway and was taxiing back in our direction.

But where was Pepper?

And then a woman screamed.

Only it wasn't just a scream, it was a string of curses:

"You bastards, I'll kick your goddamn balls off!"

"*La doctora,*" Santos breathed.

"*La doctora,*" I said and lunged forward.

The plane appeared now, moving slowly toward us, an all-black, strange-looking machine with an upjutting tail and two motors mounted on a high wing, and I realized from the whistle of the engines that they were turboprops. Its side door was open and I glimpsed a man hanging out through the opening. He was yelling something and the men on the ground were yelling back, but the engines drowned out their voices. The pilot must have seen commotion below and lights flashing and, being a cautious sort, wasn't going to cut the engines while he was on the ground and vulnerable.

Then I heard Pepper yell again.

I reached the first man in the little group and plunged my knife into his back. He twisted, gave a cry, and stumbled away, taking my knife with him.

The others turned.

And for the first time I saw her, between two of them, her hands tied in front of her.

"Alan." She mouthed my name and I saw the others raising their weapons.

I was still ten feet away and the rifles were coming up.

And then one of the men gave a cry and went to his knees, and the other two wheeled in surprise as another bale of something hard landed on them from above.

The men on the plane were off-loading their cargo, unaware of what was happening below.

I reached Pepper and pulled her to me, just as one of the men on the ground raised his head.

"*Puto*," she spat in Spanish and kicked his chin like a football.

But by now the man in the cargo door knew something was going on. I saw the moonlight gleam on something metallic and a spatter of bullets hitting the ground sent dust into my face.

The rest of the gang was running toward us from the forest now.

"*Don* Alan!" It was Santos's voice and I realized he was between us and them. "*Corre!* Get away!"

The roar of the engines was punctuated again by gunfire and Santos slumped to the ground.

I shoved Pepper back against the embankment, under the aim of the man in the plane.

The flares bathed the night with a red glow, as if we'd descended into the inferno. Frantic, I looked around.

And thought about the flares.

I reached up, grabbed one from the edge of the causeway, and then stepped out and into the line of fire. I threw it as hard as I could at the black hole of the open cargo door.

There was a yell and I pulled Pepper to the ground. Bullets from the onrushing men hummed over us and the white beam of a light picked us out.

Slowly, I raised my hands.

Would they put us aboard the plane and drop us in the ocean or just kill us here on the ground?

"I'm sorry," I heard myself saying. "I'm sorry."

But I don't know if she heard it over the engines.

I couldn't tell how many of them there were because their lights were blinding me, but I guessed there were at least five. Not that it mattered.

I waited for the thud of the bullets, trying feverishly to think of a way to make them change their minds, to explain that it had all been my fault, not hers, and that if someone had to be killed it ought to be me.

Or maybe, I thought, as the light burned into my retinas, I was already dead.

Then the light shifted away.

For an instant I was staring at a circle of bright dots, where the lights had blinded me. But then I realized the attackers were yelling and pointing at something over our heads.

Over the roar of the engines I made out the words as one of them yelled, "*Esta incendido!*"

And, as if to lend emphasis, something went flaming past us, a fireball with arms and legs that landed between us and the men. The fireball, who had once been the man in the cargo door, crawled forward, screaming, but the prop wash only fanned the flames. The men in front of him leapt back as if he were a demon, and I forced myself up, grabbing Pepper by the arms.

"Let's get out of here."

We staggered for the jungle and almost made it. But just feet before the first shadowy fronds the men behind us started firing and I heard her give a little cry.

She stumbled, then plunged forward, falling to her knees just inside the trees.

"Alan . . ."

I reached her and she stretched her bound hands toward me.

"Pepper . . ."

"I'm okay."

A light probed, hit the trees just feet away, then went dark.

"My God, look . . ."

I glanced back toward the causeway.

Flames were streaming out of the cargo door, carried backward by the wind from the propellers. The men were yelling now, pointing, while the thing on the ground that had once been a human being burned itself out.

"Come on." I helped her up and we stumbled forward.

A limb slapped my face and as I stumbled, my hand jerked away from her arm.

"Hurry . . ." It was her voice, urgent now, with a note in it I didn't recognize.

"Where are you?" I called, trying to keep my voice low.

"In here," I heard her say and wondered why her voice was so loud.

I realized it was because the sound of the engines had stopped. The pilot, afraid of the fire, had cut the motors.

I thrust my hand out to guide me, felt cold stone, and then, below it, an opening. She tugged me forward, into a tiny opening. I ducked inside and found myself swallowed by a darkness more total than any I could remember. A musty odor gagged me and I heard Pepper cough.

We were in another of the ancient buildings, one in a part of the site we hadn't seen before.

"Are you all right?" I asked.

"I don't know."

This time the tremor in her voice was unmistakable. I stretched out my hand, felt along her shirt, and stopped when she gave a little cry. My fingers touched a stickiness.

"Hell of a thing after this," she said. "We're almost out of here and I have to go and get shot."

"It's not bad," I said.

"No."

Men were crashing through the undergrowth now and a light blazed at the opening to our shelter.

"*Oye, ven acá!*"

The man with the light was calling the others over. Pepper pressed against me, shivering.

We had nowhere to go.

I fumbled for a rock, anything to use as a weapon . . .

Shots and more yells.

The flashlight shifted and as it did, an errant beam touched something in the corner of the room neither of us had seen before. It was a place where the masonry had collapsed, leaving a hole that led to the other side of the building.

"This way," I whispered, urging Pepper to her feet.

Now there was a burst of automatic fire, a fusillade of single shots and two more quick bursts.

But they weren't shooting at us.

It was the darkness. They were still confused, firing at anything that moved.

"Alan, I don't think I can—"

"Yes, you can." I dragged her forward, through the escape hole and into another room.

There was almost steady automatic fire now, from several weapons.

Then the ground shook with an explosion and pieces of masonry toppled onto us from the roof.

"We have to get out of here before this whole thing falls in," I told her, but there was no reply.

I dragged her toward the opening and into the steamy night.

A flash, another explosion, and yells. In the instant of sudden light, I'd seen we were in a second, smaller plaza, with buildings on the other side. If we could get to them, we might find better cover.

"Come on," I urged, trying to lift her, but she only mumbled something under her breath.

I tried to lift her but lacked the strength.

More running feet now, and yells, against the background of gunfire and explosions.

Our pursuers had found the little plaza, were making a systematic search of the buildings.

If I could get up, draw their attention, pull them away. But what little strength I'd had was gone. I sat dumbly, waiting, like a tethered goat.

An inner darkness, the old man said.

I remembered about Felicia now. And I knew why I'd dreamed of the *Xtabai,* the folk representation of the goddess Xtab.

She-of-the-rope. The goddess of hanging, the favorite Mayan means of suicide.

Except that Felicia hadn't tried to hang herself, because she was from central Mexico. She'd cut her wrists instead.

That was how I'd found her, lying in bed, soaked in blood. She didn't die, of course. But I blamed myself.

Just as I blamed myself now.

I'd brought the darkness. . . .

A ghoulish green light suddenly flooded the plaza from a hole in the tree cover above. Someone had sent up a flare and in its eldritch glow I saw them now, walking toward me, guns spitting fire. The bullets popped off the walls behind me and chips of stone stung my back.

But I wasn't looking at our attackers anymore. I was staring over them, at the temple that shone green in the night.

I was staring at the masks.

Then the ground split open, there was blinding light, and the masks disappeared.

Sound and movement ceased and I was in darkness.

≡ TWENTY-FOUR

It took them a while to sort things out. At first they thought we were part of the gang and then Tapia recognized Pepper and we were carried out to the *sacbé* and lifted out by helicopter. Still dazed, I glanced down at the site from the open cargo door. There were several small fires and the black bulk of the plane still sat immobile on the runway. More flares had appeared and here and there I caught the hazy outline of a temple, bathed in flickering light.

I turned my head to look at Pepper, but her eyes were closed, and when I tried to say something over the noise of the rotors to the soldier squatting beside her he ignored me. Then my eyes closed, too.

They said I slept a day. I only know that when I awoke it was dusk and I was staring at green, flaking walls while from the window a tiny air conditioner circulated a smell of alcohol.

I looked around, frantic. Where was Pepper? I pushed myself up in bed, half aware that I was in shorts and a T-shirt. It didn't matter. I had to find somebody, find out where . . .

The door opened and Eric Blackburn came in, smiling, a bottle of Presidente in one hand and a handsome, polished mahogany walking cane in the other.

"About time you woke up," he said, setting the bottle down on my bedside table. "I brought you a couple of presents."

"Pepper . . ." I blurted.

"She's fine. Got a pretty sore shoulder, lost some blood. That's why she's in the hospital. This is a motel, in case you didn't notice. You're in Chetumal. You've got a mighty hard skull. Seems like the bullet bounced right off. The doctor said there didn't seem to be any permanent damage, but he wanted to keep you awhile. Seems like head wounds are tricky. I told him we'd get you back if you went into convulsions or had a stroke or started hallucinating."

"Hallucinating?"

"Well, you were talking funny before you came around. About somebody named *don* Jildo."

I closed my eyes for a few seconds, trying to sort imagination from reality.

"What about Santos?"

Eric shook his head. "Not good. They shot him twice in the midsection. But you know how tough these *chicleros* are. He's going to pull through."

"I have to talk to him."

"You will. Right now we have to finish getting that wound of yours healed so you can start on your new job."

"And Minnie?"

"She's got blisters as big as Nebraska and she was dehydrated as hell, but she made it. She stumbled into that village just after dark and there was a man there from the government co-op with a truck." He laughed and leaned back against the wall. "Took her longer to make herself understood than it did to walk the whole damned trail, from what I hear. But he finally took her to the highway and they found Tapia's men at the roadblock. Fortunately, one of them spoke enough English to understand what she was saying."

"They took their time getting there," I said.

"You know Mexico. He had to get more troops. That meant convincing his superiors, and from what I gather he wasn't sure which ones he could trust. Tapia's a hard-ass and the rest of them were getting tired of having him yell wolf all the time. But now he's a hero, strutting around like a little Napoleon."

"I guess he earned the right."

"Sure. His soldiers killed five of those guys, including Jesus Cantu himself."

"*Don* Chucho?"

"None other. Seems like he was there to make sure the goods from Colombia got there this time, because there'd been some kind of foul-up before. He wanted to count the stuff personally before any money was handed over. Then they'd have another plane come and take it to the States."

"Nice little operation."

"Amen. He had a ranch a few miles to the west, with a vehicle trail into the site. He'd taken a hell of a chance, getting the *sacbé* cleared and widened. I guess he figured once it'd been noted on recon photos, nobody would look too hard again. And if there were a few people working near it, they'd look like archaeologists. That is, if the satellite recon even zoomed in. There's probably more than they can process as it is. The plane was even special, something the Spanish made for hauling cargo and people and setting down on short, rough runways. Called a CASA. Has a narrow wheelbase, about fifteen or sixteen feet, I understand. Range is a thousand miles. With extra fuel he could make it all the way from Colombia, or there may have been a refueling stop somewhere in Honduras or Nicaragua. Chucho was smart. Apparently thought he'd greased enough of the army brass to stay in operation, but Tapia is the rare officer who's incorruptible. And apparently there are some others he knows, who listened to him."

"Yeah." I shook my head. "Poor Jordan."

Eric nodded. "Poor Jordan, poor Abelardo Rojas."

"Who?"

"The man on the beach. He ran a little store up at Tres Cabras. Seems like he was working for Jordan, keeping his eyes open. Chucho and his people decided to make an example and left him where Jordan would find him. They knew others might figure he fell out of a boat, but they knew Jordan would know right away what message they were sending him."

Tres Cabras. The fat store owner . . . Of course. . . .

"Chucho wasn't about to let some guy from the DEA get in the way," Eric went on. "It's a hell of a scandal."

"Oh?"

"Sure. The state government's saying it was the federal police that killed him, the PAN Party says it was the kind of PRI corruption they're cleaning up, and PRI says it didn't happen on their watch. And both of them are saying the U.S. should keep hands off."

"Sounds like a train wreck."

"Yeah." Eric pushed himself away from the wall. "Look, I've got a dig to run and we're behind, thanks to this." He tugged at his beard. "And now we've got a major new site that needs to be recorded, mapped, excavated. . . ." He gave an exaggerated sigh. "Hell, this project could last for the rest of our lives."

"*Our* lives?"

"Hell, yes. You found the damn site. Now you've got to dig it." He winked. "I think you just bought us all job security."

As the door closed behind him, I lay back against the pillow and thought about an old man in the jungle: An inner darkness, he'd said. A darkness that sucked in others. He'd been wrong, of course. I'd survived. Everybody had.

Over the next twenty-four hours I was visited by the others of the crew, except for the two people I most wanted to see, Pepper and Santos, who were still in the hospital.

First came Minnie, lanky and sunburned. She leaned over the bed and kissed my cheek and I felt something wet on my skin.

"Now, look," she complained, "I didn't come here to start crying. You ought to be ashamed of yourself."

"We all owe you," I said.

"Well, as a matter of fact, you do, and believe me, you're going to pay. Eric chartered a Cessna and had them fly him in so he could see it firsthand. Now he's been telling us how it's a major find." She leaned toward me and whispered: "He's named it already: Kaax Muul. He says that means jungle ruins."

"It already has a name," I said.

"I know." She smiled conspiratorially. "But he said it would confuse things too much to go switching the name of where we're working now to the new site, because all our permits and all his publications use the name Lubaanah for the place he's been working for the last two years."

"There's some sense to that," I said.

"Still, I think Paul's up there looking down and saying, 'I told you so.' "

"Probably."

Next, to my surprise, came Tapia, alone and bearing a small box. If I expected him to be puffed up with self-importance, I was disappointed. Instead, he looked ill-at-ease, as if he weren't quite sure what to say. He laid the box on the bed and asked me how I was feeling. I thanked him for saving us and congratulated him on his success, but he only nodded, as if the whole business were a slight embarrassment.

"There's a great deal more to do," he said.

"Then you'll be busy for a while," I suggested, but he only shrugged.

"Not here. They're transferring me to Sonora."

"Oh?"

"A reward," he said, but I could tell he was not impressed by the honor.

We shook hands again and when he was gone I saw that the box contained chocolates.

It was late that evening that I was visited by José Durán. He knocked and then came in alone and I wasn't sure whether April was outside waiting or not. He stood just inside the doorway, as if he might have to leave in a hurry, and stared at me.

"Doctor," he said.

"Skip the formality, José. Come on in."

"Eric said you were weak. I wasn't sure . . ."

"Close the door, will you?"

He slowly shut the door, as if he were somehow shutting himself into hell.

"I'm very happy that you and Pepper are all right."

It sounded like he'd rehearsed it and I smiled.

"Look, José, I can save us both a lot of trouble. I've fig-ured it out and you don't have to worry."

"I don't understand."

I pointed to the bottle on the table. "Pour us both a drink, how about it? There're probably some glasses in the bath-room."

He hesitated, then picked up the bottle like it was a ticking time bomb, went into the bathroom, and came out with a pair of glasses. I watched him pour us each just enough rum to cover the bottom of the glass.

I took my glass and the bottle and finished pouring.

"You know, José, while I was in the jungle I had a lot of time to think." I swirled the dark liquid around in the glass and then raised the tumbler. "*Salud*."

He lifted his own in a perfunctory toast.

"I had some pretty wild hallucinations. I guess it was shock. The mind does funny things when it thinks it's about to shut down."

The Mexican lifted his glass to his lips, as if the gesture kept him from having to reply.

"One of the things I kept thinking about is what happened to me in these parts fifteen years ago." I took a swallow, closed my eyes, and felt the alcohol burn its way down my throat to my stomach. "Damn, that's good. For a while there, I thought I wasn't going to ever taste anything like this again. Want some more?"

"No, thank you." His eyes were fixed on me now, as if he were expecting me to spring, and maybe he was right.

"Anyway, I kept seeing the woman I used to be married to, a woman named Felicia Esquivel. We met when I was down here doing dissertation research and then we got mar-ried when I was on a big project. We lived in those same *cabañas* we're using now."

"Why are you telling me this?"

"It was the happiest time in my life," I said, ignoring his question. "But it turned into the worst time."

I picked up the bottle. "Let me put something in that glass."

"I'm fine. Now, Dr. Graham—"

"There's no need to give a blow-by-blow. I was young and immature and self-centered: All I could think about was my work. I didn't understand Felicia's needs, or the pressures she was under as a professional woman in a man's world. She started falling apart. If I'd been as sensitive as I should have, I'd have seen it, because she kept doing things to get my attention, things that were really cries for help. But nothing worked. Finally, she tried to kill herself. And instead of being there for her, I went into a kind of shock myself. I acted like she'd betrayed me by being sick. I acted like she'd let me down when I needed her support instead of being there when she needed mine."

Durán looked away for the first time.

"We couldn't keep it going after that. I went back to the States. I said I'd send for her, but we both knew the truth. She went through other men, looking for somebody to give her the reassurance she needed. I heard she ended up in an administrative position in INAH, in Mexico City. I haven't heard from her for thirteen years or so."

Durán lowered his glass, and this time when our eyes met I saw resignation in his face.

"I don't know what she told you about me," I said. "I guess at this point it doesn't matter."

"Doctor—"

"Alan."

He turned around suddenly, giving me his back. "She was very bitter."

"I'm not surprised. Felicia was never halfway about anything."

"She's a very passionate person." He turned again, as if ready to do battle. "But how . . . ?"

"Why else would you be so hostile to me for no reason? I couldn't figure it out, at least not consciously. But I think your tone of voice, your body language, the way you kept sneaking looks at me, like you were sizing me up—I think my mind was putting it all together on some level." I told him about the dreams. "It took me a while, but at some point, out there in the jungle, it came through."

"I didn't know I was so obvious."

"I guess we all are."

"*Dios*," he swore softly. He walked over to the nightstand, took the bottle, and this time he half filled his glass. "I was with her for five years."

I watched him take a healthy swallow. I'd known about Felicia's indiscretion while we were married, and I assumed she'd been with men since we'd split, but this was the first time I'd ever met one of her lovers. For some reason the jealousy I'd expected to feel wasn't there.

"She was—is—a very unhappy person."

"I'm sorry. I'd hoped—"

He shook his head violently. "*No es culpa tuya.* You aren't to blame. I used to think you were. She told me things that made me think it was your fault. I was so involved with her I hated you. How could anyone do this to such a beautiful, sensitive woman?" His laugh was off-key. "I told her that if you ever dared come back to Mexico I'd even scores for her."

I nodded. "Understandable."

"No, listen: It was more than that." He finished the glass and reached for the bottle again. "I had my own reason for hating you."

"But we'd never met."

"It had nothing to do with you. It was her. You see, no matter what I tried to do, how much I loved her, it wasn't enough. Every minute I was with her, even in the most intimate moments, you were there."

It wasn't what I'd expected to hear.

"I finally gave up with her because of that," he said. "I couldn't compete with you."

"I don't understand."

"Don't you?" An edge had crept into his voice. "Felicia still loves you. Any man she is involved with will have to live with the ghost of Alan Graham."

It was my turn to pour a stiff one.

"I'm sorry," I said.

"When I became a member of this project and met Pepper, I realized the man she kept talking about was the same man who'd been Felicia's husband. The man who'd ruined everything for Felicia and me. Pepper made you seem like a superman." He threw up a hand in frustration. "I hated you all the more. You'd ruined Felicia and now you were spreading your lies and ensnaring this decent young woman."

I thought of Pepper's descriptions of Eric and smiled as I recalled my own reactions. "Sometimes Pepper's enthusiasm carries her away," I said.

"Then she announced that you were actually coming here and I'd have to meet you." His face was red now from the alcohol. "Do you know I actually hoped that airplane would crash?"

"You can't be blamed for being human."

"I can be blamed for being stupid, for not realizing that there was more to it than Felicia had ever told me."

"I've got my share of responsibility," I said.

"Yes," he said wryly. "You're responsible for not being the son-of-a-bitch she said you were. That made it very hard for me."

The alcohol was making my head swim, but it didn't matter. "José, maybe we've both been a little blind."

"Yes, I think so."

"Maybe we were both wrong about Felicia. Maybe she's more troubled than either of us realized at the time. Maybe she brings in memories of me as a way to keep men at arm's length. Maybe no man can give her what she wants."

He nodded. "It's been over between us for two years. But I still see her when I'm in Mexico City because she works at the main office of INAH. It makes it somewhat difficult."

"I'm sure."

"She has another man now. An architect named Perea. He's old and he has a wife and grandchildren. He will tire of her as soon as a younger woman comes along."

Sadness settled over me like dirt being tossed into an open grave. I saw her as she'd been when we'd met and fallen in love and I imagined her as she was now, older, worn, with a hard set to her mouth.

"I'm sorry for her, then," I said.

Durán shrugged. "There's nothing anyone can do."

"No." I shifted in the bed.

"Well," he said with a rueful smile, "I seem to have a weakness for women with problems."

"April."

"Yes. But it won't go anywhere."

"No?"

"There's quite a difference in our ages. Not to mention cultures. And, frankly, she's a very difficult girl to get to know."

"How's that?"

"She builds a wall. You think . . ." Another shrug. "And then you find you're facing that wall. I made the mistake of telling her the pills weren't good for her and she got furious and asked what did I know. Of course, I had to tell her I didn't know anything at all, at least about her, but I was willing to listen. But she said I was only after what all men were after. And maybe I was."

"And yet most of the time the two of you seem to get along."

"Alas, my friend, I think she wants a father figure."

I laughed with him.

"In any case," he went on, "she's leaving in a couple of days. She can go back to the *Gran Disnilandia del norte,* where they grow psychiatrists on trees."

"Will you do me a favor, José?"

"Probably, so long as it isn't giving advice about women."

"Not precisely. But I *would* appreciate it if you'd help me get out of this room and drive me over to the hospital where Pepper and Santos are."

He set his glass down. "I think," he said with a smile, "that can be arranged."

And so, half an hour later, I found myself leaning on my cane, next to her bed in the little private clinic where she'd been taken. She awoke a few seconds later and smiled.

"They told me you'd be here when you were well enough," she said, "but I knew it wouldn't take you that long."

I reached down and put my hand against her cheek. She turned her head and pressed her lips against it.

"You know you missed your plane." It was all I could think to say.

"Yeah. The department will have to hold registration without me. Imagine all those students I won't get to advise."

"I was scared," I said finally. "I thought you were dead."

"That works both ways. I saw them shoot you, you know. And I didn't care what they did to me after that. Then I got mad."

"Look, this may not be the right place to say this, but haven't we been fooling around long enough?"

"Fooling around?" Her brows arched. "Is that what we've been doing?"

"Hell, you know what I mean." I cleared my throat. "I guess what I'm saying is, I can't imagine not being with you for, well . . ." I shrugged.

"Go on."

"Are you going to drag it out of me?"

"Damned straight. A girl has a right to hear this kind of thing."

"Well, the first time I mentioned it, a couple of years ago, you said you needed time."

"Two years ago is time," she said. "But what about your work with Eric? What about the site?"

"I don't know."

"I didn't think so." She kissed my hand again. "When you see Santos, tell him hi for me. They say he's on the same floor."

"Yeah." I melted away, feeling beaten, and found José in the hallway. Doctors and nurses eyed the curious spectacle as he helped me, limping, to a door at the end of the corridor. I knocked and went in.

"I'll wait here," José said tactfully.

Santos was still attached to an IV tube and his face looked drawn. I stood over him for a few minutes, watching the medicines drip from the bag into the tube and trickle down to his arm. When I couldn't stand it anymore I said his name.

His eyes flickered open.

"*Don* Alan."

"I'm sorry this happened, Santos. If there's any way I can ever repay—"

"*No le hace*," he said weakly. "Those were bad men." He managed a smile. "They said we did a good job on them."

"We did a good job, my friend."

"All I wish is they would take away these tubes. I lie here and think about beans and pork."

"I'll get you some when they let you out."

"The doctors say I may not be able to eat it again. The *balas* did something to my guts. Can you imagine that? A man not being able to eat beans and pork?"

"No," I said. "I can't imagine it."

"But maybe they don't know as much as they think, *masima*?"

"Maybe not."

"Are you going to work with *don* Eric, then?"

"I told him I would."

He looked away. "I may not be able to."

"You will. What would we do without you?"

He didn't answer.

"Santos, I need you to answer a question for me. It's about your grandfather."

"My grandfather?"

"Yes. *Don* Jildo. I told you I talked with him and he told me things, showed me his *zaztun*, cleaned my wound, fed me."

The man in the bed still didn't reply.

"One of the things he told me was about how the man Williams, the *Ingles* who came here years ago, when your grandfather was a boy, brought his own darkness with him, and how no matter what *don* Eleut, the *h-men*, did, there was no way to dispel that darkness. Finally *don* Eleut realized it was something foreign, something *don* Eleut and all his medicine couldn't affect, and that's when *don* Eleut realized the *Ingles* was going to die soon."

"Yes," Santos said finally. "My grandfather told me."

"But he also said it was the kind of darkness that only hurt the *Ingles* and not other people."

"Yes."

"And he said there was another kind of darkness, like an evil wind, that came to some other men and when a man had that kind of illness, it not only destroyed him but it sucked in the people around him."

"He told me that, too."

I took a deep breath. "Santos, do you believe there really is such an evil wind?"

The man in the bed nodded. "There is, *don* Alan. I have seen it. And there is no escape."

I stood up straight. "One more thing: Where's your grandfather now? Where's *don* Jildo?"

His lips moved and I heard the words, but it took a long time for them to register:

"My grandfather died two years ago when the last people left the old village. That is where he is buried."

Later that day, thanks to José, April came to visit and we had a long talk. I asked and she told me about the darkness.

▰▰▰TWENTY-FIVE

The next morning, against Eric's advice, I abandoned the motel and had him drive me back to Bacalar. Pepper would stay in the hospital for another day or two and Santos somewhat longer, though I was assured he was making satisfactory progress.

Supported by my new cane, I walked the beach, drank beer, retold my story to an admiring Geraldo, and bothered his workers. Eric, who insisted that I wait until my head was completely healed, whipped back and forth to the work site, tending to details that had been left hanging due to the recent excitement. Late the afternoon of the second day, satisfied that the dizziness wouldn't recur, I took the Neon onto the highway and kept going until I reached the little village of Xul. When I got back to Bacalar it was dark, and an anxious Eric was waiting to give me hell.

"Damn, are you going to do this every day?" he asked good-naturedly as I got out of the car and hobbled toward the path that led around the restaurant and onto the back patio, with the steps to the beach. "Look at you: You look like you've lost a gallon of blood, you're so white." He patted my shoulder. "I don't know if I can stand having you around, with all this excitement. I've already got a new crop of gray hairs."

"It won't happen again," I promised.

He let out a huge guffaw. "Hey, lighten up, fella. Let's have a beer."

"Don't feel like it, but thanks," I said.

"That's a bad sign." He called over a waiter and seconds later handed me a *Superior*. "Seriously, Alan, is your head still bothering you? Are you okay?"

"I will be," I said. "But it may take a while."

"I understand." He lifted his own beer and we stood by the wall, looking down on the lake, as Pepper and I had a few nights before. A few nights that now seemed like an eternity.

"Look," Eric said. "Is there anything I can do?"

I shook my head. "No."

"If it makes any difference, I've been talking to the folks at the university. I explained about the new site. I downplayed the drug business a little, just said the army had cleaned out a bunch of thugs and the place was completely secure now. I promised the dean and the chancellor I'd fly back in a couple of weeks to make a special presentation, after I've got some good slides and a sketch map. Then I plan to fly to Washington to talk to *National Geographic*. This kind of thing is right up their alley." He sipped from the bottle. "I'll be counting on you to run things while I'm gone."

I raised my own beer, started to sip, and then lowered it again.

"What are you going to tell them about Paul's theory?" I asked.

"Oh, shit." Eric sighed. "I guess he told you his ideas?"

"Yes."

"Well, I think it'd be best just to leave it alone. There isn't any real proof. The whole business is bonkers." He leaned over the wall, staring down into the darkness of the lake.

"Think so?"

He turned to stare at me. "C'mon, Alan: ancient Phoenician Christians sailing to the New World? Look, Paul was my friend. More than that, actually. He helped me over the years when I needed help. Wrote letters, made calls, pulled strings. I wouldn't have gotten hired by Houston if it hadn't been for him." He took a long swig. "But face it, Alan: Paul wasn't the man he used to be. When Marlene died it took something out of him. He had a stroke. He was in bad physical shape, but he wouldn't admit it. I think he may have had some little strokes, you know, the kind that affect the part of the brain that has to do with logic. I think that's where he got all this crazy stuff."

"He told me he'd been a diffusionist for years."

"Well, I guess we've all *considered* the possibility of diffusion from the Old World. But I suspect Paul was exaggerating when he told you that. Anyway, the point is, it's moot now. Paul's dead, there's no evidence, so it doesn't matter."

I thought about the temple of the masks. Seven of them, staring down at me from around the doorway at the top of the temple stairs. Seven masks, illuminated by a half-second flash of light . . .

"Then you didn't see anything when you went to the site," I said. "Nothing that would back up Paul's theory."

"No. Of course, I was just there a few hours. I had a bush pilot put down on the *sacbé* and that pissed off the soldiers guarding the place. I had to show my INAH permit and convince 'em it covered this site as well as where we were working, and I'd be out of there after I took some pictures. So all I could do was make a quick tour of the main groups of buildings. But it looked like a post-Classic site to me. Which argues pretty convincingly against any Phoenicians or Caananites, or whatever they were, since the post-Classic dates from about A.D. 1000."

"You didn't see any masks?" I asked.

"No. Were you expecting me to?"

"Just a thought," I said.

"Crap, Alan, I don't think we *need* Paul's bullshit to justify this as a major site. In fact, crank fantasies like his can only hurt us. You know what would happen if I brought that up to *National Geographic,* or NSF, or the National Endowment for the Humanities? They award grants through peer review. We'd get laughed out of Yucatán."

"Probably," I agreed.

"So I say we bury Paul and remember him for the good, decent man he was, hoist a few beers to him, and go on about our business. And once we start mapping at Kaax Muul, we'll name a group of buildings after him, which is what he deserved."

"Kaax Muul," I said thoughtfully.

"Yeah, that's the name I picked. A little PR can't hurt anything." He waved a hand. "I know, purists might say it should be Lubaanah and the place we've been working ought to be changed to something else, but what the hell does it matter? These are all recent names. Who the hell knows *what* the ancient Maya called these places?"

He looked down at his empty bottle. "Another one?"

"No, thanks."

He called over the waiter and then turned back to lean on the wall.

"I was thinking of bringing some people back with me from the States. Sort of a tour to drum up support. I was talking to old man Blake and he's definitely interested in coming." He smiled thinly. "Without his daughter, of course."

It was my turn to contemplate the dark waters.

"I don't think that would be a good idea," I said finally.

Eric's head jerked up. "What?"

"I said I don't think Blake should come here."

"What the hell are you talking about? The man's giving us half a million dollars, and that's just to start."

"I know."

"Then what the hell's your problem?"

"It's April's problem," I said. "I talked to her."

"She won't be here. Look, fella, talk straight. What's eating you?"

I stared into the lake, where the darkness swirled and congealed like the vortex of a tornado.

"I had a talk with April yesterday."

"You mean she was lucid?"

"Pretty much. She told me why she and her father don't get along."

"Alan . . ." He shook his head, exasperated. "What the shit do I care why they don't get along? I'm not her goddamned psychiatrist."

"She says her father molested her when she was younger.

Not just once or twice but repeatedly. She even aborted his baby."

He stared at me, eyes wary.

"That's not something I need to hear about," he said in a level voice. "It's not something you ought to be digging into, either. Do you want to see this whole damned project go down in flames?"

"No."

"Then forget what she told you. The girl's unstable. God only knows what she's dreamed up. We don't need to get dragged into her feud with her father."

"And if it's true?"

"Screw if it's true. If she's pissed at her old man, let her go to her lawyer, or the cops, or whoever handles those things. But not to us. This is, I repeat, none of our goddamned business, not yours and not mine. So drop it."

"I plan to. I mean, I agree with you, it *is* between her and her father, and maybe the law, but, like you say, it's not for us to jump into."

The other man seemed to relax. "All right, then. Jesus, Alan, you were making me nervous. You have any idea what would happen if old man Blake knew we were even *discussing* this? That anybody paid any attention when his spaced-out daughter started babbling lies about him?"

"Eric, you don't understand. April wasn't telling me this because she wanted me to do anything against her father. She hates him and she'll probably split as soon as she gets home, anything so she doesn't have to see him again. But none of this was anything she volunteered. I had to drag it out of her."

"What are you talking about?"

"I guess I'm talking about things we feel and can't make sense of on a conscious level. Things that pop up at odd times and tell us to run away from something or somebody."

"You're babbling, fella."

"Maybe. But I believe in intuition. Though I think it's usually based on little clues that are too subtle for us to recognize consciously. I once knew a woman whose father was an alcoholic, for instance. After being raised in that kind of atmosphere, she could pick up on another alcoholic within ten minutes."

"Where are you going with this?" His tone was hard now, aggressive, and my hand tightened on the cane.

"I think you know. Nobody knew why April always seemed to be sick when you stayed in camp here. There was even a rumor that the two of you were having an affair." I waved away his objection. "I know, it wasn't true. But then I asked myself, why else would she always want to be where you were? When the rest of the crew wasn't there?"

"I'm not listening to this crap."

"Suit yourself."

But he didn't move.

"April told me why. She saw things in you she'd seen in her father."

"Bullshit."

"She saw the way tension built up in you and how you had to make trips into Chetumal, and how you came back relaxed. It reminded her of the way her father was before he hit on her."

His face was a mask of rage now and his hands had doubled into fists.

"There was a girl working for Geraldo, a maid. She wasn't but twelve years old. April saw you talking to her, saw your expression, your body language. She saw you with her in your *cabaña* one night while Pepper and I were walking on the beach and she didn't know what to do. Her first reaction was to run away. Then she tried to make sure she was in camp at the same time you were. It was the only way she could think of to protect that girl or any of the others, because she knew you'd think twice if you thought she was close enough to see or hear what was going on. It's the same reason she went to that house during the *Chhachaac*. She got up from her hammock, didn't see you, and was afraid you were doing something to your godson's older sister, María. But you weren't there and María, or Xmari, as they call her, got April to go next door, to help the sick woman who had the baby. April didn't always think clearly, and her life is pretty messed up, but she has the right instincts."

"That's a goddamned lie!" He moved away from the wall and squared off, a vein throbbing in his temple.

"I wish it was," I said. "But I talked to the other help and they told me where the girl lived. That's why I went to Xul earlier. I talked to her and her parents."

"Oh, shit." His face reddened and he turned back toward the lake. "Alan, for Christ's sake, you don't believe . . ." He turned to face me again. "Look, I was nice to the girl, that's all. I joked with her a little. There wasn't anything . . ."

His words played out when I didn't reply.

"It's her word against mine," he said finally.

"Yeah. But how many were there before?"

"Before?"

"An old man told me that some people carry an evil wind with them. Usually they're the only ones it destroys, but sometimes, when the wind is especially strong, it pulls in people nearby. I thought he was talking about me." I tried to laugh, but my voice was trembling. "Actually, I think it was all just a dream, and I was trying to make sense of what I'd seen. But I didn't have April's experience."

"You're totally frigging crazy, you know that?"

"What I'm saying, Eric, is I don't think this is the kind of thing that just happened down here. I think it's been going on for a while. Is that why you're divorced, by the way? Why you don't see your own daughter these days?"

He took a step toward me and my hand tightened on the cane.

"I ought to knock your damned head in," he growled.

"But you won't. Any more than you knocked Paul's head in. Your way is more underhanded. A man who preys on young girls isn't about to face a man, even an old man in poor health." I sighed. "What was it, Eric? Blackmail? Did Paul find out your secret? Maybe bail you out of a problem at some other university? I figure it was something like that and all I'd have to do is make a few phone calls to find out."

"Damn you to hell, if you so much as—"

"So you had to tolerate him and his crazy ideas. Not that I see Paul as a blackmailer. I think it was just that he let you know you owed him. And it was too dangerous not to repay the debt. But then what did he do? Up the ante? That's how I figure it. Paul told me just before he died that you were going to publish his work in the journal you edit. I wasn't sure how that was going to work, because I knew that if you published his theories about pre-Columbian contacts with the Old World, the whole academic world would come down on you both. You could probably kiss your hope for any more grant money good-bye."

He didn't say anything, just glared death at me.

"So you tried to talk him out of it. And you burgled his house, didn't you?"

His eyes narrowed and I knew my guess had scored.

"What happened? When Paul told you about the little stone tablet you pretended not to be interested, but you knew if you got your hands on it he wouldn't have any hard evidence for his theory."

"Go to hell."

"You were scared to death of him. He *was* old and in bad health and knew he didn't have that much time left. He let you know you'd better comply." I took a deep breath because at this point I was on a tightrope.

"What did you do, Eric? Sabotage the brakes on the Rover? Or loosen the steering? You told me you'd been a mechanic, so you'd know how to do those things."

"You don't have any proof."

"No."

"So you can just get your ass out of here, now."

"I don't think so. Because if I leave now, people will want to know why. I'll go when Pepper's ready. It shouldn't be more than a day or two more."

"You son-of-a-bitch. If you go back and spread this around . . ."

"I don't have to. April said she's going to do it all by herself."

"*No!*"

The waiters turned to stare at him.

"That little bitch. Do you know what that'll do?"

"Oh, yes," I said and walked away.

"But the project!" he yelled after me. "Are you willing to lose everything?"

I got into the Neon and drove to Chetumal.

Maybe Eric Blackburn had lost everything, but I knew I hadn't.

▰▰▰ Epilogue

It was a month later. Pepper and I had flown down for a couple of days to visit José at the site of Lubaanah. The real Lubaanah, not the site where Eric Blackburn had worked for two years. A road had been cut along the trail Minnie and I had walked, and José's crew, which included Minnie O'Toole, was busy documenting the structures that had been hidden for so many generations. Only later, with the infusion of money from the central government, would excavation occur, and then, for better or worse, restoration for the sake of tourist dollars.

Santos met us as we drove into the site. He was thinner and wincing a bit, but still game. We followed him, Minnie, and José to the various small temple groups, linked now by neat jungle trails, coming at last to the small plaza group where Pepper and I had taken refuge. The air was hot and redolent with the smell of greenery, and birds called overhead. The scene was strangely peaceful, considering what had happened here just weeks ago.

"Have you heard anything from Blackburn?" I asked.

José shook his head. "He called a couple of times to say he'd be coming back. He wanted my help with the permit extension. He said he was sending some documents. But he never did."

"I thought that package you got was from him," Minnie piped up, but the Mexican just frowned.

"I think you're mistaken. If he ever sent anything, it was lost."

"He's called Pepper a couple of times," I said. "I don't know what they talked about."

"Yes, you do," Pepper shot back. "He was trying to convince me all the rumors were untrue. He threatened to sue Alan for spreading them."

"And were you?" José asked.

"No. I think April did enough without my help. That's why his funding fell through. Her father heard about them."

"Too bad," José said.

"Yes," I said, thinking of the many archaeological projects that never get written up and wondering if Blackburn's last two years would be among them.

I stared down at the place where Pepper and I had huddled when I was sure we were going to die, and then I looked out over the plaza at the temple.

Three of the masks could be seen, Mayan kings looking back at us from their places alongside the doorway. A fourth had been badly damaged, but half the head was intact. And the other two, including the one over the doorway, were missing, destroyed by the explosion.

"It's a pity," José said, reading all our thoughts. "There was a mural inside, too, but it's been destroyed, as well."

"Yes," I said and didn't say anything about what I'd seen in the brief, blinding flash before the sky went black.

But I knew I'd seen it and it hadn't been an illusion or the product of a brain under pressure: I'd seen the seventh mask, a man with an aquiline nose and beard, staring out with a faint smile curling his lips.

Santos coughed. "I brought the book," he said.

We walked with him back to the Land Cruiser with the INAH logo on the side. We drove back the half kilometer to the village, where we found the house of Santos's sister. There, on the little wooden altar table, beside a wooden cross wearing a *huipil,* was a square object covered in plastic wrapping. The sister smiled and scurried away and Santos went to the package and began to unwrap it. I saw what appeared to be a nineteenth-century ledger book, the cover worn and the pages yellowed.

We walked out the rear door, through the kitchen shelter,

and into the backyard, where turkeys and chickens pecked at the ground. At the rear of the bare space, where the house garden began, Santos stopped, opened the volume, and reverently handed it to me.

"It was my grandfather's," he said, "and his uncle's before."

The book with the old prophesies. The book John Dance Williams had seen and that Paul Hayes had only heard about.

I slowly opened it, turning the pages carefully. The writing was in a slanting, nineteenth-century script, almost all Mayan, though here and there I glimpsed Spanish words. I saw an incantation that seemed to be aimed at convincing the *colel cab,* the now almost vanished Native American bees, to give up their honey. There was a list of questions and answers, couched as riddles, which leaders had taught to their sons as a part of the initiation into the responsibilities of their office. There were nostrums, featuring herbs and leaves, useful for parturition and fevers.

And there were the chronicles.

My heart started to pound and my hand trembled as my eyes made out the ancient words:

Ti u Yaax Ahau katun cu likil kaax. Eztabalob u cahal, Ek Chhen u kaba tumen ek u ha.

" 'In Katun 1 Ahau,' " I read haltingly, " 'they left the forest. They founded their town, Black Well was its name because the waters were black.' "

Santos nodded approvingly. I read through the other calendar chronicles.

And halted at Katun 10 Ahau.

Ti Katun lahun Ahau cu tal u dzul, u yax dzul cu tal uaye ti u luum Maya uinicoob.

" 'In Katun 10 Ahau the stranger came, the first stranger to come here to the land of the Mayan men.' " I looked over at Pepper. "It's here, just like Williams said."

Zac u yich, helaan u than, u yaax dzul cu tal uaye, u yaaxil.

" 'He had a pale face and spoke a strange language, the first stranger to come here, the first or great one.' "

"But who can say what that means historically?" José said. "It could be something that happened in historical times. Each *katun* lasted almost twenty years and occurred every two hundred fifty-six years, so, during fifteen hundred years of Mayan history, we could be talking about any of five or six twenty year periods. But we're more likely talking about a *katun* that fell after the Spanish conquest, maybe even something as late as the nineteenth century."

"But wasn't there something about a great king who ruled the land where this stranger came from?" Pepper asked.

I scanned the faded letters and my finger stopped above a single word.

"There it is."

José craned his neck to see. "Are you sure?"

"Yep."

Ti u tepal u Yaax Ahau, cu tal u yaax dzul.

" 'The first stranger came from the realm of the great king,' " I continued to translate. " 'Six were the kings of the forest men then, six they were. He was the seventh and then there were no more.' " I looked up. "It uses the word *chibal,* lineage. So the Williams letter was probably right—the stranger was adopted as the seventh ruler of the lineage, probably because there were no sons."

I continued to read. " 'He ruled for many years, many were the years of his reign. Then he died *ich paa*. Within the walls.' "

"Does it say which walls?" José asked. "Does it specify the walls of this city in particular, like the Williams letter claimed?"

"No," I said. "Williams must've just assumed it was this city. Why?"

"*Ich paa?*" José said. "That's an old way of saying Mayapán."

Mayapan, the capital city of Yucatán in the fifteen century, now a jumble of ruins just southeast of Mérida. . . .

"You're right," I said, hand shaking with excitement. "The League of Mayapán ruled most of Yucatán until the middle of the fifteenth century and then there was a falling-out among the different factions. It collapsed into warfare and there was complete disunity when the Spanish arrived seventy-odd years later. But the natives still remembered the glory of Mayapán."

"So this foreign king died in the fighting at Mayapán," Pepper said. "Fantastic."

"And presumably was brought back here for burial," José said. "But who was the great king in his own country?"

"I have an idea," Minnie blurted. "Joao, or John I, the king of Portugal from, let's see . . ."

"From 1385 to 1433," I said. "He was the king who began Portugal's great period of exploration. He was the father of the man they call Prince Henry the Navigator."

"Yes," José protested. "But—"

"Katun 10 Ahau didn't just cover A.D. 140 to 160: It fell again every two hundred fifty-six years, and one of those periods was from 1421 to 1441."

"During the rein of King—well, I'm just going to call him John," Minnie said. "That can't be coincidence."

José shook his head. "Alan, my friend, I think the heat has gotten to you. Do you have any idea how difficult it would have been for a Portuguese ship—or any other European ship—to have made it to the New World in that period?"

"But Columbus did," Minnie protested. "He wasn't that much later."

"He started from the Canary Islands," José explained. "They're quite a bit farther south than the Azores Islands and the winds in that latitude can help a ship get to the New World. Before Columbus, all the other explorers who headed west left from the Azores and ended up in the Sargasso Sea."

"Then there were others," Minnie said.

"Yes, of course," I said. "Everyone knew the world was round and that it was theoretically possible to reach China and India by sailing west. The problem was that they believed there was no land between Europe and the Orient, so the ships would perish during the long voyage. Unless there was some island out there."

"Antilla," José said, arching his brows.

"Exactly. There were tales of a mythical island with seven cities, founded by seven bishops who'd supposedly fled from the Moorish invasion many years before. If they could find this island, it might be a way station to the Orient."

"But that's the point," José said. "Nobody *did* find it, because it doesn't exist. The king of Portugal sent a Dutchman named Dulmo looking for it and he was never heard from again."

"Dulmo left from the Azores, where the winds were against him," I said. "But if there was some other captain, who left from the Canaries, or who drifted west from the coast of Africa . . ."

José put a hand on my shoulder. "Show me this intrepid explorer's bones and we'll talk again."

I looked over at the demolished facade, where the seventh mask had once been.

"Yeah, you're right."

On the way back, crossing the vast, rocky field, I pulled the Land Cruiser over near the grove of poplar trees with their sinkhole.

I got out and, with Pepper beside me, walked over to the brink and looked down at the well below.

"Do you really think it was a Portuguese captain?" Pepper asked.

I shrugged. My fingers delved into my pocket and came out with the stone tablet given me by Paul. It had saved me from worse injury by deflecting the bullet and now there was an ugly gash on its surface.

"Well," I said, "it makes more sense than that these chicken stratchings are Hebrew."

"But there'll never be any way to prove it unless José finds something when he excavates, like this man's bones surrounded by Portuguese artifacts."

I nodded. "And he'd have to look in the right place. He might not be buried at the site we found. The country may have been in an uproar after Mayapán fell. His own city might have fallen. He could have been buried nearby, hidden . . ."

Her eyes followed my own.

"Do you think it's possible . . . ?"

"They blocked off the cave for some reason," I said.

"How will we ever know?"

"Maybe," I said sighing, "somebody will dig here some-day."

≡Author's Note

The literature on supposed pre-Columbian contacts with the New World is voluminous. Much nonsense has been written, invoking everything from lost continents to wandering tribes of Israelites. Nevertheless, there are respected scholars, such as David H. Kelley, Cyrus Gordon, and Betty Meggars, who point to similarities between different New World traits, artifacts, and/or technologies and those of different parts of the Old World and Asia.

Basically, the issue is whether human beings tend to develop similar cultural manifestations in similar environments (psychic unity of man), or whether certain ideas, inventions, and practices are unique, so that if they are found in two places, they must have been transmitted from one group of people to the other (diffusionism). Because a heterogeneous assortment of "evidence" has been marshaled to support diffusion, including specific cultigens, similar mythic elements, supposedly similar artistic styles, and lexical similarities, it has not been possible to develop an adequate methodology or model for explaining just how diffusion occurs. In addition, evaluation is hampered by the inability of the diffusionists to adequately explain the method of transport/transmission and why some things were diffused and others were not.

The majority of contemporary scholars in the field do not support diffusion from the Old World to the New, and the author of this book inclines toward the majority position. He

214

would be less than honest, however, if he rejected the possibility of pre-Columbian contacts outright. After all, the Vikings did it.

A different question is whether an ancient sailor, thrown up on the Yucatán shore, could have survived. Fortunately, history does provide an answer to this question: In 1511, eleven members of a foundered Spanish ship reached Yucatán in a small boat. Two survived. One, Geronimo de Aguilar, was later rescued by the Spanish, but the other, Gonzalo de Guerrero, married a Mayan noblewoman, became a trusted vassal of Nachan Can, the lord of Chetumal, and, far from seeking to rejoin his countrymen, died leading the Maya in an attack on the Spanish invaders.

Malcolm K. Shuman